TACT

TACT

JEANNIE
PENEAUX

EDITED BY MARGARET DEVERE

To my husband,
who is far superior to Mr.Darcy
in that he did not require two attempts to propose

Contents

Prologue

Miss Elizabeth Bennet cared very much for her family. The ladies of Longbourn were each, in their own ways, devoted to the well-being of one another. Even Lydia, whose character was naturally more self-focused than that of her sisters, could not be content to see one of her siblings unhappy, and being of a cheerful disposition, would then exert herself to raise the spirits of whichever of them was feeling glum.

Lizzy was under no illusions that her family were the epitome of propriety. She was aware that her mother's effusions often crossed the line between exuberance and vulgarity and that her younger sisters' high spirits occasionally led them into unbecoming behaviour. Jane and Elizabeth had once or twice invaded the sanctuary of their father's book room to entreat his intervention in their education and deportment, but he, so used to considering himself a good father if all his daughters were cheerful, well fed, and well dressed, had turned them out with sardonic quips and sallies. Lizzy had left the book room smiling in amusement but dissatisfied with the outcome of their petition.

Of all her sisters, Elizabeth had the greatest command over language. She had discovered at a young age that the correct selection of words could raise a smile or bring a tear with relative ease. Jane, who in her extreme youth had wept very easily at Elizabeth's more cutting witty remarks, had pointed out that if her younger sister had such an ability to bring joy or pain, she ought, in every instance possible, bring the former.

It had been her mother, of all people, who had clinched the matter. Heavily pregnant with Catherine, Mrs. Bennet had been confined to the house and thus had little but the squabbles of infants and the ordering of her household to concern herself with. With great wisdom, she had called her bright-eyed child to her bedside and with great care had shown her that the challenge of protecting the feelings of others was rather more difficult than the challenge of wounding them.

"It is not a sign of stupidity to be kind, Lizzy. The most intelligent lady in the land can use her charm and wit to soothe rather than rile. I wonder, my love, if you would wish to become a lady who is universally liked or one who is avoided. Pass your Mama the vinaigrette before you attend to your lessons, my dear."

Such clarity of logic had a great effect on the young Elizabeth and she consequently took great pains to modify her conversation, so that rather than exercising her quickness at the expense of others, she searched with diligence to find the least offensive and yet least dull thing to say in any social situation that she was permitted to attend. It was thus that when her cousin, who was (in all unvarnished truth) a ridiculous creature, honoured her with his proposals after the ball at Netherfield Park, that she found herself making the greatest use of this carefully honed talent.

Chapter One

"On that head, therefore, I shall be uniformly silent; and you may assure yourself that no ungenerous reproach shall ever pass my lips when we are married."

Elizabeth sat, carefully considering her response. It was very clear that whilst the advantages of an alliance between the heir of Longbourn and a Bennet daughter would be considerable, she was entirely unwilling to subject herself to such an insurmountable challenge as living peaceably with such a man until death did them mercifully part.

She sat in deep thought, her eyes lowered to her clasped hands. The hopeful suitor eventually realised that his young cousin was looking vaguely distressed by his declarations and drew his speeches to a faltering end.

Elizabeth looked up, her brows drawn together in an expression so anxious that even Mr. Collins must have been aware that joyous gratitude was not likely to be forthcoming. He waited, though, fairly confident that he could soothe away any maidenly modesty with eloquent and flowing platitudes.

"Cousin, you do me great honour with such proposals. I am sensible of the kindness and great sense of propriety that must have led you to choose me of all my sisters to speak to of such things. Your very proper decorum in paying respect to the eldest unattached sister in the household does you very great credit, sir."

Mr. Collins smiled and opened his mouth to accept these compliments and offer due flattery as to her own feminine delicacy and ladylike character. He was waylaid, however, by her rising from her chair with an elegant gesture that made apparent her agitation.

"You are aware, dear sir – you must be aware of our unfortunate situation in life once my dear father passes; your delicacy in respect to this is much appreciated and..." Elizabeth looked to the floor, managing with some small effort a blush of embarrassment, "were it only my heart, my *own* situation that I were to consider, I should even now be gratefully accepting your addresses, but," and here she glanced up to see her cousin's mouth a little agape and a puzzlement dawning in his eyes, "I cannot – nay, I must not – cruelly break my sister's heart and destroy all her hope of happiness in life even if it were to establish me so respectably."

Mr. Collins's mouth had now snapped shut and the look of confusion had progressed to decided bafflement. His fair cousin was looking at him, her expressive eyes demanding a response that would show how he understood her perfectly. He had no desire to appear slow-witted or foolish in those eyes.

It took Mr. Collins a good few minutes to collect himself. He had, of all possible responses, not anticipated this. His cousin Elizabeth seemed to be indicating, in the most delicate, charmingly modest way, that she could not become his wife on account of one of her sisters' romantic preference for his own person.

He stumbled a little through his response, deeply uncomfortable. "Y-yes? I'm afraid I was unaware that..." He floundered, eventually settling for, "Miss...Miss Bennet had such decided feelings for me. I assure you, cousin, I had no intention of engaging the heart of any young lady other than...I mean, forgive me...but I had seen no indication of...."

He trailed off and Elizabeth, faintly smiling now, helpfully rescued him. "Oh indeed, sir. No one could accuse you of trifling with her. I believe that this is why she has sought to conceal her feelings. It would be impossible, you know – to anyone other than one of her sisters to have realised – she is so very modest. It is by no means your fault that her heart had so little defence against you."

Mr. Collins, still bewildered but beginning to feel the compliment of being so apparently irresistible to a female that he could inspire her devotion without even being aware of it, stood a little taller and silently pondered how he could gather more clues as to the identity of the tender-hearted young lady without being so crass as to ask explicitly. He nodded nervously at Elizabeth, hoping to gain more time.

"Your sensibilities are a testament to your femininity, dear cousin. The bond of sisterly love is one that is shown clearly throughout scripture," he paused, racking his brains, "Mary and Martha, and...er...Rachel and Leah, to name but a few examples." He mopped his now damp brow and looked to Elizabeth, who had resumed her seat, apparently perfectly ready to continue the interview. "Perhaps, in the face of such commendable sentiments, we might, between us, find a solution? I have wished to be of service to your family since even before I arrived, I was sure, and I was quite correct that it would be entirely wrong to deprive such fair maidens of a home once your father...but perhaps the less said of this, the better."

"You are indeed good, cousin," said Elizabeth, giving every appearance of being in earnest. Her anxious expression had fled and she was now beaming at him, "It would not be right for me to speak of her feelings directly to you sir. That is for you to hear from *her*, should you wish it, and I should not in the least wish to direct you to propose to anyone not of your choosing. It is only that I was so sure that your kind deference to my seniority over her must have prevented you from permitting yourself to consider offering for her." Mr. Collins, not by any means a quick man, mentally crossed the eldest Miss Bennet off his list and graciously allowed her misapprehension to stand.

A weak "Oh indeed, cousin," seemed encouraging enough for her to continue.

"I know she is young, sir, but she has the most devoted heart and you mustn't think she falls in love easily – she is of a naturally retiring disposition," here Mr. Collins removed Miss Lydia from his list, feeling almost smug to have revised the possible Miss Bennets from five to two. To his dismay, Elizabeth rose and extended her hand to him, "but I fear that I have said more than I ought – I must not speak for my sister, even to you who have been all goodness and kindness throughout this awkward situation. Only know," and here she broke off, suddenly shy, "that even though I must deny myself the privilege of being your wife for love of my sister, I should very dearly like to have you for a brother!"

She smiled at him so engagingly that Mr. Collins squeezed her hand, not in the least bit doubtful that she would have thought him a very fine husband indeed and promptly accepting the role of a brother with neither remorse nor regret.

"My dear cousin," and here he patted her hand in a reassuring, fraternal fashion, "please do not allow yourself any anxiety on that score. You did quite right to speak of such things to me and you may rest easy in the knowledge that I shall resolve this to everyone's satisfaction."

A gleam stole into Miss Elizabeth's eyes and she laughed for a moment, presumably with relief, and murmured, "Thank you, sir. I did so hope that you would." She withdrew her hand and curtseyed, entirely unaware that she was leaving him with a now burning sense of curiosity as to which remaining Bennet sister should so dearly appreciate his addresses.

As she opened the door to quit the room, she paused, as though struck by a sudden thought.

"My sister always practices the pianoforte in the music room at this time of day. Should you wish to speak to her, she will be there until it is time for luncheon. I daresay that it would be very romantic to surprise her!"

Much moved by such Providence, William Collins respectfully bowed to his future sister and incoherently gave Elizabeth to understand that he would certainly proceed to do so.

Elizabeth, pleased with her morning work, skipped up the stairs to her bedchamber grinning. Once there she softly closed the door and flung herself on to her bed, buried her face in her pillow, and gave way to peals of uncontrollable laughter.

Chapter Two

As the door closed, the occupant of the room remained stock still, digesting the sudden turn of events. A shock, most certainly, but was it an unwelcome one? Upon reflection, probably not. The situation would turn out rather well.

What Mary very much wanted to know was how Mr. Collins's apparent inclination toward Lizzy had undergone such an abrupt change of direction. He had even now left to speak to her father, requesting his blessing for their nuptials.

Marriage!

She – plain, awkward Mary Bennet – was to be married first of all her sisters. 'Twas unforeseen to say the least. Mr. Collins had taken her quite unawares, entering the music room quietly and listening with flattering attentiveness to the last strains of Beethoven, and smiling at her start of surprise when he applauded.

Mary had been decidedly flustered, and blushed fiercely when he moved further into the room and sat near her. Her cousin did not appear to be put off by her agitation; rather, he spoke gently to her, as though she were something to be handled carefully.

"Cousin...Cousin Mary. Your diligence in practising the pianoforte is most commendable. I feel," he said with some deliberation, "that idleness in a female can lead only to ill humour and mischief. I am glad to see, for your own sake, that you have not fallen into the snare that most gentlewomen do and wasted the time and talent that you have been given."

Mary, staring at him in some surprise, said ponderously, "I believe that every character must have weaknesses that we must strive to avoid, cousin. Idleness is not one of mine – I like to be busy and I like to be useful."

It was not an elegant speech but he nodded, as though affirming something of his own thinking. "Lady Catherine de Bourgh herself is in agreement with you, Cousin Mary – or rather I should perhaps say that you are in agreement with her," he paused to shake off the mis-thought. "Regardless, your opinions are in exalted company."

He reached for her hand and held it firmly. Mary's eyebrows rose and she glanced worriedly toward the door that was ajar. She had opened her mouth to remind him of the proprieties concerning unchaperoned men and women when she was distracted by his dropping, with a flamboyant flick to the lower skirts of his coat, to one knee.

It was fortunate that he maintained his grip on her hand, as his efforts to avoid tangling the length of his garb were only partially successful, and he wobbled, requiring her assistance for a moment before righting himself and possessing himself of her other hand, looking earnestly up into her face.

"It was in fact, dear cousin, Lady Catherine herself who advised me to come to Longbourn to seek a wife. My situation at present is very comfortable but it has weighed heavily upon my conscience – this ever-looming calamity that may soon befall my fair cousins. It has long been my desire to heal the breach between our families and I am entirely decided that it must be you with whom I close that breach."

Mary flushed and felt her heart begin to beat rather fast. She had secretly hoped from the very first that his eye might fall on her, above her sisters, but she had been so sure that he favoured Elizabeth, whom she had envied and with whom she had been so curt these last weeks. How could this be?

"I feel that your good character, your usefulness, and your delicate modesty must certainly be eminently suited to the life of a clergyman's wife. Such diligence to duty can only shine forth like the brightest of gemstones and," he continued after pausing for breath and warming to his subject, "I am convinced that your maidenly modesty, which is entirely becoming in a young female, will not prevent you from feeling true gladness that the delicate situation of your sisters and mother will be secured by your acceptance of my humble addresses and thus bring true happiness to all concerned. It remains, therefore, my dear Mary, for me to assure you that my husbandly affections will be all that any young lady could wish for and that, once you accept me as your affianced husband, you will make me the very happiest of men."

Mary, looking down at the eager face of her cousin and seeing her future stretch before her, shakily removed one of her hands from his and raised it to her heated cheek. Of all the possible outcomes to her morning music practice, she had not anticipated *this*.

She of all her sisters knew her duty well enough and she would do it as a good Christian woman should. She had carefully studied the pamphlets issued to young ladies with regard to decorum and duty. It would be her honour to provide graciously for her bereaved mother and unwed sisters once her father left this earthly scene of time. She would be the mistress of Longbourn and then her duty would extend to the tenants and the poor surrounding her childhood home.

Mary smiled tremulously. It was better than she had ever hoped for, to precede all of her sisters to the altar and to do so in a fashion that would be appreciated by them and so earn their respect and esteem. Such an opportunity was not to be wasted.

"Yes, cousin. I will be your wife." she felt something else was needed and added, "I will strive to be a good one, sir."

"You have made me the very happiest of men. I am quite overcome, my *dearest* Mary! I shall go to your father immediately – I am certain that he will be expecting to see me. What congratulations will flow in unto us, such felicity we are to expect!"

He released her hand with a lingering look and a very pleased expression on his face, and quit the room, closing the door behind him.

Mary, remaining on the piano stool, quietly turned to shut her music books and close the instrument. She supposed she ought to share the news with her mother, but she would take these quiet few moments of solitude to first feel for herself the full extent of her glee. Her cousin, whom she had long considered a good man, had recognised her worth. She might be unable to account for his actions this day but she was prodigiously grateful for them.

Mary rose, shook out her skirts, and walked out of the music room with a calm unhurried stride. A lady, the manuals assured her, must not allow an excess of emotion to dictate her behaviour. She met her mother, who was lingering in the hallway, and smiled.

"Well, Mama?"

Mrs. Bennet fluttered the ever-present handkerchief that was in her grip. "Mary! Mr. Collins has gone to see your father!"

Mary was unable to meet this announcement with the due giddiness or astonishment that Mrs. Bennet clearly felt it merited. Instead, her smile widened yet further and she swallowed down a laugh that threatened to bubble up. "Has he, Mama? He said he was going to."

"But...Mary! Oh, I don't understand any of this!"

Here the laugh sprang forth and Mary reached forward to embrace her mother, "No, Mama, I don't either, but I'm quite contented.

A step was heard behind them and Elizabeth descended the staircase. Her eyes danced and she exclaimed, "May I assume that I am to wish you joy, little sister?"

The two women broke apart, Mrs. Bennet still struggling for words, contenting herself with a disjointed giggle and another flutter of the lace in her hand.

Mary, who was not without natural suspicion, held out her hand to Lizzy. "Elizabeth, can you be responsible for this? Mr. Collins has asked me to marry him and I have accepted him!"

Lizzy nodded, "Then I certainly shall wish you joy, Mary. If you are indeed happy then I am very glad of it. I hope he will continue to make you so; in fact, I believe I shall visit you when you are Mrs. Collins to ensure my new brother is treating you with all the kindness one should expect of a new husband."

Mary was not to be put off, and said impatiently, "Yes, of course, you *must* visit me, Lizzy, but...what did you *do?*"

"I? What makes you think I had anything to do with anything, my dear? If a man sensibly decides to propose marriage to one of my sisters I can only applaud his good taste. We Bennets are an illustrious lot, I believe."

She would not be drawn further on the subject, and Mary, seeing the easy good terms that existed between her betrothed and her sister in the coming days, allowed the matter to drop and very soon forgot all of the petty jealousies she had held against Elizabeth since Mr. Collins had first set foot in Longbourn.

Great was Mrs. Bennet's triumph in the engagement period during which she visited all her acquaintances in Meryton. Her future and the futures of her daughters were secured, the very real fear of the future poverty that was to be hers receded in her mind and, for the time being, at least, she was able to enjoy life without the ever-present spectre of homelessness to keep her company. It would be too much of a stretch to suggest that she became sensible, but a little of her silliness seemed to leave her and she became less liable to desperation, even facing Mr. Bingley's departure from Hertfordshire with more equanimity than she might otherwise have displayed.

The thing was done with all the pomp that Mrs. Bennet could contrive, and although Mr. Bennet offered a token complaint, he too realised the good fortune in the alliance between the families and so permitted his wife to have her way, only shrugging in resignation when she thrust the entire household into near madness in her plans for the wedding. Mr. Collins, having secured his bride and feeling extraordinarily at ease with the world for having fulfilled the duty charged to him by his noble patroness, was all that Elizabeth could wish him to be for Mary. He was still irritatingly obsequious and pompous by turns, of course, but at the heart of him, he was a kind man and he delighted in doing countless little things to please his bride, so long as he was permitted to congratulate himself at length in each instance.

As the happy couple departed Longbourn the morning after their wedding, Mary clung to Elizabeth for a moment, and whispered in her ear, "Lizzy! Do come before Easter – you said you would wish to see how well we were settled together. Come in March. Mr. Collins last night," and here she flushed from forehead to toes, "he said that surely you loved me more than all of my sisters and that I should encourage you to visit soon. He wouldn't say more. Please come."

Lizzy kissed Mary's cheek and led her towards the carriage where Mr. Collins was waiting to hand her in. "Oh certainly, Mrs. Collins," watching with amusement as both husband and wife seemed to swell slightly at the appellation, "I would be very pleased to come." She turned to Mr. Collins and said, "I need not urge you to take good care of her, brother. I am certain she will be the most cherished wife in the kingdom."

Mary's new husband nodded, rather liking the turn of phrase, and turned it over in his mind for much of the journey into Kent. By the time they drew nigh to the parsonage, he had determined that the original thought was not that of his sister Elizabeth's but that of his own designing. Being well pleased with himself for the sentiment, he set out in his mind that his dear Mary should be made the happiest of women.

Chapter Three

With the departure of Mr. and Mrs. Collins from Hertfordshire, a new normality settled over the household of Longbourn. Mrs. Bennet still visited her acquaintances in Meryton, Lydia and Kitty were still permitted rather too much free rein, and Elizabeth resumed her usual practices and patterns of behaviour, knowing that disaster had been narrowly averted by her own cleverness.

For Miss Jane Bennet, however much she had rejoiced in Mary's happiness and her mother's relief at the match, a gentle melancholy had settled upon her that seemed impossible to entirely conceal or shake off. She was a reticent lady by nature, never comfortable with the eyes of others upon her, be they either in admiration or, worse – as of recent – pity. Mr. Bingley had smiled at her and asked her to dance, and she had been lost from that very same moment. She was glad for his sake that her friends in Meryton must have known, as she did, that Mr. Bingley's behaviour was above reproach; he had left as free as he had arrived and it was only her heart that had been put in jeopardy. She could not blame him, as Elizabeth did.

Elizabeth did blame Mr. Bingley. She also blamed Miss Bingley, Mrs. Hurst, and Mr. Darcy. She felt sure she ought to feel angry at Mr. Hurst as well for his brother-in-law's cruel desertion of her sister. She felt certain that given ten minutes alone with Mr. Bingley, she could have him either writhing in shame or asking for her best advice upon when to approach her sister to propose. Probably both, in fact. It seemed a pity that he was so far beyond both her and her sister. Poor, sweet Jane! Her deep kindness was such that she tried not to burden her family with her heartbreak but it was clear to all who knew her that she suffered. Mrs. Bennet tried to cheer her with promises of other, worthier young men; Lydia and Kitty brought ribbons and bits of lace that they had purchased and handsomely offered to retrim her bonnets. Elizabeth watched her closely and waited for any opportunity she could seize upon to mend matters to everyone's satisfaction. Inspiration struck when she received a letter from her aunt in London, and Elizabeth wrote back immediately, begging that they might extend an invitation for a few weeks to her poor sister.

It was thus, in the interim, that she found herself at the pianoforte more often than had been her wont in the past. Mr. Bennet had caustically remarked that the place seemed nearly peaceful in its quietness of a morning since Mary had left them, and Jane, taking him quite seriously, said, "Oh yes, Papa, it has been so strange to spend a morning in the stillroom and not hear the strains of Mary's practice floating throughout the house. I do rather miss it." The very next morning, after her ritual exercise, Elizabeth had resigned herself to the music room for an hour and doggedly practiced the music that Mary had left behind, there being no instrument in Hunsford Parsonage. Jane noticed, of course, and, touched by Lizzy's sweetness, had summoned up more cheer at luncheon than she had recently evinced. Counting this a partial success, Lizzy had persisted and accepted music as a temporary method of consolation until she received a reply to her letter to aunt and uncle Gardiner.

The weeks passed and a long letter arrived from Mary. Some of Elizabeth's worry was alleviated by the buoyancy of spirit that flowed from Mary's pen. She wrote in some detail of her comfortable home and happy circumstances. Upon reading the letter, Mrs. Bennet paid a call to her sister in Meryton with it in hand, and returned fluttering excitedly with the gossip that Mr. Wickham had very recently become engaged to Miss Mary King.

Elizabeth found herself remarkably sanguine about her favourite's seeming defection. She even discovered in herself a startling lack of jealousy over Miss King's good fortune. She rather thought that once she did fall in love with a young man, she might very well be the jealous sort, and it was to be supposed from this that she, although liking the young man very much, Lizzy was not in any way in love with him. She smiled at him, then, when she next saw him at Lucas Lodge, and congratulated him without any ill feeling or rancour. He appeared surprised by such genuine unconcern, and then a little embarrassed to be in her company. Miss King, it seemed, was a jealous girl, and when she saw him speaking to Miss Elizabeth Bennet (who, although she might not have the benefit of great fortune, was acknowledged to be a very pretty and charming lady by all of Meryton), very soon made her way over to them and slid her arm through Mr. Wickham's.

Elizabeth was amused by this, and intrigued to see how Mr. Wickham behaved in the face of his intended bride's protective manoeuvres. She was disappointed to observe that his manners lost some of their charming openness with Miss King; his compliments seemed somehow more practiced and studied than when he had plied her with them.

Mary King did not appear to notice in the slightest, and preened at his low words in her ear. She glanced at her rival and was disgruntled to see that the charming Lizzy Bennet did not look in the least bit put out. When Mr. Wickham was summoned over to attend Mrs. Forster, he bowed to the ladies and left them standing together.

Elizabeth exerted herself and said kindly, "I have heard that I must congratulate both you and Mr. Wickham, Miss King. I wish you both every happiness. We at Longborn are only just recovered from the planning of my sister Mary's wedding so I know from experience that you are likely to be in a flurry of activity."

Unable to resist speaking of her designs in the face of such encouragement, Miss King did so at length, ending with, "But of course, before we are able to make any of these arrangements, my uncle must give his official consent as I am under age still. My uncle King is in Newcastle at present and so very busy that dear Mr. Wickham has not been able to speak to him at all, and he is much needed for his work in the regiment you know."

Lizzy thought it odd that the engagement should be public knowledge before her guardian had given consent, but said nothing, assuming that Miss King was unable to contain her excitement in having secured such a handsome betrothed. Instead of questioning the girl, she quipped, "You will be able to say with absolute truthfulness that you have the King's approval to marry – how happy a thought!"

After some moments, Mary caught the gist of Elizabeth's joke and laughed heartily. "Indeed, yes! The King's approval – that is very good." Having now warmed to the other lady marginally, she leaned closer and asked if Mr. Bingley and his party were likely to return to Netherfield soon.

Her eyebrows drawn up, Elizabeth replied that she had no more information than anyone else in Hertfordshire. "You were wishing to invite them to your wedding, I suppose," she said.

Judging by the revolted expression on her companion's face, she had concluded quite wrongly. "Oh no indeed, Miss Elizabeth! No *indeed*. Not, of course, that I have anything to say against Mr. Bingley but I should not wish to see any of the others again in town." She lowered her voice and spoke in a conspiratorial tone, "You could not know this, Miss Elizabeth – for dear Mr. Wickham has spoken only to me, as I am going to be his wife, but Mr. Darcy is not at all the gentleman he seems and he has *quite* overset my fiancé's whole life."

Lizzy, surprised that Miss King should think it such a great secret, enquired as to the nature of her information, but the lady shook her head.

"I cannot speak of it, Miss Elizabeth. Mr. Wickham said that while he remembered the father with such great affection, he could not harm the reputation of the son, even if it is richly deserved." She left it at that, and, seeing that Mr. Wickham was now in lively conversation with an equally lively Lydia Bennet, hastily made her way over to the two of them.

Elizabeth, upon being approached by Charlotte Lucas to open the instrument, drew her friend aside and enquired of her if she did not think the conversation absurdly odd. Charlotte, with her customary good sense, replied that she could not possibly expect a young man to be entirely honest with his wealthy fiancee about the secrets he had shared with other young women.

"*Think,* Eliza! Mr. Wickham has taken a rare opportunity to marry into money. He would be a very great fool indeed to inform Miss King that she is not the only lady to have heard his unfortunate tale."

This did not sit well with Elizabeth, for it appeared to lessen the integrity of Mr. Wickham, whom she herself had judged to be so honest and engaging. Charlotte smiled and teased Elizabeth that she was more put out by the implication that she had made an error than that she had been thrown over for ten thousand pounds. Lizzy shook her head and sat down to play a spirited air.

"Do sit and turn my pages for me, Charlotte, for you know I shall lose my place and I shall play the same measure thrice before finding it again." Miss Lucas did so and accused her friend of changing the subject. Lizzy laughed, "Oh very well, we shall have it your way – *he* is a deceitful wretch and *I* am a gullible fool! Really, Charlotte, I am hardly in any danger. You ought to be warning Miss King if you are so very convinced that he is a fortune hunter. Indeed, if he were a fortune hunter it makes even less sense that he should have paid me any attention whatsoever. No, my dear, I am afraid you are quite out on this and shall pay the forfeit of my being quite insufferably smug in my wisdom."

Elizabeth's surety in her judgment remained soundly unshaken for yet a week longer, until her aunt Gardiner said much the same thing as her friend. Both were women of good sense, but Aunt Gardiner had the advantage of knowing neither Miss King nor Mr. Wickham and was therefore acknowledged to be impartial in the matter. Elizabeth laughingly countered her aunt's arguments in much the same way as she had Charlotte's, and skipped off to assist Jane with her packing. Jane had consented, at Elizabeth's persuasion, to go to London for a change of scenery. Lizzy had great hopes that her sister would call upon the Bingleys and all heartache would be resolved, regretting only that she was unable to journey in support of Jane as she herself was bound for Kent in a small matter of a week.

The thought that Wickham might have misrepresented himself stayed with her, though, and she dwelt upon the facts of the matter at some length. After much thought, she reluctantly concluded that she could not be easy with his conduct, and although she would not condemn him, she was relieved that her heart had not been touched by his charm.

March came in like a lion, and it was a long and muddy journey that Elizabeth had into Kent. There was much delay on account of toppled trees and waterlogged roads and, all in all, it was a most irksome journey. By the time she arrived at the parsonage and darted inside with Mr. Collins, who had come out with an umbrella held aloft, she was entirely delighted to find herself in a warm and dry home. She said as much when she was bidden into the parlour by her sister, and exclaimed at the comfort of the room in general.

She could not have said anything better calculated to guarantee her a ready welcome in Hunsford. Mary, smiling fondly at her sister, took the compliment for herself, and Mr. Collins did likewise. She was given a hearty supper and shown about the house with much ceremony, and from each aspect of the house various areas of the garden were pointed out for her approval. She dutifully admired each in turn and was as obliging a guest as she could manage to be.

"It is a great pity, dear sister Elizabeth, that the weather is so lamentably inclement, for, on a fine day, one need only step out as far as the end of the garden nearest to the lane and look up towards Rosings. One cannot see the house from here of course, but its location is readily apparent by the smoke emanating from the chimney stacks. Perhaps we will be able to show you in the morning."

Chapter Four

Hunsford Parsonage was just the sort of home that pleased Elizabeth. It was neither too ostentatious nor too shabby. The rooms were of a comfortable size and the arrangements well thought out. Privately, she wondered how much her sister was responsible for the general air of neatness that pervaded the house and how much was due to Lady Catherine de Bourgh's influence upon her brother.

The surrounding area she took great delight in exploring, when the rain finally ceased three days after her arrival. Those three days had been tedious; being cooped up inside a small house nearly constantly in the company of two others, without opportunity for exercise, made it difficult for Lizzy to maintain her equanimity. After being called upon, every half an hour or so, to exclaim in delight over some piece of furniture or another, or being asked her advice or opinion by Mary, she had longed for a good walk.

Mary was a happy bride. It was plain to see that even should her husband never be the master of Longbourn, she could live quite contentedly in Hunsford. What was surprising, but perhaps ought not to be, was how much respect Mr. Collins gave to Mary's opinions. He sought her advice on parish matters, and it was clear, even before attending church, that Mrs. Collins had the final right of approval on whichever sermon he intended to deliver.

Lizzy took to wandering out after breakfast for a long walk of several miles, and very much admired the scenery and nature that Kent provided. The village itself did not appear so very different from Meryton in terms of the personalities contained therein, but the well-maintained buildings and the quality of the goods in the shops suggested a greater general prosperity. As Mrs. Collins's sister, Elizabeth found herself welcomed with great affability by the shopkeepers, and upon purchasing a new pair of thick gloves, for hers were quite inadequate for the unseasonably cool weather, she was pronounced to be a very welcome visitor indeed.

It was fortunate that the return to regular exercise restored her temper to its usual cheer or she might have found the initial meeting of Lady Catherine and her daughter Miss de Bourgh to quite overset her.

Receiving gracious nods from both grand ladies, after morning services, did not appear to be of particular note, except that Mr. Collins did insist upon continually exclaiming over such affability in ones so far above them in rank. Elizabeth had quietly remarked one evening, after they had all sat down in the parlour with tea before bed, that Lady Catherine's condescension was indeed remarkable but, "Perhaps, brother, her Ladyship recognises you for being the nearest person to them in rank – you are, after all the heir to an estate, you have been educated at Oxford, and have married," with her sweet smile and a nod of thanks to Mary, who had just handed her a cup of tea, "a gentlewoman."

Seeing that Mr. Collins appeared to be giving this the thought that it deserved, she let the matter drop and hoped that it might curtail his excessive humility in regards to Lady Catherine without encouraging the air of self-satisfaction that occasionally marked his conversation.

It seemed to have done some good, for, by the time the parsonage party were shown through the gates into the grandeur of Rosings Park, her brother, having pointed out the truly astonishing number of windows and whispered the cost of a fireplace or two to her, then permitted her to appreciate her surroundings in silence, trusting her to be duly impressed without needing direction from him. Elizabeth was feeling quite in charity with him, therefore, and accepted his escort – with Mary on his other arm – into the gilt-laden sitting room with a smile.

It was with pride that Mr. Collins formally introduced his wife's sister, Miss Elizabeth Bennet, to the ladies of Rosings. There was nothing to embarrass him in her manners or her birth. Lady Catherine was not, he had realised, so far above them in rank that she might disdain a connection to the Bennets of Longbourn.

Indeed, it was clear that Lady Catherine was inclined to be gracious to their pretty guest. Mr. Collins, having heeded her advice and chosen a bride from his cousins (a practice she very much approved of), was in favour with her Ladyship. If she had raised her eyebrows when he had written that it was the middle daughter, Miss Mary Bennet, that he intended to wed, all was quite forgiven when he had explained that the lady in question had quite lost her heart to him.

Lady Catherine, Elizabeth discovered, was very used to getting her own way – it was clear in her manner of address to both Mr. Collins and his wife, and also in the way she monopolized the conversation at dinner. Inclined to be amused rather than offended, Elizabeth answered even her Ladyship's more impertinent questions with graciousness, if only for Mary's sake, and by the time they had sat down to cards later in the evening, Lady Catherine was quite of the mind that her parson's family must be decidedly genteel. Her mind naturally leapt from this to the conclusion that it had been Mr. Collins's sense of modesty that described the Longbourn estate as merely small. When invited to play, Miss Bennet demurred most acceptably, but when pressed had acquitted herself well. She concluded that Miss Bennet, while clearly not of the same exalted rank as Miss de Bourgh, ought to be encouraged into conversation with that same lady.

It had taken considerable effort on Elizabeth's part to engage Miss de Bourgh in any kind of conversation at first. Miss de Bourgh did not play, neither did she particularly like to read. No, Miss de Bourgh was not at all fond of music, but she did, apparently, find great interest in being ill. Had Miss Bennet ever been afflicted with megrims? Upon finding out that her sympathetic companion had not, Miss de Bourgh proceeded to enjoy the conversation prodigiously. Elizabeth was subjected, in great detail, to the list of Unfortunate Ailments that so plagued that lady. She was to be congratulated, it seemed, upon having the delightfully robust constitution that so characterised the lower classes – oh no, Miss Bennet must not be offended, indeed it was a true blessing for her – but Miss Bennet could not possibly understand what it was to be delicate.

Miss Bennet understood very clearly three things. Firstly, Miss de Bourgh was as capable of dominating a conversation as her mother – her lineage was very evident; secondly, Miss de Bourgh was not in the least interested in hearing suggestions or even talk of any cures for her ailments that might rob her of any distinction; and thirdly, such tedious conversation must be borne with since every other occupant of the room was entirely delighted with Elizabeth for managing to draw Miss de Bourgh out.

Elizabeth wondered if she could successfully petition her father in her next letter to command her return home with expediency.

The very clear success that Elizabeth had with Miss de Bourgh pleased Mr. Collins immensely – Lady Catherine herself had remarked that good manners and breeding were clearly to be seen in his new sister and that her advice to him to marry into that family had been excellent. Lady Catherine was pleased, Mr. Collins was pleased, Mary was pleased, and Elizabeth was pleased when the carriage was called for their return home.

One morning, over a fortnight after Elizabeth had first come into Kent, she was astonished, upon returning from a walk to the village, to find Mr. Collins walking very swiftly to meet her, hand on hat to prevent it from flying off in his haste. In any other man, this would have not been so surprising, but Elizabeth had established very early on in her visit that Mr. Collins was about as fond of strenuous exercise as Mary was, which was to say – not at all.

She hastened her own step.

"Brother! Is aught amiss? Has the pig escaped its confines again?"

She waited for Mr. Collins to regain his breath as he turned with her towards the house. "No, dear sister, that calamity has not befallen us since we undertook Lady Catherine's suggestions for improvement to the sty. I came to bid you return quickly for Mr. Darcy has arrived for his annual visit to Rosings, and with him he brings Colonel Fitzwilliam, who is, I believe, the youngest of the sons of the *Earl* of Matlock, and even now, Elizabeth, they are awaiting us at the parsonage. Come!"

Lizzy did not have any particular desire to meet with Mr. Darcy again. She had not at all liked him in Hertfordshire and therefore did not consider that she would like him that much more in Kent. He was, however, as Mr. Collins explained, Lady Catherine's favourite nephew and by all accounts his opinions had a great influence over hers, so he must be greeted, and greeted with great politeness, said her brother firmly.

Elizabeth had turned to him at this, quite surprised. Seeing her quizzical expression, he said, "My dearest Mary has told me of your opinions of that gentleman and that he quite insulted you at your first meeting – believe me, sister, I know all, but you must refrain from laughing at him as Mary says you did at home. In your father's house, how you conduct yourself is quite his business, but in mine, where Lady Catherine's favour is greatly to be wished for, you must display that excellence of deportment that I know you possess."

He spoke kindly, but Elizabeth was offended and wished heartily that she could deliver Mr. Collins a very well worded setdown for daring to criticize her manners. Seeing clearly, however, that much damage could be done should she do so, she nodded tersely and set a rather more rapid pace to the house than her sweating brother could have wished for.

It was as the maid assisted her in taking off her outer garments and she stepped upstairs to swiftly change into her indoor slippers that Elizabeth was able to dispel her anger and to think rationally. If Mary's comfort depended on her husband, and Mr. Collins desired the continued good opinion of Lady Catherine, who in her turn was directed by her nephew – then for the sake of her sister she must comply with Mr. Collins's request. Perhaps her brother was not so great a fool as she had thought him.

Such a thought could not help but make her smile as she presented herself in Mary's parlour. At the sight of her, the two gentlemen rose and bowed – a courtesy which she returned in her own fashion. She took the opportunity to catch her brother's eye and smile slightly, lest he be in anxiety that she might disgrace him. He was visibly relieved and permitted Mr. Darcy to gravely present his cousin, Colonel Fitzwilliam, to the ladies of his household.

The colonel was not a handsome man but he had a great pleasantness about him that made engaging him in conversation not at all arduous. Elizabeth found very quickly that his rather plain features were softened by his affability of manner. He, quite struck by Mrs. Collins's pretty sister and quite burningly curious about any young woman of whom both his aunt and his cousin approved, exerted himself to please.

It was a surprisingly lively quarter of an hour that they spent. Elizabeth, responding to the colonel's charm, became quite spirited and demanded of him his opinions on the best walks to be had in the area.

"For I have been here nearly three weeks, Colonel Fitzwilliam, and have had to discover for myself all the best haunts. You know, my brother and sister are not at all fond of walking so I quite depend on your advice!"

The colonel was entirely ready to give it, and even went so far as to embellish his directions with any connected anecdotal tales he remembered being told as a lad.

He was deeply engaged in telling Miss Elizabeth of a delightful walk that might take her to the ruins of the original abbey that had been burnt down a hundred or so years ago before Rosings Park was built to replace it when Mr. Darcy stood and walked over to them. He had limited his conversation with her to the barest of civil necessities early in the visit and instead punctiliously congratulated Mrs. Collins on her recent marriage.

The colonel broke off and looked inquiringly at his cousin, "I say, Darcy, is it time to leave already? I do not believe I have ever paid a call that flew by so fast."

Mr. Darcy shook his head, "Not yet, Fitzwilliam." Then, addressing Elizabeth, he quietly asked her if she would accompany his cousin Miss de Bourgh out in her little phaeton one morning if the weather was deemed fine enough. "Lady Catherine bade me encourage you to accept, for my cousin is not much in the way of seeing other gentlewomen and would undoubtedly value your company."

Astonished, and much very disinclined, Elizabeth paused momentarily before speaking, hoping that there could be some way of avoiding the engagement. Alas, she could not conjure any plausible excuse and, as all of the other occupants of the room were waiting for her answer, she was forced to respond positively. "Thank you, sir. I should be quite willing to ride out with your cousin." This being as enthusiastic as she could manage without actively telling a falsehood, Elizabeth was relieved when the colonel suggested that the ladies drive up as far as the old abbey, for it enabled her to show some real interest in the excursion.

Mr. Darcy, ever determined to be disagreeable, said that he thought it would not do, "for the road is not at all suitable for a lady to navigate and Anne dislikes anything akin to adventure – should the ladies run into difficulty, the footman would have to leave them quite alone. Miss Bennet, I daresay, would prefer to walk." He said this last with a slight curling of his lips and Elizabeth read contempt in his faint smile. She was prevented from responding by Mr. Darcy's turning to Mr. Collins and assuring him, lest he be unduly alarmed, that the footman who would be accompanying the ladies was a faithful retainer who had been serving the de Bourgh family for quite some time.

Mr. Collins bowed in gratitude and instantly forgot that such a thought as escort had not even entered his head. "Oh *certainly*, Mr. Darcy, yes, yes indeed sir. A most *fitting* choice of a servant to protect Miss de Bourgh, I am sure."

It was then that Colonel Fitzwilliam, who clearly had little notion of when to keep quiet, said reproachfully, "I am sure that you shall be glad to know that Miss Bennet will be safe too, Mr. Collins."

Mr. Collins, it appeared, had not considered the matter. He asked Mr. Darcy (to Elizabeth's disgust) if he thought it necessary that his young sister should not venture out without a male escort.

Lizzy deemed it necessary to intervene. "'Tis very good of you, brother, to think of me, but I assure you my father has never curtailed my walks at home and I must cheerfully bow to his authority in this."

Mr. Darcy frowned and addressed her brother. "I should not permit my sister to wander about unattended."

This, it seemed, was quite enough for Mr. Collins to categorically forbid his sister from stepping out beyond the garden without company. Elizabeth, irritated beyond measure with Mr. Darcy but regrouping admirably, replied archly that a Miss Bennet was quite a different kind of female to a Miss de Bourgh or a Miss Darcy "and indeed," she added with shameless flattery, "Miss de Bourgh herself paid me the compliment of noticing my robustness. I am sure that Mr. Collins is entirely capable of judging for himself how to care for those of us in his care – after all, he does so with Mrs. Collins quite splendidly, does he not?"

Deeply appreciative, Mr. Darcy blandly suggested that Lady Catherine's advice be sought on the matter.

Elizabeth closed her eyes in temporary defeat.

Chapter Five

When both the weather and Miss de Bourgh's health permitted the drive, Miss de Bourgh, swathed in shawls, arrived outside the parsonage shortly after the breakfast things had been cleared away by the maid. The lady was clearly disposed to talk and after Elizabeth asked in the most general terms after Miss de Bourgh's wellbeing, she was subjected to an uninterrupted dialogue on the very latest symptoms she had suffered only two nights previously.

They headed toward the village of Hunsford, Miss de Bourgh assuming that Miss Elizabeth would very much wish to be seen in her company. Elizabeth, swallowing her affront, replied cheerfully, "Certainly, Miss de Bourgh, I do not have the least objection to driving through – it is a very fine town. I beg that you would not underrate yourself, however, for your company is quite its own reward." Not a trace of sarcasm was to be detected in Elizabeth's tone and the gentlewoman beside her had her eyes on the road ahead. Pleased by her response, Miss de Bourgh, who was not in general guilty of an excess of humility, nodded and forbore to insult Miss Elizabeth's character any further that morning.

They did not venture away from the wider thoroughfares, Miss de Bourgh resentfully informing her that Mr. Darcy had told her that she ought to keep to the main roads. Elizabeth took enjoyment wheresoever she might find it, and, due to her cheerful disposition, was appreciative of the views from the height of her seat. There was some advantage to being able to see above the hedgerows, she supposed.

By the time the full hour had ended and the ladies had drawn up outside Rosings, Elizabeth felt queasy in her stomach both from the driving and the conversation. Miss de Bourgh was met outside the house by Mrs. Jenkinson and bade Elizabeth a civil farewell that might almost be thought of as warm, before quite rudely deserting her upon being ushered in by her companion. Mrs. Jenkinson met Miss de Bourgh outside the house and anxiously ushered her in, leaving time only for an almost warm farewell from the suffering lady to her long-suffering audience. The groom had handed the reins over to a waiting stable boy and Lizzy took the opportunity of requesting his escort to return to the parsonage.

She was overheard by Colonel Fitzwilliam, who, having seen the phaeton return, had come to bid the lovely Miss Bennet a good morning. He noted that she was looking somewhat paler than previously and offered her his arm to the parsonage, asking her gently if she would be willing to accept him in place of a servant.

Lizzy was very glad of his offer and they commenced the short stretch back along the main drive of Rosings.

"Did you enjoy your morning, Miss Bennet? I daresay you did – I find Kent a very pretty country in general, myself."

"Oh! We went through the village and looped back through the countryside surrounding it. We did not go much further than I have already explored, but I did enjoy the views."

"And what did you think of my cousin's phaeton? It was designed especially for her, I understand; Lady Catherine insisted that Darcy select the horses himself. I believe driving is one of Anne's favourite activities. She is unable, you know, to exert herself very regularly."

"I think both the horses and the equipage very handsome, Colonel. Although…" and here she broke off with great artistry.

"What is it?"

"I would not in the least wish to criticise Mr. Darcy's ability to pick a horse; I am no horsewoman myself, you know, but it seemed to me as though one horse was rather faster than the other. Miss de Bourgh had constantly to be adjusting our speed to compensate, with great skill, I might add. Perhaps Mr. Darcy might like to drive with Miss de Bourgh one morning and see what might need adjusting. Doubtless, it is something minor, such as a strap that has been set too loose by a groom or some such thing."

Colonel Fitzwilliam, who was considered to be something of an expert in horseflesh by his friends, was extremely amused by such ignorance but far too much a gentleman to show it. He said with an unsteady voice that he would certainly suggest that Darcy do so. Privately, he thought that he might tease his cousin at length about his shoddy judgment of cattle, and had to turn away momentarily to conceal his grin.

Elizabeth, satisfied that she had engaged Mr. Darcy to suffer as unsettling an hour as she had just endured, smoothly changed the subject to that of the colonel's travels. He was very used to speaking with single young ladies who were far more interested in Mr. Darcy than in him – rarely if ever did they evince any interest in his own life unless it was concerned with his relationship to the master of Pemberley, so he found her attention especially flattering.

He told her one or two of the more amusing stories from his active service, heavily edited of course, and found his estimation of Miss Bennet's mind restored by the general intelligence of her conversation. By the time he delivered her back safely into her sister's home, they were equally pleased with each other and they parted on the most cordial of terms – in a fair way to becoming fast friends.

The inmates of the parsonage were bidden to dine at Rosings Park the next evening. Mr. Collins, thrown into transports of delight, had burst into the house with the invitation. "You must not, dear sister, feel at all uneasy about needing to wear the same dress twice – you cannot have anticipated such graciousness in being invited so many times to dine at her Ladyship's table."

Lizzy laughed lightly. "Oh, not at all, brother. I quite believed you, you know, when you spoke of such things at Longbourn and so I made sure I should not be taken by surprise should such an invitation occur more than once. Should her Ladyship invite us many more times, though, I fear she may see a repeat of my most favourite gown. Mary, my dear, might I beg your assistance with my hair for the Event?"

Almost as soon as they entered the salon in which Lady Catherine received them, they were greeted with the news that Miss de Bourgh was not at all feeling the thing that evening and so the party would be deprived of her company. Mr. Collins lamented at length at such ill tidings, Mary occasionally added a remark in support, and Elizabeth managed to look disappointed at their depleted number.

Lady Catherine, waving off Mr. Collins's eulogy to her daughter as one would an errant fly, spoke over him, "Yes, yes, Mr. Collins, we must endure as best we can. My daughter is of a delicate constitution and thus we are to expect her occasional absence." The butler entered and solemnly informed her Ladyship that dinner was waiting to be served at her pleasure. "Good, we shall go in now. Fitzwilliam, you will escort me. Darcy, take Miss Bennet in. Mr. Collins, you will have to make do with your wife."

Thus Elizabeth found herself seated next to Mr. Darcy, who, annoyingly, had no notion that she was still vexed with him over the matter of curtailing her solitary walks. He saw her properly seated, and with due diligence ensured that her plate was amply filled and her glass brimming. Elizabeth thanked him with cool civility and, once her Ladyship had picked up her fork, commenced sampling her meal with great concentration.

It was unfortunate, given Elizabeth's plans for retaliation, that Mr. Darcy seemed as content to ignore her as she was him. Consequently, there was little speech between them throughout the meal save that which pertained to the food. Elizabeth nearly lost her icy politeness when he offered to water her wine for her and responded with more sharpness than Mr. Collins would have desired, had he but been able to overhear from his position lower down the table.

"Thank you, Mr. Darcy, I am almost at the age of attaining my majority and have not needed to have my wine watered for many years now, but please," and here she gave a comforting pat to his forearm that rested on the table, "should you wish to do so to yours, do not feel in the least bit ashamed of it. My own father, you know, suffers from gout occasionally so I realise that when gentlemen get older it is often necessary to not imbibe quite so much as they did in their youth."

Having let her shaft fly, Lizzy smilingly took a swallow of her drink.

The man sitting next to her watched her do so, his eyes narrowing after a moment before he turned his head to his left and with very deliberate calmness addressed his aunt.

"Miss Elizabeth and I were having an interesting conversation a few days ago, Aunt Catherine. We wished to seek your opinion on a matter of convention."

Lizzy set her wine down with a snap.

Pleased, her Ladyship bade him elaborate, and Mr. Darcy, with what Lizzy could only describe as malice, threw her a provocative look as he did so.

"It is merely that there seems to be a sad tendency in modern society to neglect the care of young ladies. Very often it is considered quite unexceptionable for them to scamper unprotected about the countryside. I do not think it at all seemly."

Lady Catherine was quite adamant that young ladies of rank ought to be treated with the greatest of care; why, she herself as a young girl was never even permitted to leave the house without a male to ensure her wellbeing. "It is quite shocking, Darcy, the amount of licence that is allowed these modern young women. It will certainly not end there, you may depend upon it. Why, I heard only the other day from dear Lady Metcalf that her daughter, who is becoming quite the bluestocking, you know, had asked her father if she might not attend Oxford with her brother. Her Ladyship seemed to think it was a matter of great amusement."

Her guests paid due attention to Lady Catherine's strictures on the matter, Mary looking quizzically at Elizabeth's flushed cheeks.

"Of course, that is not to say that a woman's education ought to be neglected. I myself was educated at a very select seminary," finished her Ladyship, with great satisfaction, not at all concerned that she had wandered from the point.

Sadly, her favourite nephew was not in a pleasant humour that evening, for he returned with a sally that made her grimace.

"I cannot see that it is at all necessary to educate a female so well while their prospects are so narrow. It seems a waste of funds and resources when the most that will be required of them is to run homes for their husbands and rear children."

Lady Catherine stared at him. Mrs. Collins threw him a look that almost amounted to contempt and then directed it at her husband when she saw him nodding thoughtfully. Colonel Fitzwilliam frowned at him.

It was Miss Bennet, carefully setting down her knife, who was provoked, as perhaps Mr. Darcy had intended, into responding.

"I quite agree with you, Mr. Darcy." Four sets of brows were raised and Elizabeth's eyes sparkled. "If one is to judge the usefulness of learning only by the use to which it is put, then it is a waste to educate those who have no use for it. Especially when, as you have pointed out, there is a lifelong occupation that is destined for them once they have reached adulthood." Elizabeth cast a glance at her hostess and the surprised expression on Mr. Darcy's face before continuing, "In fact, in accordance with your opinions, I see no necessity at all of educating eldest sons – what need have they of expanding their minds when their destiny is clear? They ought only to be schooled as far as is needed to adequately run an estate."

Over Colonel Fitzwilliam's crack of laughter, Elizabeth's eyes met those of Lady Catherine's, wishing to gauge the level of offence she might have caused with such a saucy speech.

Lady Catherine de Bourgh, quite unmistakably, *smirked.*

Chapter Six

Once the dinner guests had departed, Lady Catherine and her nephews returned to the drawing room. Mrs. Jenkinson was summoned to give an account of how Miss de Bourgh fared, and reported that she had been feeling very unwell indeed, and recommended that the doctor be sent for in the morning if there was no improvement overnight. Her Ladyship nodded briskly before dismissing the woman for the evening and offering tea to Mr. Darcy and the colonel.

They sat in companionable silence for a while until Lady Catherine was once again seated and stirring her tea pensively.

"Miss Bennet reminds me very much of myself when I was a young lady. Before Sir Lewis offered for me, I mean. I am quite pleased with her and should be very glad to assist her in settling well. She wants only a little push and she should do very creditably. It is only a pity she is not better dowered. Mr. Collins seemed to think there is not much to divide among the Bennet girls after Mr. Bennet dies."

Mr. Darcy, who was clearly not as favourably inclined towards assisting Miss Bennet's matrimonial prospects as was his aunt, forbore to break his silence, finding instead a fascination with the intertwined floral patterns on his teacup.

Colonel Fitzwilliam, throwing his cousin a reproachful laughing glance, obliged his aunt by entering into the spirit of usefulness which she so enjoyed.

"I agree, Aunt, she is entirely charming, but I cannot immediately think of any of my acquaintance that would do for her. I daresay she would be glad of any introductions you could secure for her if indeed she is lacking in portion. Mr. Collins ought to know if anyone does, I imagine, but I should not like to see her matched with anyone unworthy, or too elderly."

"Too true, Fitzwilliam. She needs a young man; that is quite plain." She sipped at her tea, satisfied that it was perfectly brewed to her requirements. If there was one thing in which Lady Catherine excelled, it was attention to the smaller details in life. "Clearly, the fellow ought to be a gentleman – the girl has breeding, it is evident. I deplore seeing fine young women with excellent lineage married off to tradesmen simply on account of a lack of funds. It has led to a sad decline in families with unbroken noble lineage. What of Lord Bath? He is young enough and wealthy enough to be able to afford her – last I heard he was on the lookout for a wife, and he is of a good age to begin a family."

"*Stodge!*" exclaimed the Colonel, "oh no, dear Aunt. The lovely, vivacious Miss Bennet with *such* a slow top? I wonder that you could countenance it. He wouldn't understand above half of the things she says and she'd run circles round him to boot."

Mr. Darcy was evidently paying some heed to the conversation for he smiled at this.

"A fair point, nephew," graciously conceded the lady. "What of Mr. Aldridge then? He is young, wealthy, and lively enough for Miss Bennet. I was goddaughter to his grandmama, you know. His mother was a fine woman, and so very amiable. It is a pity her last confinement ended so unhappily. She has not been the same since and I am very much afraid that she mollycoddled her son as a result."

"No," said Mr. Darcy succinctly, entering into the subject at last. "He is not suitable."

"And why, pray, would you say such a thing? I know of no ill against him." Lady Catherine had a wide enough circle of gossiping acquaintances to feel that if she was unaware of tonnish news it must be either very recent or untrue. "What have you to accuse him of? The Aldridge estate is worth a clear seven thousand, from what I understand." This, it would seem, provided significant defence against untoward behaviour.

Colonel Fitzwilliam shook his head, flushing slightly. "I'm afraid Darcy is quite correct. He would not do at all."

"But why, Fitzwilliam? I must *insist* on knowing."

His mouth set in a grim line, Mr. Darcy looked even more severe than usual, and every bit, thought Lady Catherine irrelevantly, like his father. "I'd be the worst sort of reprobate to sully your ears with the truth about Matthew Aldridge, Aunt Catherine. Neither I nor Fitzwilliam will speak of it."

Quite burning with curiosity on the subject, Lady Catherine opened her mouth to argue but was prevented by the colonel.

"I declare! Miss Elizabeth could do little better than to take up with a dashing soldier," smiled the colonel modestly. He was only half jesting.

"Out of the question." This from Mr. Darcy, and said in such acid tones that his cousin marvelled at his severity.

"Well now, how serious you are, cousin! I daresay *you* have a better notion."

A gleam in her eye, Lady Catherine mockingly supposed that Darcy thought Miss Bennet required a husband who could do something about that tongue of hers.

Mr. Darcy blushed, and his cousin, having a brain that clearly operated in a similar male fashion, murmured, "I'd not mind making the attempt." To which he received a stern glare from the gentleman, who did not, apparently, think that such things should be insinuated in front of one's aunt.

Her Ladyship, resolutely ignoring her nephew's impertinent attempt to protect her tender ears, rose and announced that she had remembered that she owed a letter to her godsister, and that she would retire to her rooms for the night. She directed them to the library, in which she had ordered the decanters replenished.

Happy to accommodate her, the gentlemen rose, bowed, and bade her have a good night's rest.

Once in the library and seated with his drink, the colonel sprawled on a small settee by the fire. Mr. Darcy stood, glass in hand, staring at the dancing flames.

"I can not help but wonder, cousin, why a man who well-nigh bludgeoned Matlock into setting up a schoolhouse for disadvantaged girls would suddenly hold such strong views against female education – particularly when even a simpleton could see that not one of the females at table would be best pleased."

Darcy did not deign to respond at first, so Fitzwilliam, the germ of an idea now growing in his head, continued, "Miss Bennet looked ready to thrust her knife at you."

Darcy shrugged and said haughtily, "The lady thought to punish me by ignoring my existence. It was necessary to put her in her place. I'd have done the same to any dinner companion of mine that treated me so."

"Hmm," said his cousin, not quite convinced. "One also cannot help but wonder why a young man who by all appearances is quite indifferent to Elizabeth Bennet's considerable charms would be so against the suggestion that she might like to wed a military man."

Here Mr. Darcy dragged his gaze away from the fire. "It would be insupportable, Fitzwilliam; that is all."

"Come now! You cannot object to the lady, surely. No one could. If you do not consider her a suitable wife for a common soldier such as myself, how much lower must the poor girl look for a husband?" he waited for some minutes for a response and had to content himself only a level look in reply. "Or – is the question one should ask, how much *higher?*"

The next morning found the inmates of Rosings occupied with their own tasks. Lady Catherine was seeing her steward, Miss de Bourgh was still abed, and Mr. Darcy was much occupied in writing numerous letters, the recipients of which he refused to reveal to his cousin.

Colonel Fitzwilliam, feeling quite bored, wandered over to the parsonage to see if Miss Bennet could be persuaded to accompany him on a long walk.

Miss Bennet, it turned out, had been longing for a ramble that morning, but, the manservant and Mr. Collins being too busy, had been unable to get out of the house. She fetched her coat and bonnet in a trice and very soon they had set off, at Miss Bennet's request directing their steps toward the old abbey.

The sky was cloudy, but every now and then the sun broke through the cover and gave of its warmth. There were signs of spring about the countryside. Crocuses and hyacinths were trying to shake off their winter slumber and burst forth in colour. They were late this year, but it would not be long before they bloomed.

Miss Bennet was a good walker, the colonel discovered; there was only a small adjustment of pace needed for them to be quite comfortable together. Her face reddened slightly with the exertion but there was little sign of fatigue, even after they had covered a mile.

He remarked on it.

"You are a true countrywoman, I see, Miss Bennet. I know of many women in town who insist that they love to walk but, when put to the test, rarely live up to the challenge of anything more than a slow trudge across the park."

His fair companion laughed at him. "Am I under scrutiny, Colonel? Shall you have me court-martialed if I fail to obey your marching orders with sufficient energy? I am fond of walking; at home, it is my invariable practice to walk a couple of miles before breakfast or I find myself unable to manage myself for the rest of the day. I become, according to my sisters, quite intolerable if I wake up to discover heavy rain...Oh!"

She stopped short where she was, in delight. They had until then been compassing a coppice, and having just entered through the gate to cut through, discovered that within the shelter of the trees a blanket of bluebells had thrived. Dappled light broke through the deep green canopy and lit up, in patches, the thick carpet of purple.

Miss Bennet dropped her voice and sighed in contentment. "How utterly enchanting. I think I shall come here at least a dozen times more while I am in Kent and still not be satisfied that I have seen it enough. What a pity it is that I do not paint!"

She was an engaging creature, thought the colonel – lively and pretty and...but he would not think of such things. Instead, he gallantly decreed in pompous tones that the coppice should now be called "Miss Bennet's coppice," but if she would be so good as not to mention to Lady Catherine that they had stolen it from her, he would be obliged.

Elizabeth, laughing again, was quite prepared to tease him mercilessly on the subject of a soldier's cowardice when confronted with an upset aunt, and did so at length as they journeyed through the bluebells. Emerging from the other side, she had mercy on him and instead quizzed him on the ruined abbey that now lay before them.

"Darcy and I used to play here as boys, Miss Bennet; we would walk along the tops of these ruined walls and pretend to be pirate ghosts and all manner of nonsensical things."

"Pirates haunting an abbey, Colonel Fitzwilliam? Nonsensical indeed. Did you never venture up here at the dead of night, dressed in monks' robes to frighten each other senseless? I am disappointed."

"Had we left our beds at Rosings in the middle of the night we should have been senseless – if our aunt didn't catch us, our uncle would have.

Sir Lewis de Bourgh, Miss Bennet, was not a man to take pity on two young miscreants."

"Ah, you have not had the advantage then, of being raised with sisters. Should we have engaged in such mischief, we should have taken very great care not to be caught. Now do tell me, Colonel, am I now standing in the chapter house or the kitchens? Should I be intruding on a monk's sleeping quarters, do inform me and I shall vacate them immediately, for I should not at all like to scandalise the dead."

They spent some time wandering around the ruins, Miss Bennet graciously accepting his vague answers to her more historical questions. She was noncommittal when he advised her that Darcy was really the man to ask about family history, he having a very good memory for the accurate retention of facts.

When the colonel completed his explanations and they retraced their footsteps, Elizabeth mused smilingly that she had not enjoyed a morning half so much since she had come into Kent – no, not even that first morning when they had all needed to catch Fat Martha in the pouring rain.

She was begged earnestly to share the details of their escapade and did so, the two of them laughing heartily at the picture she painted of herself and the Collinses – so ridiculous in their incompetence at returning a naughty sow to her sty.

Colonel Fitzwilliam rather thought that she was the most companionable woman he had ever encountered, and while he would need to hint gently to her that he was in no position to offer for any woman who was not very wealthy, he was quite determined to take what enjoyment he could from her company for the little while he had left in Kent.

Chapter Seven

Mr. Darcy, at the same time his idle cousin was out walking with Miss Bennet, was sitting with Lady Catherine de Bourgh in the smaller of the sitting rooms that overlooked the front entrance of the main house. Having just bade farewell to the family doctor, they seated themselves together to discuss Anne.

Lady Catherine sat gravely still while Mr. Darcy, his elbows resting on the arms of his chair, steepled his long elegant fingers together, deep in thought. She was not able to bear the silence for long.

"Darcy, Anne has been showing signs of this since last year."

"Yes," replied he, in measured tones. "I know it."

"*How* can you have known it! I have not told anyone," she cried, indignant.

"You will recall I was the one who engaged Dr. Langham. I told him I wanted to be kept informed and he did."

"Darcy! That is most officious of you. I am shocked."

"Madam, this is rather beside the point. It is hardly astonishing that I should want to know of the state of my cousin's health." Lady Catherine was annoyed, but very soon her shoulders slumped again and her mood turned from outrage to unhappiness. Her nephew, unable to sit still when feeling helpless, rose and began to pace.

"I do not think she has the strength of will in her to even want to recover, Darcy. I tried every means within my power to engage her interest in living, in her future, but she appears to have no desire to think of anything but her present suffering. It is partially why I tried to direct her thoughts towards you, but to no avail. Even a prettily painted future at Pemberley failed to rouse her interests."

He bowed, "I am flattered that you thought it might, Aunt Catherine. I gather that Dr. Langham's belief that she could not successfully conceive a child is accurate." At her mute, miserable nod he gentled his tone, "It would not have done, madam; you know that it would not have answered well."

She sighed, "You cannot blame a mother for trying, nephew." She rallied. "I do not intend to be defeated, Darcy. I shall continue to do battle against this illness in my daughter, even if she will not. I do not lack the will."

Moved, Mr. Darcy stood beside her and kissed her hand. "No indeed, you do not. Mama was the same; I suppose it comes from my grandmother the countess." He returned quickly to the point, "My wife must have strength of health as well as strength of purpose. There is a great deal that must be put on her shoulders. I could not have served my cousin such a turn as that…" he paused, deliberating, "nor ought I forget what I owe to my dependents."

Lady Catherine was more astute than many gave her due credit for. "I suppose you are speaking of Miss Bennet." She sounded resigned. "Well, I cannot fault your taste, I suppose – if Anne may not marry, at least you have chosen a gentlewoman with character – I should have been very disappointed in you had you fallen for a pretty-faced idiot."

He faltered. "Her mother is quite dreadful. I can bear her position in society and her lack in terms of dowry, but the connections in trade and the vulgarity of some of her relations are untenable. As much as I…as unobjectionable as Miss Bennet is, I fear it would be a mesalliance. It would be wrong of me to subject Georgiana to them."

Lady Catherine raised her brows, surprised. "You need not acknowledge them, Darcy – I am sure she could not possibly expect it of you!"

"Yes, that thought has some merit. If the situation were made plain at the beginning, she could accustom herself to the notion." He nodded thoughtfully. "Yes, I think that would do." He frowned. "She would need considerable help adjusting. Could I count on your assistance?"

Lady Catherine smiled, though sadly, at her elder sister's only son and found herself promising to be as useful to him as she possibly could be. "I shall be glad of the occupation, I should think – I am not one of those weak-willed women who are driven into the depths of despair by a death in the family. I know my duty; I am a Fitzwilliam by birth, after all." She swallowed, blinked several times, and briskly changed the subject. "Well then, I shall need to be driven over to the Snowes' farm in half an hour or so. They cannot seem to get along without being told what to do as if they were infants – you or Fitzwilliam shall drive me."

The colonel, having properly returned Miss Bennet to her brother's protection, was still smiling to himself when he encountered Darcy coming down the stairs just as he had put his foot on the carpeted bottom step.

"Where have you been?" asked his cousin. "Lady Catherine wants one of us to drive her out to a tenant this afternoon. There is some quarrel over the boundary line."

"I have been taking Miss Bennet on a stroll up to the abbey. She really is a delightful young lady – I am quite enraptured."

Darcy stilled, his hand resting on the smooth oak of the bannister, and looked down at his cousin. "Fitzwilliam, do be serious."

"I must say," continued the unrepentant colonel, "if it were not for her ignorance when it comes to horses, I might really be in considerable danger of the parson's mousetrap."

"Of what are you speaking?" asked Darcy impatiently.

"Oh! I had meant to tell you, Miss Bennet charged me to make you drive out with Anne in her phaeton one day. She seemed to think that one of the horses had been badly chosen." He laughed at the memory.

"What? I do wish that you would not speak in riddles. What exactly did Miss Bennet say?"

"Merely that one of the horses appeared to be naturally much faster than the other and thus Anne had trouble maintaining an even pace, for which naturally you are to be held accountable."

Darcy grinned, and he momentarily looked more like the boyhood pal that had explored the ruins of Hunsford Abbey with him than the staid master that he was becoming more and more. "She was teasing me, again." He sounded satisfied, as though Miss Bennet's ignorance gave him pleasure.

"Eh?"

"You had better turn around, Fitzwilliam, and take our aunt out. I have other things to attend to."

"What? Oh, very well then. This is my comeuppance for spending such a pleasant morning, I suppose, while you slaved over your mysterious correspondence."

Mr. Darcy, after dutifully handing his aunt into the carriage and informing the colonel that he had better drive more steadily than his wont, wandered round to the parsonage. He was admitted by a harassed-looking maid who neglected to announce him into the parlour.

He found Miss Bennet oddly posed. Her arms were outstretched, with a measuring tape in one hand and pencil and paper in the other, apparently attempting to gauge the width of the room's sole window but finding herself lacking in arm span to complete her task. Her back was to the door and she, busy as she was, did not turn to face him when she spoke.

"You must not ask me what I am doing, dearest, for it is a secret. I shall not tell you even if you promise me your prettiest new bonnet."

Mr. Darcy supposed, aloud, that Miss Bennet had not been intending to address him and was greatly amused to see her start and drop her tape.

She flushed pink and stared at him in dismay before she belatedly responded to his bow.

"I...I beg your pardon, Mr. Darcy. I thought you were Mrs. Collins returned from Rosings. I wonder that the maid did not announce you." She watched him, a light crease between her brows, as he closed the door with a click.

He then walked over to the bay window and picked up the tape from the floor next to her foot, indulging himself with her closeness for a moment before withdrawing. Miss Bennet looked, as she was doubtless very aware, like the epitome of loveliness with the sunlight shining in through the window and embarrassment lightly staining her cheeks the colour of a rose.

He indulged himself yet further and could not resist a tease. "I cannot promise you my new bonnet but perhaps you will tell me without bribery what it is you were hoping to achieve. May I assist you? I will measure it for you – it is not beyond my reach."

He did so and was rewarded with a faint confused smile, as though one so humble as she could not have foreseen such gallantry. "Thank you, Mr. Darcy. It is only a secret from Mary, and Mr. Collins too, I suppose. Do let me write down the number or I shall forget it. The depth too, if you please, thank you."

Having done so in neat small numerals, she slipped her paper into her pocket and relieved him of the measuring tape. "Would you care to sit down? I am afraid Mr. Collins is out on parish business and my sister has walked around to Rosings a little over half an hour ago; I was rather expecting that you were she. I am afraid you find me all alone this afternoon, sir, but I am certain Mrs. Collins would not mind if I called for the tea tray a little early."

He chose the chair opposite hers and shook his head at the offered refreshments. He patiently waited for her to reveal the reason for her odd behaviour when he had come in.

She sat awkwardly clasping her hands and looking anywhere but at him before doing away with her air of mystery. "I suppose you will only tell my brother and sister of my freakish starts if I do not tell you what I was doing. I was not up to mischief or anything of that nature, not really, anyhow." She hesitated and grimaced a little. "I am intending to use the full extent of my feminine wiles to persuade Papa that he wants to purchase a little pianoforte for Mary, one that will fit snugly into that little casement."

"I do not suppose your father will prove too difficult to persuade, Miss Elizabeth," said Mr. Darcy, thinking that Mr. Bennet probably delighted in indulging her – he himself would have difficulty refusing her when – *if* – he did decide to wed her.

She corrected this false impression with a head shake, smoothing down the loose tendrils of her hair as she did so. "You are unaware of my father's dislike of parting readily with his money, sir," she laughed. "It often takes me considerable effort to persuade him to give me what I want – but very often it is a worthwhile challenge."

"I daresay that a husband might give rather more readily than a father with five daughters to oblige. Perhaps your practice will prove useful." He cursed himself as soon as he had said it, for she looked both self-conscious and bewildered, and despite having spoken with his aunt that afternoon, he did not wish to commit himself before he was entirely sure how he would act. It would be unfair to raise her expectations and hopes further than he already had with his attentions.

They heard the sound of the front door being opened and Darcy hastily stood, "I had better return to Rosings. Good day, Miss Bennet." With that he hurried out, encountering Mrs. Collins on the way as she stopped to remove her cloak and bonnet. He bowed very civilly to her while the maid fetched his gloves, but would not stay any longer. As he passed by the open parlour window, he heard Mrs. Collins voice drift out.

"Elizabeth! What can you have done to poor Mr. Darcy?"

Chapter Eight

"**N**ot a thing, my dear, not even when I was nearly provoked into making sport of him for having such an unnecessary length of arm," replied a startled Elizabeth to her sister. "He is the *oddest* man; I do not think I have met anyone so capricious in my whole life." She shook her head as if to clear it of the strange behaviour Mr. Darcy had inflicted on everyone. "When does Mr. Collins return, do you suppose?"

Mary quite refused to accept the change of topic. "Yes, but Lizzy – you will try not to provoke him, won't you? Mr. Collins is quite right when he says that he is not a man for us to make an enemy of. Lady Catherine is very fond of him and while she cannot withdraw Mr. Collins's preferment now, it could make life very...very *awkward*, if she were to take up against us."

"Mary! As though I should do anything that I thought would cause you discomfort. Besides, my enemies need not be your enemies. I am sure Mr. Darcy and his aunt are quite aware that Lizzy Bennet's wild temper and desire for a good argument are not shared by the – what was it your husband called you again? – the incomparably useful Mary Collins."

Mary smiled happily. "You may laugh at us, Elizabeth, but if Mr. Collins had attempted to praise my beauty or lovely nature we should both know he was lying. He is honest in his compliments. I find that I do not mind at all. Other women may enjoy having their eyes compared to stars, or...or their hair likened to a raven's wing – it is not for me. I should probably shake my head if anyone attempted it."

"I cannot deny that you are well suited to each other. I am glad I came; I shall not find it necessary to poison my dear brother after all – he does take good care of you and you are happy, I think." Her familiar mischievous twinkle lurked in her eye. "If only your dearest, most favourite sister would cease to find Mr. Darcy quite so offensive, I daresay you should be incandescently happy in your wedded bliss!" She went to fetch her book, still laughing, but Mary, though exasperated, knew that her words had not been carelessly discarded, and was able to greet her husband with perfect ease, in the knowledge that she had done as he would have wished in speaking to her sister.

The next morning the sun rose up in the sky, quite determined to coax all the earth to bloom in happy response to its light and warmth. Lizzy nigh on skipped down the stairs to breakfast. "How strange the weather is in Kent, Mary. Good morning, Mr. Collins – if you can spare me Dawkins for an hour, I shall be very much obliged to you. Why, only yesterday I felt the want of my warm coat and thick gloves, but today it is as though summer has come already."

Mr. Collins was unable to do without the manservant immediately but apologetically promised her that she should have her walk that afternoon. Lizzy was disappointed but directed her annoyance at Mr. Darcy. Had he not suggested that she ought not to go out unattended, she was certain it would not have even crossed her brother's mind that her liberty was unusual.

An opportunity for defiance came soon, however, when both the Collinses were summoned suddenly to the bedside of one of the parishioners – Mrs. Garron had been taken very ill and was not expected to survive another night. Mrs. Collins was needed to give practical comfort where she could and Mr. Collins was wanted for the spiritual.

The two made great haste with their breakfasts and hurried off. Elizabeth was left quite alone.

She comforted herself, as she put on a coat and bonnet, that she was not given to grand gestures of contrariness as a general rule and that – *had* Mr. Collins truly thought himself of issuing orders as pertained to her safety, she should have obeyed him as her temporary guardian, even if the obedience would be grudging.

Really, she mused, as she danced down the garden path and out through the gate, she was not ignoring her brother so much as she was ignoring Mr. Darcy, who clearly deserved to be ignored if she was not permitted to quarrel with him openly.

Elizabeth made her way quickly to the bluebell copse, intending to see it swiftly and then sneak back to the parsonage before she could be caught out.

She was prevented in this by a tall gentleman already being there and hailing her before she could turn and withdraw.

"Miss Bennet!"

"Colonel Fitzwilliam."

"I thought I should venture up here again to see the bluebells – I see we are of like mind, Miss Bennet," he said cheerfully.

"I could not resist the call of such weather, sir. I am afraid you have caught me in my misbehaviour – the Collinses were called out this morning to Mrs. Garron's deathbed and I have exploited the opportunity for a ramble."

"Ah. You may depend on me, Miss Bennet; I shall not breathe a word."

"Thank you, Colonel – I am so much more comfortable breaking rules when I can be sure that I will not have to bear reproach for it."

He grinned at that and said that she had much in common with some of the officers he had commanded in the past.

They walked together through the wood once again. Elizabeth was as pleased with it the second time as she had been the first. When they had looked their fill and finished breathing in the warm fresh scent that pervaded the wood, they turned back together and naturally made their way back. The colonel's easy, friendly manner put Lizzy greatly in mind of Mr. Bingley, and not for the first time she wondered how it was that such an unpleasant gentleman as Mr. Darcy could hold the friendship of two such amiable men as him and the colonel.

"Are you at all acquainted with the Bingleys, Colonel? Mr. Bingley leased a house near to my home last autumn and they were a welcome addition to the neighbourhood."

"Not well acquainted, I am afraid, Miss Bennet. He has been friends with Darcy since Eton – they are of an age, you know. I have heard much of him but have not been much in his company. He is a pleasant-mannered man, I understand."

"Oh yes! I liked him, I do not think it possible not to like Mr. Bingley – he is so very affable, you know. It makes one wonder how often he is cheated by his servants –I cannot imagine that he is known for being severe upon dishonest ones."

"No, nor I. I believe Darcy feels it his duty to protect Bingley from those who would take advantage of his good nature. Darcy," he added laughingly, "has no compunction in dealing with errant servants."

Lizzy smiled. "You astonish me, Colonel. I should have thought Mr. Darcy and his sister were nigh to the poor house simply on account of him being so famous for his liberality."

He acknowledged her sarcasm with a grin but replied, "No, Miss Bennet – although I must say that he is a liberal master at Pemberley, he has the good sense for the sake of my ward not to give away his whole income to the undeserving poor."

"Your ward, sir? I thought that Mr. Darcy stood as guardian to Miss Darcy. Perhaps Miss Bingley was in error."

"Oh, it is not commonly known, although certainly not a secret. It was thought wise that there should be two trustees for Miss Darcy's affairs and I was appointed the second."

"And does your charge give you much trouble? Is she often found flouting her brother's orders and walking out alone?"

The colonel shook his head. "Miss Darcy is of a retiring nature and, quite rightly, would not even think that her brother's requests could be ignored. She is a very dear girl, Miss Bennet, though perhaps a touch shy."

In her mind's eye, Elizabeth pictured a docile creature who lived in fear of displeasing her severe brother. Her brow wrinkled at the thought that the colonel's description of Miss Darcy was not at all in keeping with Mr. Wickham's account of the matter.

"Do you know of Mr. Wickham, Colonel?"

To her surprise, he halted in his walk and the contented, genial expression vanished from his face. In a moment, his demeanour changed and he bore a strong resemblance to Mr. Darcy.

"I beg your pardon, madam?" he spoke with barely restrained anger in clipped, hard tones. "What can possibly have prompted such a question so soon after discussing my ward, I wonder. I am afraid that I must demand a full answer."

Made decidedly uncomfortable by the sudden transformation, Lizzy glanced about her. They had not yet reached a populated part of their walk; the lane was yet some distance further down the hill. She could just see the gate that would lead them to it.

"I am afraid I do not have the pleasure of understanding you, sir. I cannot comprehend what it is I have said that has led to such offence. I asked, simply because it occurred to me that your description of Miss Darcy was not at all in keeping with the way in which Mr. Wickham spoke of her. I am attempting to reconcile the two." There was now a measure of reserve in her tone, a defensive note that had crept in at the accusatory way in which he had spoken to her.

If anything, he seemed to be made angrier at her words. "Given my knowledge of Wickham's character, Miss Bennet, I do not suppose that they can be reconciled. Do enlighten me as to what that man has said about Miss Darcy."

It was not a request and Elizabeth stiffened yet further, intending to remind the man that she was not accustomed to being addressed in such a manner, nor would she tolerate it – but before she could do so her companion huffed out a breath of air and stalked off a little distance from her. She did not approach him, being so annoyed herself and understanding the wisdom in a little distance to collect one's thoughts. She found herself a conveniently fallen tree and sat, composing her response as he stared off into the distance, his back to her.

He turned back in a short while and seeing her seated, occupying herself with a small bunch of daisies, approached her log.

She spoke before he could, as neutrally as she was able. "Mr. Wickham has spoken but two sentences to me regarding Miss Darcy – firstly, that she is, or was, but sixteen. Secondly, that although he devoted many hours to her amusement, she has grown very like her brother in terms of pride. Mr. Wickham has said much against Mr. Darcy's character but little against the lady. Does that satisfy your demand for information, Colonel Fitzwilliam? I should like to return to the parsonage very soon if it does."

He looked chagrined. "I apologise, Miss Bennet. I am, I believe, a reasonable man but regarding Mr. Wickham, I have little command over my temper. I ought not to have spoken to you thus – I am sure you are blameless. You are not the first young woman, nor will you be the last, whose ears he has courteously filled with falsehood. I beg your pardon. I will, of course, take you back immediately."

Elizabeth remained sitting on her log. "I suppose there is some great mystery afoot here that I am to know nothing about. How vexatious." She held up her chain of white flowers and thoughtfully straightened the odd stem to her satisfaction. "I suppose, then, that Mr. Wickham's words concerning Mr. Darcy disregarding his father's will were slander – no, you need not answer that. It becomes clearer to me now – why else would he have only told the odd acquaintance, not spreading it abroad until Mr. Bingley and his party had left Netherfield? I shall not pry, Colonel Fitzwilliam, but I should like to demand an answer of my own now since I answered *your* demand."

He raised his eyebrows, promising nothing.

"Is Mr. Wickham a dangerous man?"

He kicked a clump of dirt with his boot and toyed with it. "He is not a violent man, Miss Bennet, but neither is he at all trustworthy. He is not at all well received in Derbyshire on account of his dishonesty and poor character."

"Very well then. We shall speak of pleasanter things."

"Will you first accept my apology for frightening you? Darcy will have my head if I have seriously upset your peace."

"Mr. Darcy! I shouldn't imagine it would bother him a whit, Colonel! I am well able to cope with the occasional lapse of manners in your relatives, sir – I daresay it was too much to hope that you would be exempt from the more obvious family traits. You may, since you have begged my pardon so nicely, consider yourself forgiven and the incident shall be cast into the furthest recesses of my mind, only to be resurrected whenever you put me out of humour." With that, she hopped off her log and started down the hill toward the lane.

He laughed again and followed her, as she had intended him to, but said, "You are quite out about Darcy, you know – he takes very good care of his friends and I believe you are counted to be one of them from what I gather in his conversation. In fact," he said, hoping apparently to raise Mr. Darcy in her opinions, "he takes such care of his friends that he was recently forced to intervene in Mr. Bingley's affairs. The poor man was quite in love with an unsuitable lady. My cousin had to say quite plainly that she was after his fortune, for Bingley was quite blinded by his own feelings. Darcy told me weeks ago that he congratulates himself on having saved Mr. Bingley from such an imprudent match."

They had by this point, reached the lane that led to the parsonage and Elizabeth could see the gate that led to her sister's house. Her voice sounded unnaturally loud in her ears when she asked the colonel, in a trembling voice, what right Mr. Darcy had to be the judge of any lady's feelings.

He looked at her curiously, wrinkling his brow. "I would imagine he observed her carefully, Miss Bennet. He is a fair man. I do not suppose the case makes any difference to you or me. Perhaps I ought not to have mentioned it – all this occurred last year when he was rusticating with Bingley in one of the southern counties. I do not even recollect that he told me which one. You are inclined to think his interference officious?"

Elizabeth raised a hand to dash away the angry tear that had spilt onto her cheek – heat suffused her face and her heart was beating very fast. Righteous fury was infusing her every bone and she laid her other stiff-fingered hand on the parsonage gate to open it.

The Colonel saw the tear and his eyes widened.

"I say, Miss Bennet – I do not think...."

"Hertfordshire," she said, succinctly. "The mercenary, unsuitable, heartless young lady was from *Hertfordshire*."

With that, she fled indoors.

Chapter Nine

Mr. Collins attributed the low spirits of his favourite sister-in-law to the sad passing of Mrs. Garron. Clearly, Elizabeth was a young lady of such delicate sensibility that she could not help but be quite cast down by the cruel reality of death. He attempted in his awkward but kind way to condole with her, and congratulated himself that within a quarter of an hour her sweet smile had returned and she bravely attempted to be cheerful again. She said that she was very weary that night and retired early. The Collinses were confident that a night's repose would soon mend her.

Yet Elizabeth was decidedly not herself the by the time morning had come, and even after they had partaken of their luncheon it was apparent that she was still decidedly out of spirits. Mary began to worry when her sister had rejected the possibility of a walk that afternoon – Mr. Collins, thinking to offer up Dawkins to the cause of Cheering Elizabeth Up, had said that she might go with his blessing. Instead Lizzy asked if she might sit in the parlour and reread a few of her letters from Jane in the quiet. Her head, she said, was plaguing her although she would not hear of the apothecary being sent for – Lizzy was certain that quiet and solitude would soon mend her.

The solitude was quite easily arranged, for Mrs. Garron's affairs must be taken care of, and as she had no remaining family, that task naturally fell to the Collinses. They walked off down the lane together, arm in arm, with the assurance that should Elizabeth require them, she should send the maid to fetch them immediately.

Elizabeth soon realised, after spending some time dwelling on Jane, her misery, and Mr. Darcy's culpability, that her headache was not at all diminished by such morose thoughts and as her character was not one that naturally embraced ill humour, she made an effort to lift her own spirits by beginning to pen a letter to her father.

She had not written much more than the preliminary greetings when the door opened and the maid announced the man Elizabeth least wanted to see.

Mr. Darcy entered the room, bowed, and waited as she stood to curtsey. Once she had done so, grudgingly, he put his hat and gloves down on a little table and sat down at her civil invitation.

He did not look quite so calm and cool as he ordinarily did, and Elizabeth wondered if the colonel had told him of his blunder. Clearly, Mr. Darcy did not relish her knowing of his interference, perhaps thinking she would call him to account for it. He was incorrect on this score, for although she would not avoid the subject should he raise it, she could do no good by flinging his abominable conduct in his face.

Unable to resist needling him, though, with ponderous courtesy Elizabeth enquired after the health of his aunt, Miss de Bourgh, Mrs. Jenkinson, and lastly his cousin the colonel.

Never particularly forthcoming in his civilities at the best of times, Mr. Darcy's impatience with the polite necessities of civilised behaviour was readily apparent by the time she had gently led the conversation to the health and whereabouts of the last in the list of his tactless relatives.

"Fitzwilliam? I've not seen him since yesterday, Miss Elizabeth. Lady Catherine desired him to head over to Mrs. Garron's cottage today in order to assist with the necessities."

They then fell into the familiar awkward silence that so often existed between them. Elizabeth thought of at least three different avenues of conversation that she could rescue him with but was disinclined to aid him in the matter. If he wished to annoy young women by visiting them only to waste their time with silence, she would not discourage him. It must be borne for Mary's sake, apparently. However little she desired his company, she would not do as she wished she could and rail against him for his despicable behaviour toward the sweetest sister in all the world.

He stood abruptly in another minute and strode toward the door, only to return in quick paces once he had reached it.

"In vain I have struggled. It will not do; my feelings will not be repressed. You must allow me to tell you how ardently I admire and love you." Elizabeth, having half risen from her chair to see him, as she supposed, out of the house, sat back down with a gasp of astonishment.

Mr. Darcy appeared to think this sufficient encouragement to continue. "I know that I must have surprised you, forgive me – I was not even certain until this last week that I would ask you. I have tried to shield you from false hopes. You are not an unintelligent creature; you know – surely you must know of the struggles I have had to overcome in order to ally myself with your family. I thought in Hertfordshire that I should forget all about you once I was away, but seeing you here again in Kent has made my efforts to remember my duty to my name entirely futile. Were it only my inclination I had to answer to I should have spoken to you sooner, but I have a younger sister, whom I trust that you will love as dearly as I do, whose future may be affected by the circumstances of your upbringing and the behaviour of most of your family. It cannot be helped."

He stopped speaking for a moment and looked at her pale astounded face and sighed. "I do not mean to embarrass you, Miss Bennet. I have every intention of caring for you to the very best of my ability – you need not fear to be made to blush by my relatives nor by my lineage, and materially speaking at least, you will be very well situated. My ancestors have been landowners in Derbyshire for more than three hundred years." He paused and glanced down at his fingers, considering his next words. "Should you, as I hope you will, accept my hand in marriage, there are conditions that must be required of you. I do not think you will struggle at all to make new friends, nor do I think you will find it hard to care for your new relations but – it will be necessary at first to minimise communication with Hertfordshire and then to end it completely once Miss Darcy makes her come out. I believe that I have now said all that I must on the subject and wait only for your answer."

From the time that Mr. Darcy had begun to speak to the time he eventually ceased, Elizabeth's countenance had changed colour several times. Pallor to redness, and then finally back to white again. Her amazement was boundless. She did not believe that excessive modesty was an affliction with which she suffered, but that this man, of all men, should express a desire to wed her was beyond anything she could have imagined. Given that her ire was increasing with every ill-judged word he spoke, she tried to compose herself to refuse him with great patience, not merely due to a desire to avoid his anger but also because she could not help but feel compassion for him, even above that which she had felt for poor silly Mr. Collins. Mr. Darcy at least believed he loved her – how else could he have lowered himself so very far (as though she were a scullery maid!) to speak to her thus. Thinking of Mr. Collins made her consider briefly if a similar answer to the one she had given *him* might assist her. Could she reasonably convince Mr. Darcy that one of her sisters was pining for him and thus she could not in all good conscience accept him? She quickly sifted through, and as swiftly dismissed, the possible suitability of Lydia or Kitty.

It would not do. Whatever his many faults, this was not a stupid man – nor was he an easily led one. It was decidedly inconvenient. Tact in its most delicate form would be necessary for every word she spoke if she was to conclude this unpleasant interview on civil terms with him. To do so without incurring his resentment was possibly even beyond her skills but the effort must be made.

"You have honoured me, Mr. Darcy – I...I confess that I did not expect this. I, as you have pointed out, had not considered that one such as you would have even looked at me twice, let alone wished for my hand in marriage." Elizabeth kept her eyes on her fingernails, her hands clenched tightly together – both wishing and dreading to see his face change as she uttered her next words. She tried for humble tones. "I am not worthy to be your wife, Mr. Darcy. I am flattered, beyond anything, that you should have considered me and I truly thank you for the compliment of your affection, but I am not so low in rank, sir, that I cannot comprehend what is owed to a family name. The Bennets have been in Hertfordshire for only a hundred years, but I should not disgrace them by wedding a stable boy, or a carpenter and that is as much a degradation as a wedding between us would be to you. I am sorry, sir, that I was not better born and I sincerely wish you every happiness. I do trust," she added with a tremulous smile, "that the next young lady so fortunate to receive your addresses will be of sufficient rank, wealth, and dignity that you might speak to her without any struggle or self-reproach that might mar your future happiness."

He was not a slow man. The import of her words sunk in very swiftly and a curious mixture of agitated disbelief was apparent in his features. He had been successfully caught in the noose of his own pride. Merely by agreeing with him, she had refused his hand with his own reasoning. There could be no fault found in her logic; it was his own argument after all – how could a reasonable man be angry in the face of such kindly spoken words?

Mr. Darcy ran his hand through his hair, sending it into disorder. He appeared to be thinking very seriously, for he was frowning prodigiously as he loomed over her, still on his feet. It took him some three or four minutes to speak, Elizabeth in the interim wishing that she were anywhere else but there and marshalling her defences if he should press his suit, but praying that he would not.

When he did reply, he sounded very grave and very serious. "I have misspoken, Miss Bennet, and I have done so disastrously, it would seem. I had not thought that your response would take this form."

To her dismay he approached her and sat beside her. She edged away, ready to stand but he gestured that she should remain. "No, please remain seated, Miss Bennet – this conversation is not likely to be a short one – I do not mean to alarm you. Forgive me; I fear that I am making very little sense." He smiled a little when she nodded in affirmation. "I have been thinking of recent that I should prefer it if you would agree with me a little more often. I have discovered that I am quite wrong; it is far less agonising when you do not." His mouth returned to severe lines. "I beg your pardon, Miss Bennet, for having in my declaration, made you feel in any way unworthy of anything. I think you deserving of every good thing that life can give you."

Elizabeth, unexpectedly feeling very sorry for him, steeled herself and pressed home her advantage. "No no, do not reproach yourself, sir. You are entirely correct – I am not your equal. Let us simply forget this all happened and part with all charity and no ill feelings. I promise that I shan't tell anyone."

Mr. Darcy's displeasure was very evident. His mouth twisted downwards in a grimace and his eyebrows drew down low on his forehead. She could not tell whither his displeasure was directed.

"I have done a great deal of damage, I think," he said, sounding guilty. "Miss Bennet, I ought not to have addressed you in such terms. I cannot think what possessed me."

"You did not stray from the truth, sir," she said, stiffly.

"It does not excuse me." He checked himself and spoke again. "If I am able to convince you that you need not refuse me so for my own sake, will you reconsider your answer."

Elizabeth swallowed, averted her eyes, and shook her head.

Very gently he spoke again, "I am in earnest, Miss Bennet."

Nervously she glanced at the closed door and tried to put a little distance between them.

He frowned and inwardly she quailed – perhaps she wasn't so accomplished an actress as she had thought.

"I cannot fathom why you would not withdraw your refusal, nor can I quite comprehend why you are looking as though I am a thing to be feared. I have been clumsy, yes, and I ought not have made you think you are my inferior but that does not explain either fact."

"I have no wish to anger you, Mr. Darcy. I am well aware that your influence could make the lives of my dear brother and sister difficult. Do let us cease this talk – it does not do either of us any good. You have said my family is objectionable, I have agreed, let us part."

"Anger me! Miss Bennet, I am not so vindictive as to punish the family of the woman I love for my own stupidity in expression."

Elizabeth rather doubted this.

He exhaled and dropped the hand that he had, seemingly without realising it, reached out to her. "If I give you my solemn word, Miss Bennet, that I shall not do any harm to you or any of those that you care for as a result of this interview, will you speak plainly? This situation must be mended. I cannot endure the thought of you docile and believing in your own inferiority, then civilly sending me on my way as though we were indifferent acquaintances. I must be permitted the opportunity to rectify this."

She could think of no good reason, other than her desire for peace, to deny him. At her nod, he looked relieved.

"Very well, then, tell me."

Chapter Ten

She regretted it almost immediately. Her tight rein upon her temper was already under strain and the grim, unbending determination on Mr. Darcy's countenance did not bode well for a brief explanation.

Reluctant though she was to prolong this private interview with Mr. Darcy, Elizabeth knew that to deny him any explanation would not make him desist from pursuing the subject. He was not a stupid man – it would not take him long to realise that she had a myriad of other reasons, especially if Colonel Fitzwilliam later revealed to his cousin the contents of their conversation the previous morning.

"As you wish, sir," she said softly. "In truth, I do not know that I could trust myself to your care as your wife."

"I beg your pardon?" exclaimed he, clearly offended. "What evidence have you that can possibly support such an opinion?"

Elizabeth lifted her hand in a placating gesture. "Mr. Darcy, this conversation may cease just as soon as you wish it to. I am entirely willing to forget the whole."

"You cannot make such an insulting assertion and then leave it unexplained. I have never harmed a woman in my life, Miss Bennet – such behaviour is beneath me."

"I did not suppose you to be a violent man, sir."

He relaxed marginally. "Explain then, if you please."

She hesitated. "I do not think I can properly explain to you what it is to be a woman entirely at the mercy of a man. When I marry I shall be entirely dependent on my husband. He may beat me, speak unkindly to me, neglect me, or isolate me, and be entirely within his rights as a husband. If, as I have so often observed, a young husband's infatuation fades and his admiration wears thin as the years pass…. One might reasonably expect a man in the first flush of love to be the very best example of what husbandly kindness he is capable. Indeed some men are well-nigh *blind* at first to every fault a woman possesses. If you, the honour of your addresses notwithstanding, are able to speak to me, even whilst proposing marriage, of my faults, and to wound my feelings by speaking so of my family's defects…. I cannot see any possible happiness for me in years to come when my youth and tolerable beauty deserts me and I am left with only your resentment for what I cannot help. If I am to be dependent on my husband's tender care for me, I must see some evidence of tenderness where it is most usually found."

As she spoke, Mr. Darcy coloured and began to look ashamed of himself again. Elizabeth added wearily, "You must see, sir, we should not suit. I am sure that you are deserving of some paragon with everything to recommend her."

Mr. Darcy shook his head in denial but he surprised her by quietly asking, "And what, Miss Bennet, do you suppose yourself to be deserving of? You have said that I surprised you, for which I am at fault, but what sort of man must one be to win the hand that I so covet?"

Here Elizabeth blushed hotly at such frankness. "I had not thought of it. I ought not describe an imaginary being. He does not yet exist except as an ideal." He winced and she pitied him. "Oh, some honest-hearted, kindly squire, I suppose. A good man who adores me. There! Is such a list excessive? Truly I am a vain coward, Mr. Darcy. I think far too well of myself to settle for less and am too afraid of my future to marry simply because I am asked."

"You underrate yourself, Miss Bennet," said Mr. Darcy matter-of-factly. "What other reasons have you to refuse my suit? Come, this is not a comfortable experience for either of us but I must know if there is anything insurmountable."

"We are at cross purposes, sir. I speak of these things to convince you of my sincerity, not to provide you with the twelve labours of Hercules that you must complete."

He was thoughtful. "If your refusal is due to doubt in my ability to care for a woman under my authority, I have the means to provide you with tangible proof to dispel it. You had better meet my sister. I will arrange it."

"Mr. Darcy!" exclaimed Elizabeth, visibly annoyed, "I should not wish to give rise to the speculation that would cause. I daresay that Miss Darcy is everything delightful and if this were my only qualm it might answer."

"Name them."

"Sir?"

"Your qualms, reservations, doubts, and worries that are preventing you from accepting me – name them. If there is aught that I cannot lay to rest, then I shall leave you in peace with only my regret for my failure. It could not be worse than the regret I should feel if I were to retire now while I might secure, with some effort, my happiness for my entire future."

Elizabeth was beginning to find Mr. Darcy extremely tiresome.

"If your sister, sir, of whom you reportedly take such care, came to you with the information that a man had most reluctantly proposed marriage to her but that it was conditional upon her never seeing any of her family again, I wonder what advice you would give her. I daresay that you would be within your rights as her guardian to wonder why you had not been applied to first."

He was pale now. "I can only apologise then, Miss Bennet. I have gone about this wrongly. Your points are sound. Honesty compels me to admit that any man addressing Miss Darcy in such terms and without my approval first sought would find himself ejected from whichever of my properties he had made a nuisance of himself in. It was wrong of me to speak so to you, Miss Bennet. I was so intent on minimising the potential damage to my sister that I have inadvertently hurt you. I am exceedingly sorry."

"It cannot be undone, sir. You are not able to return to the past and properly write to my father nor seek an interview with my brother. Please, let us part and be done with this." She stood, glancing at the mantel clock as she did so.

"Are you unable to forgive me?" he asked bluntly.

Put in such terms, Elizabeth, who had taken two steps to the door, turned to him once again. "Able to? Certainly. I do not believe I am guilty of implacable resentment but...do you not see that such disrespect is no inducement to accept you? If this is your beginning, what would your ending be? My demurral is not based on fanciful imaginations that you can dispel with pretty apologies, Mr. Darcy. Will you not accept my answer, knowing that I have not given it to insult or anger you but to safeguard my own happiness? Is this not a woman's sole right? The only power we have is that of refusal."

"You have a good deal more power than merely that, madam. Have I then, in one atrocious morning, destroyed any hope of success? It cannot be. Do you mean to tell me that there is nothing that I might do that will suffice – even if I should write to your father, this very afternoon to lay before him every instance of my fault and offer my apologies?"

Her eyes widened but she remained silent.

"Would you accept my word that I do respect you?"

"I do not know," said Elizabeth, now feeling quite out of her depth. She had not anticipated this, that such a proud, haughty man should offer to take such a humiliating course of action.

"Miss Bennet, only tell me what I must do and I shall do it, but I beg you – most fervently – that you will not condemn me to a life of heartache and misery on account of what may be atoned for."

So sincere were his words, so unhappy was his tone that Elizabeth found herself rapidly revising all that she knew of the man. She had not ever thought that he might be the object of her pity nor had she considered that he could speak to her in such tones. Solemnity was in his voice but his eyes were fixed on her with something akin to desperation. She would not accept him, to do so would be foolhardy – but perhaps good might be achieved this day that might heal those who had been hurt.

"Mr. Darcy, I cannot possibly marry the man who has injured one of my sisters," she said at length, "yes, I *do* say injured. I shall not bandy around the thoughts and feelings of my dearest sister for public speculation, but suffice it to say that your actions in persuading Mr. Bingley that my sister is a fortune hunter have caused her significant pain. If...if you will repair your fault in this – I do not say that you must whisk Mr. Bingley off to call on Jane and force him to declare himself – but if you will correct the misimpression you have given him of my sister's character, then I will consent to a courtship once you have my father's leave to ask it of me. I do not know that I will, even then, be willing to accept you – even if you do not change your mind, but...."

Thunderstruck, Mr. Darcy nodded at once. "A fair resolution. I do not know whether to be impressed by your astuteness or to wonder how you could have known...."

Elizabeth sighed. "Colonel Fitzwilliam."

"What?! I cannot see how...."

Elizabeth impatiently explained, "Of *course* not. He did not know I was Jane's sister." She wondered if she ought to cease speaking but then burst out, "How *could* you have hurt her so? She is the sweetest and the truest hearted woman in all the earth, never even dreaming that a gentleman could treat her so shabbily as she has been treated – I have known her all my life so I ought to know!" She angrily dashed away a tear and groped for her handkerchief, turning away to dab at her eyes.

"Do not...Miss Bennet, please do not. I have erred – you must know better than anyone the hidden feelings that I have clearly misjudged...I admit my fault freely but I...."

Almost against her will Elizabeth felt the stirrings of amusement in the face of Mr. Darcy's panicked expression and, testing a theory, permitted a small sob to escape and muttered an excuse that she had evidently missed too many walks of recent.

"Miss Bennet, please. I can bear your reproach but it pains me that I have been the cause of your distress. I shall amend all." He rose to his feet and paced. "I must." He made a circuit of the room and knelt at her feet.

Amusement vanished.

"Mr. Darcy, do get up, sir. I am merely overwrought and my head is aching. If the maid or the Collinses come into the room I shall be very hard pressed to dream up an explanation."

He rose and studied her face. "I do not think I have made such a mull of things in all my grown years," he murmured, musingly. "I shall leave you now, Miss Bennet. I have your permission to call upon you in Hertfordshire?"

She nodded, "Provided you rectify the situation with Mr. Bingley, yes, you may call."

"And once I have done so, I may request your father's permission to court you?"

" If you still wish to by then," said she, thinking that a few days reflection might bring her a reprieve. Mr. Darcy might easily regain his confidence in his own superiority and congratulate himself upon his escape. She would certainly not be hoping for his call.

He almost smiled then and his eyes held a curiously tender glow that she could not comfortably bear, "I will still wish it, Miss Bennet. I am quite determined. I shall do all that I can, use every resource that is within my reach, and learn every painful lesson well. I will not give up until I have won you."

Chapter Eleven

It was a far humbler and wearier Mr. Darcy who left the parsonage that afternoon. The confident young man who had knocked on the door less than an hour ago seemed a hazy dream. He departed through the threshold with less hope than he had expected to feel, yet at the same time felt less despair than was rightly deserved.

Once he was in the lane that led him back to Rosings, he swung his gold-topped cane at an errant flower, and crimson-hued petals sailed through the air, over the parsonage wall and out of sight.

His disappointment was great and his regret acute – he had expected, with a certainty that now shamed him, that they would walk this route slowly together to tell his relatives the good news. He had not considered her relatives, nor had he dwelt upon the proper order of things – that her male relatives ought to have been informed first....

Another cheery crocus met its end by his stick.

It was irrelevant for now to think of what he had wanted. It had been inconceivable for a young woman in Miss Bennet's position to refuse him. He had not thought it possible.

She surprised him constantly, had done almost from the first, in fact. Miss Bennet did not behave or speak as he was used to a lady behaving or speaking. There was an almost mannish intelligence about her, a brilliance that he had never before encountered in any of her sex. He found himself constantly wondering what sweetly coated conversational cannonball she would next launch. Elizabeth Bennet was never boring. A tender half-smile crept across his face, swiftly replaced by a grimace.

The worst of the situation was that he could not reasonably blame her for refusing him. His guilt felt heavy on his own shoulders. He had not behaved well, neither had he spoken well – it was little wonder that she had looked so wounded by the end of his botched and ridiculous speech.

By the time she had answered him, he had formed a desperate resolution to evade, at all costs, an absolute refusal. It was imperative that Elizabeth Bennet become his wife. The thought of her living in the world without being constantly in his society was intolerable. He set about persuading her, with the same logical reasoning that had served him well at university, that he ought to be given the opportunity to try again.

His anger at his own wretched stupidity had been temporarily pushed aside – the time for self-castigation would come, but that precious opportunity for private, frank conversation with such a woman was not to be squandered.

Darcy reached Rosings rather more quickly than he had meant to, so lost in his thoughts as he was. His mind was a jumbled mess that needed to be put in order before he decided upon a definite plan of action. Mr. Bennet must be written to, Bingley must be dealt with, not to mention Aunt Catherine….

He was interrupted in his musings by Colonel Fitzwilliam coming out from the library and calling him in. His cousin did not look at all pleased.

"Darcy, a word in private if you will."

" Now, Fitzwilliam? I have many things to do at present."

"Yes, I think now," said he, with decision.

"Very well, but only for a few minutes – I have important letters to write."

"What I have to say will not take long."

Curious now, Darcy followed the colonel into the room and waited expectantly.

With very straight shoulders, his cousin faced him squarely. "Miss Bennet."

Guardedly, being made by this much more uncomfortable than he would care to admit, Darcy responded cautiously, "What of her?"

"Miss Bennet was the young lady you separated from Charles Bingley during the winter."

Wondering what more he would have to face before the day ended, Darcy spoke. "Yes. I misjudged the situation. She did not appear to care for him."

"I must tell you, Darcy, I was most put out with you yesterday for putting me in such a...in such an awkward position as to make such a sweet young lady as Miss Bennet weep on account of my own errant tongue. She was greatly upset. It was abominable.'

"Was she? I am sorry for it. She informed me that I had been incorrect in my assumptions just this afternoon."

"Oh," said the colonel, feeling as though he had arrived at the close of a battle rather than the beginning. "Well, it was very bad of you, Darcy."

Darcy nodded, almost absently. His mind was on other matters and it infuriated his cousin.

"Darcy! You *must* give this matter your attention! You simply cannot be so blasé about reducing a gentlewoman to tears; I know *I* am not. She deserves better."

"Yes, that is certainly true. I did not think she would be so upset. She knows I cannot bear to see her cry."

"What! Explain, man! Can it be possible that you have feelings for the lady, then?"

Mr. Darcy responded in haughty tones, "It is hardly your business, Fitzwilliam, but yes, as a matter of fact, I have asked her to marry me."

"Wha-at?!"

"Do lower your voice, cousin."

"Oh!" he exclaimed loudly once again, then reduced his volume as requested. "You have astounded me, Darcy. Er...you do not appear to be...that is...I mean...."

"She refused me."

"Oh," said the colonel, deflated. Then, "How *extraordinary*," he said slowly, "On account of the Bingley business?"

"Partly, yes. I did not...express myself well."

"Well. I suppose natural nerves and...I'm sorry to hear it, cousin. She's a marvellous woman, of course, can't say fairer than that." Realising belatedly that praising the female who had rejected his cousin was not a good idea, the colonel attempted to be comforting. "I ...er...daresay some fish don't want to be caught, eh? I'm sure there will be another young lady in a few months time and...."

"No," said Darcy, shaking his head decidedly. "I shall convince her to change her mind. She must."

"Darcy, if she's not wanting to be caught by you, then that's that. Some trout will come for a bit of dry bread but some need to be baited better with a nice fat worm, such as your humble servant. In fact, I have been considering myself...."

"Fitzwilliam," spoke the master of Pemberley with terrible finality, "there are two things of which you ought to be aware. Firstly, that Miss Bennet is not a fish and even if she were, this hook is very well baited, I thank you. Secondly, if you have any intentions towards her, you had better bid them farewell."

Nettled, Colonel Fitzwilliam responded, "Darcy, simply because she didn't accept you does not mean she would refuse me – I am considered to be very charming, you know."

"You can't afford her," returned Darcy bluntly, his mood quite soured by jealousy and a smarting conscience.

The hallway clock struck the hour, the deep chime echoing into the room. Fitzwilliam waited for the echoes to fade.

"Is that not for her father to determine?"

"He would very quickly determine that you could not adequately support her once I put a stop to your annuity and bought up your debts."

The colonel laughed at the fine jest. "You are forgetting how well I know you, cousin. You aren't a vindictive man; you didn't even do as much as that when Wickham earned your disfavour."

A certain malicious savagery was present in Mr. Darcy's face as he answered very carefully and clearly so as not to be misunderstood. "I don't think you quite understand the matter, Fitzwilliam. If you take so much as one metaphorical step in Miss Bennet's direction save as her eventual cousin by marriage, I will very deliberately arrange matters so that there could be no possibility of you being considered eligible."

"Hold now, steady on, Darcy," said the colonel, a little alarmed at such uncharacteristic ferocity. "I am your kin, man! You'd not do it. Come – I shall cry friends and withdraw from the field. I wasn't really serious anyhow."

Very quietly, so that his cousin had to lean in a little to hear him, Mr. Darcy made it evident that though the colonel may not have been serious, he was. "I doubt very much that there is anything I would not do, Fitzwilliam – if it meant that she could be brought to marry me."

"I beg your pardon, sirs. I am seeking out Lady Catherine – I was informed that she was on her way to the library. I must have missed her."

Not having heard the library door opening, both men started visibly at the soft, nervous tones of Mrs. Jenkinson, who appeared as though she would rather be anywhere else in the world but in this room seeking out her mistress.

Recovering first, Mr. Darcy gestured with his hand. "As you see, madam, she is not present. May I assist you?"

"N-no, sir. It is just that Miss de Bourgh wishes to see her mother and the footman said that he had seen her come this way but ten minutes ago. I shall ask elsewhere. Forgive me for having disturbed you; it is merely that Miss de Bourgh was adamant that her Ladyship be summoned to her rooms."

"Do not distress yourself; you were right to enter. Fitzwilliam, you are the nearer – pull the bell. The butler will be able to enlighten us as to Lady Catherine's whereabouts. There can certainly be no necessity for you to tire yourself by seeking her out all over the house. Do be seated, Mrs. Jenkinson."

The butler, being summoned, was indeed able to impart the needed information, but, having helpfully done, so was not congratulated upon his professional efficiency.

"Her Ladyship departed approximately five minutes ago in the carriage, sir. The hour had just passed, I believe. Having exited the library, she bade me instruct the stable that they must make it ready immediately. A matter of some urgency, I gather."

Perplexed, Mrs. Jenkinson looked to Colonel Fitzwilliam, who in his turn was looking in open-mouthed dismay at his cousin. Mr. Darcy's eyebrows were raised high on his noble brow. He dismissed the butler politely and shot a warning glance at the colonel, who was evidently feeling unwell, for he started to babble incoherently.

"Do you think? I suppose...I mean, surely…oh *dear*."

"Quite so."

"Should we…?"

Mr. Darcy did not choose to answer the bedlamite; instead, he bowed to the worried Mrs. Jenkinson with great elegance. "I beg you to return to your charge, madam. Colonel Fitzwilliam and I shall seek out her Ladyship and return her to you as shortly as possible."

The two gentlemen left the library with great alacrity. Colonel Fitzwilliam was the speedier in retrieving his hat and gloves and making it out of the house. Mr. Darcy, who had the longer stride, soon overtook him and the two cousins hastened their way on foot towards the parsonage.

They were admitted by the maid, who was seen to be in a state of great excitement at the goings on, and upon nearing the parlour they heard with dread the strident tones of their aunt carrying clearly throughout the house.

"...absolutely insist that you immediately retract your ill-thought refusal even though I cannot for the very life of me fathom *why* my nephew should wish to be allied with a silly little miss who cannot see what is best for her own future."

Mr. Darcy, pale of face but steady of hand, pushed open the door to the parlour to see Lady Catherine de Bourgh and Miss Bennet facing each other with great hostility.

"I cannot either, Lady Catherine." said Elizabeth Bennet, very drily. "I am afraid that he quite neglected to say."

Chapter Twelve

As she finished uttering those blighting words, the door to the parlour swung open to reveal Mr. Darcy, Colonel Fitzwilliam, and a very interested maid. The maid was easily dealt with by a raised eyebrow and direct stare; the other occupants of the room were not, alas, likely to be so quickly dismissed.

Elizabeth knew a moment of shame when her eyes met Mr. Darcy's – the expression in them was one of wounded feelings. She felt that she was hardly in a position to complain of him hurting her pride if she went about trampling over his. Mr. Darcy raised an eyebrow as if to offer aid. She quickly made a decision to accept any ally available to her, but hoped he would not see her current need of him as encouragement. Had it just been herself and Lady Catherine, she could have quite possibly managed the woman with a little stretching of the truth and a great deal of circumspection.

Sadly, Lady Catherine had arrived at the parsonage in high dudgeon, most indignant on behalf of her favourite sister's only son, at the same time that the Collinses had returned from their duties in the village, so the little parlour was quite overcrowded.

Neither her brother nor her sister was likely to be the least bit of help – Mary was looking too astonished even to speak and her brother was in the decidedly uncomfortable position of being torn asunder in his loyalties. With some dark amusement, she considered the effect of reminding the assembled gathering that no man can serve two masters at once. Perhaps not, although whatever his faults, she suspected that Mr. Darcy might understand the quip.

"Ah! Mary dearest – you are positively inundated with callers today; here are Mr. Darcy and the good colonel. It is not strictly the hour for calls but I daresay I can hunt down the cook if you wish me to?" said Elizabeth, with great sweetness, hoping to rouse her sister out of her awkward stupor and into her duties as a hostess.

Mrs. Collins started and began to stammer. "Oh. Yes, I mean. No, Lizzy, I shall go myself, thank you. I am sure there are some biscuits to s-serve with the tea." Then, recollecting herself, curtsied to the gentlemen, "I beg your pardon; welcome to you, Mr. Darcy, and you also, Colonel Fitzwilliam. Do sit down; I shall be back directly. Lizzy, you will not mind sitting on the stool by Mr. Collins, will you? I fear that there aren't enough chairs in here at present." With that, she quit the room, deeply regretting that etiquette manuals did not cover such a situation as one's elder sister rejecting the richest man of their acquaintance who also happened to be the nephew of one's irate patroness. It was all very awkward, and for some reason she could not quite name, she felt decidedly annoyed that she had been put in such a position.

Elizabeth, feeling as though she were in a farce, nodded at the men and retreated from the field to sit on the low stool beside Mr. Collins's chair. Mr. Collins looked down at her worriedly and opened his mouth once or twice before opting for neutral silence. Fond of his sister-in-law he might be – indeed he believed her the embodiment of every admirable feminine virtue – but he felt quite unequal to the task of calling Lady Catherine to task for her (he was forced to admit it) uncivil behaviour.

Lady Catherine consented to be led to the most comfortable seat in the parsonage by her military nephew, and Mr. Darcy went to sit beside her.

He took a moment to draw a fortifying breath and began. "You have been misled, Aunt Catherine. Miss Bennet has most kindly given her consent to my calling on her in Hertfordshire pending her father's permission. There is also a matter that I must amend in town before I can do so. No fault lies with Miss Bennet for her refusal – I was precipitous."

This was a very charitable speech, coming from Mr. Darcy, thought Elizabeth. Having blamed only himself, he had rescued her brother from Lady Catherine's ire. Poor Mr. Collins was sat beside her not knowing what to do with himself. He did not know if he ought to look cross with his sister or defensive on her behalf. How did one reprove a lady that Mr. Darcy himself approved of? One did not. He gaped again and grunted, hoping it might pass muster.

Mr. Darcy aided him at a pleading glance from Elizabeth. "Miss Bennet was most indignant on your behalf, Mr. Collins, that I should have paid my addresses to her without first seeking your consent as her temporary guardian. I apologise, sir. I can only offer my regrets that I did not consider it."

Mr. Collins graciously waved his hand, which was supposed to indicate that any apology from such a great gentleman as Mr. Darcy was entirely unnecessary. "No indeed, sir; I would not have you give it a moment's thought."

Deciding that Mr. Collins ought to be cultivated, Darcy turned to address his aunt. "I do not think that this conversation ought to take place with so large an audience, madam. I am sure that if you will return with us to Rosings, I can allay any concerns you might have without imposing on the hospitality of the Collinses or causing Miss Bennet any more upset than she has endured already today."

"I came to speak with Miss Bennet on your behalf, Darcy, and I shall not go away until I am satisfied with the outcome. If your natural modesty has caused you to underrate yourself in your propositions, then the situation must be rectified. My dearest sister would wish it, I am convinced."

Glancing at Miss Bennet, who had bitten her lip at the thought of Mr. Darcy being considered modest, with a questioning look and receiving a minute nod, Mr. Darcy turned his head to address Mr. Collins once more, just as his wife entered with the tea tray.

Tea was poured and thoughts were collected in a civilised fashion. Lady Catherine even unbent so far as to commend Mrs. Collins on the preparation of the blend. Mrs. Collins replied with the mundane details, and Colonel Fitzwilliam, having felt rather useless in general, leapt in to aid the polite topic along.

Mr. Darcy sat near Elizabeth and spoke to her in a low voice, with Mr. Collins at her other side pretending that he was quite deaf. Doubtless he would one day make a most excellent chaperone, should he be blessed with daughters.

"I must again beg your pardon, Miss Bennet. I had thought that my conversation with my cousin was a private one. I fear that Lady Catherine wished to advocate for me and instead has had quite the opposite effect to the one she has intended."

Elizabeth sipped her tea thoughtfully. "I daresay, sir, that we can both be blind to the faults of our relatives on account of our great regard for them. You need not apologise for the doings of others, Mr. Darcy."

"I see."

"If you think that permitting Lady Catherine to present her case, or your case, as it were, will soothe any ruffled feathers and so make things easier for my sister and brother, then I am willing to listen. I will not make wild promises to her once she has done so, but perhaps if we were in a more private setting...."

"You are a very kind woman, Miss Bennet," he said sincerely. "I ought to have said so sooner, I think. Do not concern yourself; I believe

I may manage my aunt once she has climbed down from the rafters. We had better go into another room."

Elizabeth blushed. and Lady Catherine, looking over at that moment, looked pleased and said something in a low voice to Colonel Fitzwilliam. Mrs. Collins went to fuss over the tea tray and the two were left to themselves.

Mr. Darcy quietly asked Mr. Collins if he might have the use of his book room to speak to Miss Bennet with his aunt present. Apparently unable to deny Mr. Darcy anything, the clergyman readily agreed, apologising profusely for its smallness but pointing out its excellent view of the road in compensation.

The three of them left Mrs. Collins's parlour and once again caught the maid loitering in the hallway. When faced with the displeased stares of Lady Catherine, Mr. Darcy, and Miss Bennet, she did not feel so much like enjoying the situation and she bobbed a hasty curtsey.

Darcy held open the door for the ladies and, with a pointed look at his aunt, ensured that the latch was properly clicked shut. To her credit, Lady Catherine merely raised a brow at him, shrugging elegantly, and addressed Miss Bennet.

"Well now, Miss Bennet. I make no apology for my intrusion into your sister's parlour this afternoon, much as my nephews might wish I would. My own sister, Miss Bennet – the Lady Anne Fitzwilliam – considered herself pleased to accept the Darcys of Pemberley as the quality family that they were – indeed as they still are. If the daughter of an earl – a woman of considerable intellect and character – did not spurn such an alliance, what possible reason might you have to hesitate?"

"I have explained my reasons for my reluctance to Mr. Darcy, Your Ladyship. I am very aware of the very great honour that Mr. Darcy has bestowed. I hope I did not give the impression, sir, that I found you in any way lacking."

"Miss Bennet, there can be no reproaching *your* conduct," said he, very gently.

"Well then! That shows some sense at least. I am glad that my estimation of you was not far out, but then I am so rarely wrong in these things. You could not find a finer man than my nephew, Miss Bennet. You may think me a partial old woman, and perhaps I am, but I will say this for him – he is not at all like some of the other, less worthy young men you might find of similar rank and station. I cannot think of any woman of marriageable age that would not leap at the opportunity to step into my sister's shoes at Pemberley and yet you will not. Why? There can be no fault found in my nephew."

Gravely, Mr. Darcy thanked his aunt for such a lively defence. The sarcasm was completely lost on her and she accepted his gratitude as her due.

Elizabeth slowly defended herself. "I confess myself most confused, Lady Catherine. I would have thought that you would baulk at the suggestion I should be married into your...er...*august* family. I have heard from more than one source that you had intended Mr. Darcy to wed Miss de Bourgh. I do not say this to bandy about idle gossip, but as we are speaking so frankly at present I can see no harm in it. I should not in the least wish to supplant Miss de Bourgh."

"From whom can you have heard such a thing?" exclaimed Lady Catherine, blithely ignoring the truth of the gossip.

Unwilling to damage her brother's standing with his patroness and having learnt from the colonel yesterday that Mr. Wickham's name was not one to be uttered, Elizabeth searched in her head for an acceptable answer.

"From Mrs. Garron, I believe." said she, after the briefest of hesitations, feeling secure in the knowledge that Lady Catherine could not possibly vent her wrath on a dead woman.

Mr. Darcy looked at Elizabeth penetratingly and she lowered her gaze to her lap, afraid that she might be caught out. She was reminded once again that this was not a stupid man who would readily believe anything a young lady might say. He said nothing, however, but returned his stare to the other occupant of the room, who was presently ignoring the commonly held belief that one ought not to speak ill of the dead.

Once having exhausted that train of thought, Lady Catherine returned to her subject with all the single-mindedness of a harrier after its prey.

"I suppose you are to be commended for your consideration of my and my daughter's feelings, Miss Bennet. I am able to assure you that there is no such intention and you are therefore free to marry my nephew with my blessing. A better match you could not wish for, I am certain."

Alarmed at the satisfied finality in her voice, Elizabeth responded quickly, "Your Ladyship is very generous. I am sure that once I am able to speak to my father, he will advise me what is best to be done. I do not feel that such a...a momentous decision should be rushed into. Mr. Darcy must excuse me from committing myself before I have considered all of the ramifications."

He was beaten to excusing her by his aunt.

"Hmmm. I suppose that shows wisdom. Too many young girls nowadays rush headlong to accept the first offer that they are given and give no thought to how they will cope with the demands of being a wife. When you *do* accept my nephew, you may be assured that I will be *most* willing to guide you."

Her eyes wide, Elizabeth looked vaguely panicked and managed to stammer out her thanks. Mr. Darcy, evidently feeling that Miss Bennet had endured enough that day, stood.

"Let us leave Miss Bennet to her thoughts, Aunt. I am sure that you will be wanting to see Anne immediately. Mrs. Jenkinson sought you in the library – she was asking for you, I believe."

Curious, Elizabeth silently observed Lady Catherine's now pinched expression and the comforting hand Mr. Darcy laid on her shoulder, and drew her own, fairly accurate, conclusions.

They returned to the parlour to take their leave of the Collinses. Lady Catherine, now pleased with her measure of success, did so with gracious condescension. Mr. Collins, evidently relieved by this, regained his tongue and took the opportunity to pontificate upon his dear sister's good nature and obedience.

"Such a docility of spirit is sadly *rarely* seen. Why, I recall that in this very room, she has often been required to give up her walks, which my dear Mary says she prizes dearly, and has not once even murmured at the difficulty it leaves her in. Not the smallest *particle* of defiance is in her, I am *sure* of it."

Elizabeth, on edge, shot a glance to the colonel, who looked ironically amused but shook his head at her. This silent exchange was not lost on Mr. Darcy, who shepherded him out of the room to hand his aunt into her carriage. Before quitting the room himself, he addressed Elizabeth.

"Have you, in truth, been obliged to walk out less than you would wish?"

"I have done so less than I am used to at Longbourn, yes, sir."

He sighed, "I see. I will have a man sent over every day to escort you while you are here then. I did not consider that there would not be a manservant readily available. It is little wonder that you were so quiet at Rosings that evening."

"You do not think that I was merely overawed by the exalted company in which I found myself, sir?"

Unexpectedly, he laughed quietly and bowed over her hand in farewell, "I stand corrected, Miss Bennet. I had forgotten the small matter of your docility of spirit. What time do you habitually take your walks? I shall add it to the very top of my list of things that must be done in order to please Miss Bennet."

Feeling more in charity with him than she had ever done, she smiled and told him, and then he left.

Those who lived at the parsonage returned to the room once their visitors had left them, feeling they had emerged from a very dangerous ordeal relatively unscathed.

Mary looked at the too innocent expression on Elizabeth's face.

"Lizzy," she said ponderously, "do you not suppose you could…."

"No," said Elizabeth, very firmly, "I most certainly could not."

She went to bed that night with her thoughts in no better order than when she had awoken that morning. Her mind was crammed full of more bewildering information than she could possibly deal with at once – it must be sifted through, as Lydia did her ribbons to decide upon the prettiest.

First, and most important – Mr. Darcy apparently loved her.

Second – she had narrowly managed to avoid enraging her relatives and his in the process of heading him off. She would have to find a way of getting him to accept a refusal at some point. That could be thought of later.

Third, and most surprising of all – Mr. Darcy had a very pleasant laugh.

With that, Lizzy closed her eyes and knew no more until morning.

Chapter Thirteen

The time that Elizabeth had remaining in Kent seemed to her to pass with all the speed of Mrs. Garron's funeral dirge. There was too much to be done, yet at the same time too much time was left to idleness.

Mr. Darcy was true to his word and a man was sent every morning to accompany her on her walks. She did not know whose servant he was; they did not engage in conversation. He was there, said Mr. Darcy, to ensure her safety as she went wherever she was pleased to go. As a result of this, Elizabeth found herself, in the last week of her visit, able to see more of the beautiful countryside than she had in all the previous days she had been there.

The return to regular exercise did much to cheer her and she found that when they were once again invited to dine at Rosings, she was able to bear the experience with greater equanimity than she might otherwise have done.

Mercifully, the subject of Mr. Darcy's strange affection for her was not audibly raised by anyone, yet the air was heavy with the knowledge of it. Whilst it was never openly discussed, it was clear that expectation was present; it was apparent for example, in the way the gentleman escorted her into dinner without so much as a blink from anyone else there, in the proprietary manner in which he pulled out her chair for her to be seated, and in the knowledgeable way he pressed her favourite dishes upon her notice – evidently he had been studying her preferences every previous time they had been together. It made her feel uneasy.

The expectation was clearer than ever when the gentlemen from Rosings came to take their leave a few days before her own departure. Colonel Fitzwilliam was his usual affable self, but knowing of his cousin's interest, was a little more reserved with his charm than on previous meetings. He at least, like his aunt, clearly considered a marriage to be a foregone conclusion. Mr. Darcy was at pains to better himself in her estimation and seemed to recognise instinctively that the courtship period had not yet begun and therefore ought not to be discussed before the actual fact. She was gently civil to him in return for his forbearance and she even went so far as to tease him lightly about the long competitive race to London that he was likely to have with his cousin. Such lively conversation from her seemed to please him immensely.

Elizabeth felt a measure of flustered anxiety when he bowed solemnly over her hand on that last visit and pressed it between his own fingers as he straightened, looking down at her face as though she were something worthy of fascination. She ruthlessly chided herself for being so susceptible to the flattering attention of an important man. Really, she thought, it was far preferable when she had assumed that he held her in contempt.

The last day, sans Mr. Darcy, was spent packing her trunks, willfully ignoring Lady Catherine's advice on the correct way to do so, and taking leave of the few acquaintances she had made in Hunsford itself. She had become quite a favourite with the shopkeepers, being friendly enough despite her obvious quality, and any new face in a confined and unvarying society must be looked upon with great favour.

She called also at Rosings, to take her leave of Lady Catherine and her daughter, Miss de Bourgh now being well enough to sit quietly by the fire again, and she knew a pang of remorse at her own glib thoughts of that young lady. Self-obsessed she might be, but looking at that pale drawn face and the sunken eyes that spoke of pain, Elizabeth despised herself for her lack of compassion. How could she have not seen it before? She was learning rapidly that her judgment was not so sound as she had thought it, but how was it that the clear signs of illness, not merely in the lady's conversation, had so escaped her?

She had blindly seen what she expected to see in a wealthy young lady related to so proud a man as Mr. Darcy, and it shamed her. She exerted herself that last morning to enquire, in her sweetest voice, as to the wellbeing of Miss de Bourgh, earning herself such a speaking look of approval and gratitude from the mother that she found herself shamed twice over.

If she found the resultant enthusiastic monologue tiresome, she valiantly concealed it and felt that had she comported herself so from the beginning, she might have been prouder of herself. It was a lesson that she resolved to learn, even if it was a difficult one.

Miss de Bourgh, when they rose to leave, was moved to extend a thin, shaking hand and wish her very well. "I have heard, Miss Bennet, that you may well become kin to us. I am glad of it – fresh healthy blood is what is needed in our family even if I may not benefit by it. I do not know if I will see you again so I must offer my felicitations in advance of them being necessary. No, don't look so very embarrassed, Miss Bennet – I am merely finding that my mother's plain speaking is occasionally necessary as time grows shorter. Should you wish to write to me, I will be glad to read any letter you send. You will forgive me for not seeing you to the door; I must retire to my room again. God bless you, Miss Bennet."

Mrs. Jenkinson escorted her charge out and Elizabeth found her eyes wet. Lady Catherine nodded briskly at her and turned away to mop her own eyes.

"You will write, Miss Bennet – a lively, happy letter for my daughter? I am certain she will enjoy that."

There was naught Elizabeth could do, no wrangling words she could utter, to avoid it. It was impossible to do anything other than promise that she would – her smarting conscience would not permit her even to try.

The next morning, a carriage awaited them outside the Hunsford parsonage. Mr. Collins and Mary were to accompany Elizabeth back to Meryton – no other escort was available and Mary had shyly and privately expressed a wish to her husband that she might consult her mother on one or two things. Mr. Collins, after a lengthy silence and a little more oblique hinting, had eventually understood what was *not* said, and caught his wife up in his arms with an exuberant joy that startled and delighted her.

The trio of travellers did not converse a great deal on the journey home, too preoccupied with their own thoughts and feelings to desire entertainment. They passed the known landmarks with little more than a comment or two and then lapsed into companionable silence.

They were met on the steps of Longbourn by Mr. Bennet, Mrs. Bennet, and a giggling Kitty and Lydia. The Collinses were very civilly made welcome and Mary made much fuss of by her mama. Mr. Bennet, having dismissed his married daughter with a pat on the cheek and a "Well well, my Mary – he has been taking good care of you, has he not? You are looking quite...quite pretty, my dear. Ah! Elizabeth…" and here he waved a sheet of closely written paper, "you will be able to spare your aged father a few moments of your time in my library once you have refreshed yourself, I daresay."

Curious beyond measure and half suspecting the identity of the writer of the letter in his hand, Elizabeth curtseyed with great formality and obsequiously assured him that her joy was to do his bidding as soon as was humanly possible.

Mr. Collins, overhearing, nodded approvingly, and Mr. Bennet – upon whom sarcasm was not lost – chuckled and sent her on her way.

She hastened to change out of her travelling clothes, and entered her father's private sanctuary with a light knock that belied the trepidation she was feeling.

"Well, Papa, have you had numerous letters from the lords and dukes of London begging for the honour of Jane's fair hand?"

This opening volley earnt her a smirk and she began to relax.

"Not this time, my dear, although such epistles would surprise me *considerably* less than the one I received yesterday morning. I do not suppose you would care to guess who would write me such an astonishing letter, would you, Lizzy?"

"I fear my poor guessing abilities would only serve to disappoint you, but I can fetch Mama if that is the sort of entertainment you desire. Doubtless you will enlighten me as to your meaning before dinner this evening, sir?"

"Hmmph. Mr. Collins and Lady Catherine de Bourgh haven't managed to cure you of your impertinence, I see." He attempted to look stern but was never proof against the mischievous sparkle in his favourite daughter's bright eyes. "Ah, very well. Mr. Fitzwilliam Darcy of Pemberley has written to me. There now, it is time to be serious."

"Is his name Fitzwilliam? I had not heard that it was." Was all Elizabeth would say, though she was now burning with curiosity.

"Lizzy, you aren't going to pretend ignorance, are you?" asked Mr. Bennet, sounding disappointed. "I had rather thought you above such feminine ploys."

"Did you, Papa? 'Tis a dreadful thing to have one's daughters demonstrate their more female faults, I am sure."

"Yes," he said testily, "it can be quite irksome. Let us speak plainly now, if you please. Mr. Darcy has written this letter to me wishing to express his sincere contrition for his *conduct* and I require an explanation if you please. Has he harmed you?"

"What?!" cried Elizabeth, exceedingly distressed. "No, Papa! He proposed to me in a less than flattering manner and that is all really. If he has described his manner as ungentlemanly then he has grossly exaggerated his faults. I am all amazement – did he indeed write such a thing?"

"He proposed to you," said Mr. Bennet flatly. "Is that all?"

"Y-yes. I do not know what he was about; I daresay he would offer a servant a position in his household with more charm – I was offended, of course, and meant to refuse him outright but his aunt is Lady Catherine, you know, so it was necessary to speak to him calmly. He appears to have listened."

Mr. Bennet tossed the letter on his desk. "Very well then, your reports align. We may proceed with the matter knowing that I have the truth of it."

"Oh," said Elizabeth, feeling affronted at having been managed with such skill. "Would it not have been easier to just ask me, sir?"

"I attempted to, Elizabeth – but *you* were being evasive."

"I beg your pardon then, Papa. It is a Gordian knot I have got myself into. So he didn't actually write that he had behaved in an ungentlemanlike manner?"

"Not in so many words, no, but I believe he meant to communicate that he has been raised to speak to a young lady with rather better manners than the ones he has shown you. No, I shan't hand it over for your perusal, my dear. Perhaps one day. I will instead read you whichever passages I feel you would find helpful."

Elizabeth raised her brows at this and dropped the hand that had crept of its own volition across the desk. She did so dislike being coerced without knowing the point her father wished her to get to.

"What do you advise me to do then, Papa? I have told Mr. Darcy that if he does not change his mind...I beg your pardon?"

"Not a thing, Lizzy."

"Really? I was certain you were attempting to speak."

"No, no," returned Mr. Bennet with equal gravity, "Do carry on – this is most entertaining. You were about to convince me that Mr. Darcy is a flighty, capricious young man who proposes to a young woman of limited connections and wealth at the drop of a handkerchief. Having done so and being put off, he writes a very proper letter to her father and then...then simply abandons his case? Do I have the right of it, my love?"

Elizabeth opened and shut her mouth a few times before loftily ignoring the bait and continuing with dignity. "*Should* Mr. Darcy elect to come into Hertfordshire, and pending your *gracious* permission to court me, I have told him that he might do so but that I would make no promises as to the outcome."

"Ah. Very fair of you."

"Is it? I have no intention of marrying the man but I cannot see how he can be put off permanently without causing grave offence."

"You had better allow him to make his case then." Mr. Bennet's eyes were twinkling. "He is an intelligent fellow if I am any judge – which I *am* – and clearly very motivated."

"And when I reject him? What then?"

"You are so very sure that you do not like him?"

"I...well, of course, I do not yet...."

"Yet what?"

"Yet I am afraid that my judgment is not so accurate as all that. The evidence against him is...well I do not think it to be entirely sound."

"So new judgments must be formed," said Mr. Bennet, still vastly entertained but with a certain sternness in his face now.

"I suppose so."

"You suppose so? Lizzy, I should not wish for you to wed a man you cannot respect, but to throw away a *good* man – of good sense and good character – on a whim is not what I think best for you."

"What was in that letter? It must have been a fascinating read if you are able to draw *such* conclusions from its contents. How do you know he has not misrepresented himself to you?"

"Do you think the man a liar?"

"I was not saying that at all, sir." Lizzy grumbled, outmanoeuvred once again, "No, of course I do not. If anything he is a little *too* honest."

"Ahh. Now we come to the salient point. He has trampled on your pride and so he must needs be the worst of all men."

Elizabeth was silent as she digested this. "'Tis a very lowering thought, Papa." she said after a while in a small voice. "Have I been blinded by my vanity? It is possible, I suppose, but I do not see how I could have accepted such a proposal as the one he tendered."

"Yes, I should rather enjoy an account of that one day. My little Lizzy, you need not accept any man merely because he speaks eloquently and well of his all-encompassing passion for you – in fact such a man is probably very well practiced at making such speeches to other young ladies…."

"Papa!"

"But that is by the by. If Mr. Darcy, who I can assure you is *not* accustomed to demeaning himself by writing letters of apology to minor country squires, is able to humble himself in order to mend his bridges with you…surely that must speak in favour of his suit when he offers for you again."

Chapter Fourteen

T he next morning, it was a matter of some importance for Elizabeth to walk out, once breakfast was finished with, to call upon her friend Charlotte at Lucas Lodge.

Charlotte was ever a fount of sensible, rational advice that Elizabeth valued greatly, and in her current state of uncertainty, she had set herself the task of gathering as many opinions from her loved ones as possible. Of all people, her friend had her best interests in mind and perhaps would present some argument either way that would aid her to come to a clearer understanding of her own mind in regards to Mr. Darcy.

She was given a very ready welcome by the Lucas family, with whom she was quite a favourite and by whom she had been much missed. Lizzy patiently answered many questions regarding her visit to Kent, and by the time she had fully satisfied Sir William's curiosity regarding the grandeur of Rosings she was very willing to accompany Charlotte to call upon the Brown family, who relied much upon the good works of the wealthier families in the neighbourhood.

They set off, with Elizabeth commandeering the heavy basket on the short walk that took them to the overcrowded little cottage on the outskirts of town.

"Oh how pleasant it is to be home, dear Charlotte – you cannot imagine how I have wished to see familiar faces this last week."

"And you with such a spirit for sightseeing, Eliza. Was Kent so very dull then?"

"I protest such a poor drawing of my character, as though I should only miss those who are dear to me if I am suffering ennui. Surely my absence must have been a relief if I am so very shallow."

Smiling, Miss Lucas slipped her arm through her friend's and matched her pace along the path.

"You have been much missed, as well you must know, but I had been quite set in my mind that you should be so satisfied in exploring parts unknown that your father would well-nigh have had to order your return. I confess you have surprised me with your fondness for the familiar."

"Oh, Charlotte, I will yet surprise you more. Mr. Darcy – I believe I mentioned that he was in Kent – is desirous of marrying me."

Charlotte's hand slipped from the crook of Elizabeth's arm and she stopped walking abruptly.

Enjoying her friend's astonishment immensely, Elizabeth waited patiently for the information to sink in properly.

With her customary good sense, Miss Lucas did not seek clarification of that which had already been said, nor did she require reminding as to the specific gentleman being referenced.

"I see. How...how delightful." Then, resuming her steps, "I suppose you have not yet answered him?"

"Now how can you possibly know that, oh wise Charlotte?"

"You would not tell me if you had refused him, and I daresay you would have announced an engagement to such a man in a much grander fashion."

Elizabeth acknowledged this with a nod. "He is to return to Hertfordshire soon, I believe – he wishes to court me."

"And?"

"And I am inclined to permit it."

"You are inclined--Elizabeth!" cried Charlotte, sounding offended.

"What is it?"

"Have you *no* comprehension of your good fortune?"

"Oh! Well yes. I am very flattered, of course. It is just that it has been a very odd couple of weeks for me. I don't believe I have felt so wrong-footed before in my life. I am in dire need of counsel."

"Well, if you would like my humble advice, you will say, 'Thank you kindly, Mr. Darcy,' and grasp a secure future with both hands."

"Would you?" asked Elizabeth curiously.

"*Obviously.*"

"Before knowing, *truly* knowing, his character? I accept, and I will tell you why presently, that I have been sadly blind as to Mr. Darcy, but it doesn't follow that I know enough of him to wed the man."

Charlotte almost shrugged, "If you know enough of him to be sure that he is respectable, I do not see a reason for hesitation. I daresay an engagement period would suffice to give you a more thorough painting of his virtues and his failings."

Elizabeth smiled and shook her head. "I suppose I am to brand myself a jilt then, in the eventuality that I discover something I do not like in him."

Her friend had little patience for this. "Eliza, how many married people do you suppose think each other the very pattern card of perfection for the entirety of their lives? Infatuation fades – you know that it does; if you can respect your spouse based on the entirety of their being rather than loving them for their few temporary virtues, I daresay you will have as much chance as anyone to live a contented life, and as Mrs. Darcy you would have a respectable position and income to aid you in that contentment."

She would not be moved in her opinion, and Elizabeth quickly gave up trying to show her friend why the prospect of marrying a man she knew little about frightened her so. It would not, she believed, be so very bad if he were a lesser mortal – a humble parson for example, but to become the wife of Mr. Darcy seemed a greater risk somehow than marriage to another man might be. Perhaps when Jane arrived on the morrow, she might be brought to understand and take her part.

Charlotte once again freely dispensed her advice to Elizabeth before they parted company and suggested that with regards to Mr. Wickham, her father might be appealed to on the matter if Mr. Bennet would not bestir himself as his daughter half suspected he might not. The ladies bade each other farewell once Mrs. Brown had been visited and the basket of groceries delivered.

Upon returning home, having enjoyed wandering familiar paths in the warm sunshine, Lizzy went directly to her father's study. He was deep in a Greek text when she entered but he bade her come in and sit herself down when she requested admittance. Encouraged by this great fatherly sacrifice on his part, she did so.

"Papa, I am once again in need of your advice – this time in regards to Mr. Wickham."

"Wickham, eh? I had heard that he was engaged to Miss King, though not officially by all accounts. Has he been making up to you too? You will soon have a score of suitors if you do not decide upon Mr. Darcy, my dear – perhaps this is why you are in such a quandary over the man. Did Miss Lucas not give you suitable advice?"

"Nothing of the kind, sir, although I am deeply touched by your apparent faith in my popularity. I am to attribute such bias to paternal affection, I suppose."

"That, or senility. Out with it, Elizabeth – my tolerance is not so high as all that."

"I have had it from two separate sources that Mr. Wickham is not a man to be trusted – that is to say, he is not at all *honest*. The sources are, I am coming to believe, reliable. Before I left Hertfordshire it was hinted that Miss King has been told a similar tale to the one Mr. Wickham had related to me – a tale concerning his past dealings with Mr. Darcy that I now understand to have been slanderous."

"And you want me to bar him from the house or run the man out of town based upon this string of suppositions?"

"You could if you wished to, sir, but I was rather thinking you might prefer to investigate the matter more thoroughly – given your most excellent advice to me yesterday afternoon regarding the collection of evidence and forming good judgments."

Mr. Bennet put down his book and sighed. "Do you know, Lizzy, I suspected from the very first that you would cause me great tedious exertion one day. Very well, my dear, you may rely upon me to seek out information. I don't suppose it will stop you and Miss Lucas wangling Sir William around your little fingers but yes, I will make enquiries when I have the time. Off you go now, my love."

"Yes, Papa, of course...but...."

"What is it *now*, child?"

"Kitty and Lydia, sir. Charlotte says that she was alarmed on their behalf last week at the assembly on account of their familiarity with some of the officers."

Mr. Bennet laughed. "*No*, Elizabeth. Your mother was there to supervise them; it has nothing to do with me. I should think you would be encouraging their silliness yourself if it would drive Mr. Darcy off and save you the effort of having to make use of your assessment skills. Leave me in peace, Elizabeth – Odysseus is in as lively a quandary as you are, except with Scylla and Charybdis."

Elizabeth retreated to her bedchamber to change from her outdoor clothes. Once done, she sat upon her bed in deep thought, staring out of the window for the space of ten minutes.

Hearing the sound of giggles from the room that Kitty and Lydia shared, she reached for the small paper-wrapped parcels she had brought from Kent and went to find them.

They bade her come in their lively, good-humoured way and she paused at the threshold before doing so. Her sisters made a pretty picture together, sat at the window seat, Kitty holding up two pink scarves in the light for Lydia's approval.

"Oh, the one on the left, Kitty, certainly; the peachier pink would turn your complexion to sallow as soon as you put it on. The rose is far superior."

Mulishly, Kitty complied and tossed the ill-favoured peach scarf back on the bed. It was a trial to her, but Lydia had an eye for colour; it could not be denied.

Elizabeth came forward. "I bring consolation, Kitty dear, for all that Lydia is correct. Here is a small trifle I have brought you from Kent. I did not shop overmuch but there was a delightful little haberdashery shop there that you would probably impoverished yourselves in. Also for you, Lydia – I did think the blue for you – yes, I see I was correct."

Never was a Bennet sister so popular, never was family harmony so apparent as when a traveller returned with gifts. Lydia and Kitty exclaimed with delight over their new gloves; Lydia received a delicate powder blue pair and Kitty a soft pink. Lizzy received their fond embraces and sat upon their bed awaiting their attention.

"Are you going to scold us now, Lizzy?" asked Lydia pertly, "Charlotte did threaten to snitch on us."

Lizzy laughed lightly, "Am I your keeper, Lydia? You are clever enough to avoid stepping into *outright* improper behaviour – not least because it would quite ruin your own chances at snaring a respectable man."

"La! What a dull thought. I daresay I shall wed an officer after all, you know."

"That would be a waste of your charms, Lydia. If I were you I should wait for at least a colonel or a man of higher rank to propose – you would not like to live on a smaller income than Mary, I am sure of it."

Lydia, listening even as she admired how dainty her new gloves looked on her hands, snorted at this.

"Lizzy! How can you compare me to *Mary!*"

"It is a good comparison. You have the same background, even if your characters are so different – but even Mary, now that she is Mrs. Collins and on a comfortable income, must make do with a maid, a cook, and a manservant – she has to help with the household tasks, you know."

"Scrubbing floors!?" asked Lydia, clearly struck with horror at the very thought.

"Nothing so drastic as that, but she has found it necessary to help with waxing the furniture and the like."

Lydia's mouth dropped open. She was a bright girl and quickly arrived at the point Elizabeth wished her to. "And an officer would be even less likely to have more servants, would he not? Horrid thought. What a pity it is that the dashing young men must be so poor. I suppose you are right, Lizzy – it would be a waste. I do not at all wish to do servants' work."

Kitty, who had been listening intently, joined the conversation. "But surely, Lizzy, we do not all need to marry clergymen like Mary."

Elizabeth grimaced and hoped Mr. Collins and Mary had gone out. Longbourn's walls were not the thickest between the bedrooms.

"Mary made a very *good* match, Kitty. Mr. Collins is a clergyman with the prospect of inheritance – it is only for the duration of Papa's life that Mary must make do as she does now. After that she will be the mistress of this estate."

This thought sobered the girls and Elizabeth thought her point had been driven home amply.

"Speaking of marriage, I have news to impart to you, and advice to ask."

They were all rapt attention.

"When I was in Kent I received a proposition that I am considering."

Kitty squealed and Lydia burst out, "Oh, you sly thing! To keep such a thing from us until now – who is it?"

"It is a secret."

"Well, we won't tell anyone!" exclaimed Kitty, with all the confidence of a young woman who had never kept a secret for more than two days together.

Lydia giggled.

"You must not tell anyone, Kitty," said Lizzy, firmly, "for if you do and word gets out, then I will be quite committed and unable to do anything but marry the man. I do not yet know if I want to."

Kitty nodded seriously, and Lydia, still giggling, assured her that she would not say anything that might cause Elizabeth difficulties.

"Very well then. It is Mr. Darcy."

Lydia picked up the discarded peach scarf and threw it at her sister's head.

"Wretch! I truly thought you had some delightful secret to tell. How can you tease us so?"

Amused, Elizabeth threw the scarf back. "Peach does not at all become me, thank you, Lydia. I am indeed in earnest. Mr. Darcy, the very same Mr. Darcy who was here with Mr. Bingley in the autumn, was visiting his aunt, Lady Catherine, and has asked to court me."

The scarf dropped to the floor.

"Elizabeth! He is so *rich!*" cried her vulgar youngest sister.

"His wealth is entirely beside the point if I do not marry him – it affects us not at all."

"What on earth can you want our advice for, Lizzy?" asked Kitty, shocked.

"I am undecided as to what to do. On the one hand, as you so helpfully pointed out, Lydia, he is very wealthy and I could secure the futures of all of my dear sisters and aid them in finding good matches for themselves. On the other hand – he is so very strict in his notions of proper behaviour…. I should not wish to burden you – who are so charmingly high spirited – with behaving in a dull, decorous way."

Kitty was much touched by this and said so, but Lydia cried, "Why on earth should your marrying such a strict man affect us? I am sure I do not care in the least what Mr. Darcy might think of *me*."

"Because if he approved of you and your conduct, he might permit me to invite you to town for a season."

"London! Oh what a promise of fun! Lizzy, do you mean it?!"

"Acquit me, I have not promised. Neither to you nor to Mr. Darcy. If...*if* I decide to marry him – and I am inclined to think some good could come of it if I did – it must necessarily alter your behaviour – the sisters of Mr. Darcy would have a very great advantage but I strongly suspect that he would much rather cut you off entirely if he thought you might embarrass him. I do not say he is right, you understand, but one cannot explain these things to men very easily. They do not understand how boring it is to always be polite and kind and not shout or run or jump or...well, you know."

Shrewdly, Lydia commented, "Are you telling us that if we behave ourselves as you and Jane do, you will invite us to town for a season of balls and parties."

"If I am in a position that I am able to, *yes*."

The girls looked at each other and quickly came to an accord.

"You had better tell us exactly what you want us to do."

Chapter Fifteen

The Gardiners returned with Jane the following afternoon; they and the children all tumbled out of the carriage weary from the journey. There had been much rain on the way, and consequently the roads had been a trial, particularly for Mrs. Gardiner who was once again in an interesting condition.

Jane stepped forth into the embraces of her sisters looking in every way calm and unruffled; not a hair was out of place and her dress had nary a wrinkle. Had Jane been less incomparably good, Elizabeth rather thought she might be able to accuse her sister of vanity. In truth, Jane gave very little thought to her face and figure but had a strong desire for order and neatness in her appearance. It did not trouble her in the least, though, to have her clothes crushed in a close, affectionate reunion with her little sisters.

"Oh, Lizzy! It is so very *good* to see you. I have missed my dear family sorely, however charming it has been to spend time with our aunt and uncle and the children. Mary! You look very well – my brother is to be commended; marriage suits you very well."

Mary did indeed look well. Her skin glowed with clear good health and her once lank dark hair looked thick and lustrous. The sullen expression that used to be so often seen on her face was replaced with a soft smile and an air of general contentment. The neighbours who had called upon them at Longbourn in the recent days had said as much, and each time compliments were given, Mary would blush and Mr. Collins would beam with husbandly pride.

Mrs. Bennet hurried them all inside the house, fluttering and very much enjoying the large gathering of visitors. "Come in, come in, and rest yourselves – the clouds are gathering and I am sure we are due for a storm to come just as we are standing outside. We will be very cosy this night, for dear Mr. Collins and Mary are to leave us in the morning. Jane, you must share with Lizzy tonight and thus we will make do very well. We shall be a merry party at dinner – the Lucas family are bid to join us. Cook is feeling harried by it all, of course – not everyone is blessed with my patience, I fear – but I do think she will enjoy it more once it is over with."

Such a busy time was had that Elizabeth got barely a single moment alone with Jane, however eager she was to impart her news and to ascertain if her dearest Jane's heart had healed enough for her to be comfortable. The rain started, as per Mrs. Bennet's predictions, and they could not even venture as far as the garden to escape company. The house was as full as it could stand, and whatever room Elizabeth went into, there was always someone else present.

The Lucases arrived by carriage later on and they soon all sat down together to dine. Mrs. Bennet, whatever silliness or faults she might have, was an exemplary hostess. The menu was perfectly designed to please her guests and no expense had been spared on the quality of the food offered. Elizabeth was put in charge of pouring out the tea once they had all assembled in the drawing room, and found a moment to speak to Sir William Lucas about her concerns regarding Mr. Wickham. Charlotte, well aware of her friend's ability to charm her father into anything, sat by and listened with appreciation.

"Sir William," Elizabeth began, with wide innocent eyes and a tilted head, "I wonder if I might seek your advice, given that you are an upstanding member of Meryton society and far more familiar with how one must go about treating the aristocracy than I."

Predictably, Sir William stood a little taller and gallantly offered to assist Miss Eliza in whatever it was she wanted him to do. Miss Eliza did not hesitate.

"It is a case of some delicacy, sir. I have heard from both of the nephews of *Lady Catherine de Bourgh* – I daresay you are already known to her – that Mr. Wickham, who has been residing here in our happy town, is not a man to be trusted. I am very much afraid that to have a dishonest man in our midst might harm us in some way." She waved her hand expansively. "I do not care to *think* of the details of what might happen, but I am sure that you know well the disadvantages that such a man may bring. I know that I am probably being overly sensitive – it is the way of my sex, I fear – but I am almost *sleepless* in my concern for dear Miss King. I thought that you would know who to inquire of about such things and that you, who have been to St. James's Court, would know to heed such accusations against Mr. Wickham, given the exalted circles from which they originated."

Sir William Lucas, very properly concerned by such tidings, promised Eliza that he would do all within his power first thing in the morning to make enquiries about Mr. Wickham. He patted her hand and told her that she had been quite right, quite correct in bringing this matter to him, the magistrate. He assured her that he would write to Miss King's uncle and sort the thing out. "If Mr. Wickham is an honest man he need fear nothing, my dear, but I cannot see how he can be, given the rank of the gentlemen who have spoken to you. Leave it with me, my dear."

Elizabeth, with a warning glance at Miss Lucas, who looked to be on the verge of laughter, thanked him very prettily and handed him his tea.

"Clever Eliza!" remarked Miss Lucas, once he had moved away and she, in turn, received her cup. "I wonder how soon people will start to realise that you are the fabled piper – piping the tune that we all dance merrily to."

Lizzy laughed,."Oh, I think this will please you immensely. I have never had so much difficulty getting my own way than with Mr. Darcy."

"It does. I foresee great amusement when he returns, in fact. He is still much on your mind then, my dear?"

Lizzy nodded to the next guest who had come for tea, her aunt Gardiner. "Yes, I confess that he has taken root in my mind and I cannot at all be comfortable until I have decided upon a course of action."

"Must you have a motive? Can you not simply behave as other mortals do and see if you cannot like him enough to...." She trailed off, aware that Mrs. Gardiner, while the very soul of discretion, was listening with interest.

"Oh, do not stop on my account, Miss Lucas. If a gentleman has caught Elizabeth's fancy, I daresay it will not be at all long before we all hear his identity. Speaking of great mysteries, however, is aught amiss with Kitty and Lydia?"

Elizabeth suppressed a grin and looked politely interested. "Not that I am aware of, Aunt. Lydia at least enjoys very robust health."

"What makes you ask, Mrs. Gardiner?" asked Charlotte, not at all fooled by the innocence in Elizabeth's expression, nor by her careful answer.

"They have quite transformed, since I last saw them, into the most delightfully mannered young women. It is as though the vestiges of childhood have almost entirely left them. I really thought I could have been talking to a younger livelier version of Jane earlier on."

"The transformation must have been quite recent, I must suppose," said Miss Lucas, looking significantly at Lizzy and remembering the last assembly ball in Meryton.

Elizabeth became quite enraptured by the state of her teapot and the other two ladies raised their eyebrows as their glances met over her head.

By the time the Lucas family left, well fed and fully satisfied as to the superiority of Mrs. Bennet's table, the remaining inhabitants of

Longbourn sat down together in the drawing room; the little children had been sent off to bed much earlier and only the adults remained. Even Mr. Bennet, in a mellow mood, deigned to remain with the rest of them. A soft, pleasant hubbub filled the room, each conversation indistinguishable from the rest unless one actively made the attempt to decipher the words. Elizabeth took a moment to sit beside Jane.

"Oh, my dear, I have so much to tell you of – we must have a talk later, you and I, unless you are too tired. It has been a weary day for you, I gather."

"Of course, Lizzy; we shall speak later. I shan't fall asleep mid confessions, I promise you. I am a little tired, of course, but not so fatigued as our poor aunt; she was quite unwell earlier on account of...well, you know." finished Jane, blushing.

"Ah, poor Aunt Gardiner. Perhaps we might find a cunning way of sending her off to bed early then...."

Elizabeth was unable to complete her sentence, for Mrs. Bennet, who had been speaking to Kitty, had let out a small shriek and was even now staring at her second daughter with wide, shocked eyes.

Mr. Bennet began to look amused and it did not take Elizabeth very long to hit upon the reason for her mother's outburst. She sent Kitty a glare and did not feel in the slightest bit sorry for her sister when she looked guilt-stricken and her shoulders slumped.

"But, but...I do not at all understand! Elizabeth, how can this *possibly* be true? Your father would *surely* have told me of an engagement."

Lizzy heard Jane gasp beside her and she quickly shook her head. "I daresay he would do so, Mama – *should* such an engagement exist."

"Then...then...Kitty was only funning – Mr. Darcy did not *actually* propose to you?"

Silence descended upon the company. Elizabeth collected her wits together, regretting that an outright lie would be quickly corrected by Mr. Collins or Mary.

"He has requested permission to court me, Mama," she said quietly, heartily disliking that such a private conversation should be taking place so publicly and feeling her neck flush hot with embarrassment.

Mrs. Bennet let out another little shriek. "Elizabeth! Oh, you clever, *clever* thing. You will be so...I mean...such *consequence!*"

Mr. Bennet took pity on Elizabeth, seeing her red-stained cheeks. "Thank you for that helpful evaluation, Mrs. Bennet. Shall we defer our discussion on the subject until a later time? It is fortunate that we are among family, who I am sure would not dream of spreading such gossip about that Elizabeth might be forced to decide in a manner she may not wish to."

"Not wish to?! Not – *wish* to marry such a handsome, well-connected rich young man as Mr. Darcy? Do not even consider such a thing, Mr. Bennet!"

Elizabeth quietly suggested that it was entirely possible that they would both conclude that they should not suit one another.

"Not suit?" echoed Mrs. Bennet, aghast, as bitterly disappointed now as she had been ecstatically surprised but moments ago. "Let me tell you this, Miss Lizzy, if you set your mind to convincing him that you are the ideal wife, he won't think any such thing. You *could* not throw away such an opportunity! I do not think I could forgive such a waste."

Annoyed, Elizabeth retorted, "Madam, I am fairly certain that the laws of this land permit a young woman the power of refusal – if Mr. Darcy *does* propose to me again, I shall give him whatever answer seems best for the both of us. To do otherwise might doom us to a lifetime of misery."

Mrs. Bennet was not a bad woman, but she was a simple-minded one, and most of the people in the room knew that her anger once roused was hot but it burnt out swiftly and that she very rarely meant what she said when in a temper. "Elizabeth, if you drive Mr. Darcy and his ten thousand pounds away through sheer *stubbornness,* you may as well consider yourself homeless, for *I* certainly shall not provide a home for such an ungrateful girl and what is more…."

Mrs. Bennet was unable to say whatever else she wished to in the height of her disappointed anger, for, in a move that quite astonished them all, Mr. Collins intervened.

"My sister Elizabeth," he said slowly and carefully, "will *never* need to consider herself homeless as long as *I* am alive to offer her a place to live. A more selfless, loyal, morally upright young woman I have very rarely encountered." He crossed the room to her as he spoke, intending to reinforce physically what he wanted to communicate. William Collins would stand by her. *He* had not forgotten the noble sacrifice she had made for the happiness of both himself and his dear Mary. Elizabeth had told him on that very occasion that she so much wanted a brother – well, she should have one now.

Elizabeth, surprised as much by the lump that had appeared in her throat as by the loyal defence given by Mr. Collins, reached for her brother's hand and pressed it gratefully.

"Oh! My dear brother," she said, and burst into overwrought tears.

Chapter Sixteen

"You know that she did not mean it. Mama was simply so very – surprised – by hearing of it so very suddenly. From her perspective, she had been granted her very dearest wish, that her daughters should be well settled and in the next moment was fearing that it should not be after all. Do not heed it, *dearest Lizzy* – Mama truly loves you – all she does is for our wellbeing. Oh, Lizzy, do not cry. You must be quite overwhelmed."

Elizabeth, having burst so suddenly, so mortifyingly into tears at Mr. Collins's defence, had fled the room with her bewildered elder sister hard at her heels.

Having begun to cry, it seemed as though she could not stop – the events of the last few weeks had finally caught up with her and her already tangled thoughts and feelings needed to be let out on the shoulder of a gentle Jane.

Sweet Jane, however weary she might be, however burdened her own heart, was eager to be of some comfort to Elizabeth. It was rare that such a service was necessary for this particular sister; Lizzy was such a cheery soul in general and quite clever enough to defend herself in an argument – Jane would have been hard-pressed to think of a time when she had sobbed quite like this.

Eventually, the weeping ceased and Elizabeth's breathing slowed from short hitched gasps to a steadier gentler rhythm. From vast experience of comforting Kitty and Mary, Jane knew that the words would soon spring forth and they could speak profitably.

"Forgive me, Jane; I do not at all know what came over me – it is not at all like me."

Jane stroked away the wild hair that was tickling her chin and once again rested her cheek upon her sister's head.

"I know, my dear; it is a sign of how concerned you have been. I am here now – tell me all."

And with that, Elizabeth imparted to Jane all that had transpired since she had gone into Kent. She hesitated in telling her about Mr. Bingley, but the slow steady stroke of Jane's hand on her head was so soothing and the desire to speak unhampered truth, without agenda or fear of consequence, was so strong in her that she spoke until all of it was out.

If Jane's arms tightened involuntarily for a moment when Lizzy mentioned Mr. Bingley, she did not say anything, merely listened attentively as the tale unfolded.

When Lizzy was done, they half lay together on the bed in silence. Eventually, Jane sighed and whispered, "Poor Mr. Darcy."

Elizabeth gave a watery chuckle. "No, my dear – rich Mr. Darcy; therein lies the problem."

Smiling at her sister's wit returning, Jane said, "I do not suppose he has ever considered that it might be an impediment before. Why do you, my dear? You have long known that we must marry well. I do not quite understand."

"If he were less than he is, I might consider him in as carefree a fashion as I did when I thought he disliked me. I do not like feeling foolish, and when I think of how I should have liked to dismiss him...it would not have been a sensible thing to do. I am at war with my own inclinations. I do not usually struggle to determine what it is I want; ordinarily, my mind is too busy fathoming out how I can get it."

"Do you feel bound by duty to encourage him?"

"No-o. I am not afraid of Mama's wrath, if that is what you mean, nor do I fear that Papa would try to coerce me, however much that letter has put him in favour of the match." She wriggled off the bed and started to take off her evening clothes, a flash of a smile appearing when Jane frowned at the way she pulled at the buttons to undo them. "It is more that I know full well how good a match with Mr. Darcy would be for my family. Kitty and Lydia have already shown a willingness to better themselves and I know how much worry it would ease in Mama for me to be secure but...."

"You do not love him," came the simple rejoinder.

"No," said Elizabeth, finally free of her dress. "I do not. I do not know if I can even like him. That is...I do not dislike him any more; he has shown some excellent qualities, not least the ability to admit when he has erred and to make amends – very few men are capable of such, I believe. If he is a good man, which I think he may be, however ill favoured his manners in company, it must be wrong of me to marry him with such an imbalance of affection, surely? We have always said that we wished to marry for love, have we not?"

"I hardly think we were expecting these exceptional circumstances, Elizabeth," said Jane ruefully. "I do not suppose this can be sorted out until Mr. Darcy comes into Hertfordshire. He will call on you and you will decide if you like him enough to marry him and then things will become clearer. If you cannot like him nor respect him, then on no account must you accept him."

Elizabeth's head popped up through the neck of her nightgown. "Jane. Will you be glad to see Mr. Bingley again, if he comes?"

"Certainly," she said with great calmness, neatly hanging up her dress. "I am sure I should be glad to see any neighbour of ours return to the area – it is so melancholy to see a home empty of its occupants."

"Jane!"

Miss Bennet sighed. "I fear I may be as confused about Mr. Bingley as you are about Mr. Darcy but for different reasons. You are considering if you can marry without love to a man you believe will make a good husband and I – I am wondering if I am in love with a man who might make a very bad one. We neither of us will know until the gentlemen come, if they come."

They both climbed into bed, tired in body, mind, and heart, glad of the comfort they could give and receive from each other. Jane blew out the candle and they lay in the silent darkness, their thoughts clarifying in their minds now that they had spoken them aloud.

"Perhaps…" said Lizzy, sleep slurring her voice, "perhaps we had better end old maids after all and live like this forever. I can think of worse fates than to live with my dearest sister all my life."

A soft snore answered her.

It was a sheepish Mrs. Bennet who came into the girls' room the next morning. The two young ladies had slept later than their wont and were hurrying with their toilettes before the breakfast bell was struck.

"Good morning, girls."

"Good morning, Mama," chirruped Jane, who woke each morning with the cheerful thought that a new day was a beautiful thing.

Elizabeth, trying desperately to shake off the slow fog of sleep by doing battle with a face cloth and freezing cold water, made a noise somewhere between a salutation and a grunt.

Mrs. Bennet came further into the room, instinctively reaching to hold back the lock of Elizabeth's hair that was in danger of being drenched. It was an office that she had often performed for her daughters – holding their hair back when ill or when washing. Motherly gestures of love did not vanish simply because her daughters were grown.

Elizabeth raised her head from the bowl and met the eyes that were so like her own.

"I did not mean it, Lizzy," said Mrs. Bennet, troubled that her heedless words had so upset her most unflappable daughter.

"Oh, I know it, Mama. Do not fret – I shall try very hard to like Mr. Darcy. Perhaps it will not be so hard as I imagine it."

"Oh, my love!" said Mrs. Bennet, returning to cheerful excitement. "Such a fine thing! Will he come soon, do you think?"

"I cannot tell you, ma'am."

"Well, I suppose gentlemen never do come when they ought to, do they? It is a trial, to be sure. Let us go down to breakfast – the Collinses are to leave us soon after. Mary will want to take the journey in easy stages; you may depend upon it I shall tell Mr. Collins how to manage it. I was quite, quite dreadfully ill with my first and the very thought of a long carriage ride on bad roads...well! By the by, I do not suppose you could assure your brother that your Mama is not so dreadful a human being as he seems inclined to think?"

Elizabeth, submitting to Mrs. Bennet's deft hands putting up her hair as she rattled on, winced as a strand was pulled a little too tight.

"I am sure he knows that a dearer mother never existed, Mama, but I will be sure to tell him."

It was apparent, by the time Mr. Collins and Mary sat at breakfast, that in his ready defence of Elizabeth he was now regarded by all as quite one of the family. Mr. Bennet especially seemed to speak to him with a greater measure of respect, and Mary, when she was not steadfastly looking away from the fish on his plate, looked at him with what may have been adoration in her eyes.

He smiled when Elizabeth came into the breakfast room arm in arm with her Mama, more convinced than ever that the epitome of generous, forgiving womanhood was present in the room. Should she marry Mr. Darcy, she would be entirely deserving, he thought, of the rank and privilege that would be bestowed on her. He flattered himself that he had seen her exceptional qualities almost as soon as he entered the house and that where William Collins's high opinion was warranted, surely Mr. Darcy need not think twice about courting such a woman. Indeed, one might almost suggest that he himself had aided the match, not that he would ever be so crass as to say so in public, of course.

The Collinses parted from the Bennets with great satisfaction. Mr. Collins was pleased to have been of service to his dear sister, and his confidence was much bolstered by the increase in familial feeling toward him after what had been uncalculated instinct on his part. He held no ill will toward Mrs. Bennet – if his sister Elizabeth could forgive and forget with such readiness, so too could a Humble Reverend. His thoughts were quickly focussed by his dear Mrs. Collins leaning heavily on his arm to ascend into the carriage and he was put in mind of the last time he had handed her up as his bride. He marvelled that his regard for her had increased so much in what was such a short time. She was an excellent woman, so practical and so ready to aid him in his work.

The promise of motherhood suited her, he thought, as he settled himself into the carriage, smiling fondly at the faint smell of ginger that pervaded the enclosed space. She reminded him very much of a painting he had once seen of her namesake – the very essence of maternal beauty.

Seeing her husband regarding her with such undisguised admiration, Mary briefly forgot the churning of her stomach and blushed.

"Mary, my dear," said Mr. Collins, "what think you of the name Catherine Elizabeth?"

Chapter Seventeen

Two complete days after the Collinses had departed from Longbourn, Mrs. Phillips made haste up the drive, eager with news and excitement. She communicated that Mr. Bingley, who had so suddenly left the country in the autumn, was to return on the morrow.

Mrs. Phillips was very fond of her nieces, the two youngest in particular, but was sorely disappointed at the lack of reaction that her gossip met with amongst the ladies of Longbourn. Jane she had not expected to give much away – she was such a reserved thing (although so well mannered), but she rather thought that Kitty and Lydia might have let slip some detail of their sister having met Mr. Bingley in London and that she was the reason he was returning. Alas, she left the house with no further gossip to spread around Meryton, the Bennets having expressed mild pleasure that the great house at Netherfield would not be left empty and that Mr. Bingley was quite permitted to come and go as he pleased without requiring their sanction.

The weather having turned dry again, Elizabeth walked out in the gardens with her aunt Gardiner, who after the extraordinary information imparted last evening was very anxious for a tête-à-tête with her. Her niece would have infinitely preferred a muddy trudge up to Oakham Mount but Mrs. Gardiner, her hand resting lightly on her stomach, laughingly requested that Lizzy not walk her weary body to exhaustion.

"I cannot tell you how surprised I was last night, Elizabeth. The Darcys are a family that I know of; they are from Derbyshire, you see – Pemberley is very near to the little village where I spent much of my girlhood. Of course, I could not claim an acquaintance with them; they moved in very different circles from us."

Elizabeth listened with interest. Here was yet another source of information from which to collect the pieces of the puzzle that made up the whole of Mr. Darcy.

"Mr. Darcy's aunt, Lady Catherine de Bourgh, resides in Kent. Rosings Park is very grand – I suppose that Pemberley must be also."

"It is certainly the *largest* house in Derbyshire, Lizzy, but you must not think it ostentatious or gothic. I do not know when the house dates from but it is a very charming property. I daresay *you* would be more interested in the grounds – I have never seen any to rival them, though I am admittedly very partial to the scenery in that part of England."

"And the family – are they well reputed?"

"A very *steady* family. They have been landowners in Derbyshire for – oh, a very long time, several centuries probably – but there is a very great loyalty amongst the tenants and farming folk – or at least there was when I lived there when old Mr. Darcy was still alive. I do not think that I have heard of the son as being reckless or wild, but you would know more than I of that."

"Three hundred years, I believe, Aunt. Mr. Darcy mentioned it once," said Lizzy, her thoughts elsewhere. "He is not wild, no. I have accused him in the past of being very proud, too proud to bring his family name into disrepute by behaving badly. It is no wonder that he is a little conceited if his ancestry is all that I have heard."

"The grandson of an earl? No, I should think it more surprising if he was not."

Elizabeth sighed. "His conceit is not overt, not really; it is more that he clearly has an expectation of everyone else in a room already knowing how very grand and important he is. I do not think he at all sees the need to make himself agreeable to others."

"Is he above being pleased?"

"Clearly not," said her niece with a wry smile, "else he would not have found himself at all pleased by me when I gave him no encouragement.

"I cannot fault his taste, Elizabeth," replied her aunt fondly.

Elizabeth attempted a nod of agreement but ruined the effect by laughing. She stooped down to pick a bright daffodil.

"What a great pity it is that our merchants cannot replicate such a gay shade of yellow, Aunt; you ought to bid my uncle look into the matter – I should wear it in an instant."

"I should rather think that bright a hue would wear *you*, my dear," said Mrs. Gardiner, quite willing for her niece to redirect the conversation. Then slyly, "A gentler shade might make a very pretty wedding gown."

Lizzy coloured and the offending flower was indignantly tossed away. "You dare to tease me, Aunt?"

"I should not have the courage if you were Mrs. Darcy, but I feel I may torment plain Lizzy Bennet without much fear of repercussion."

A laugh that was not entirely amused was forced from the younger lady. "Oh, yet another reason to add to the list of why marrying Mr. Darcy would be a Good Thing To Do. I am quite fatigued with the subject – I almost make up my mind in one direction and then the very next moment find an equally good reason to decide in the opposite manner. Forgive me, dear Aunt. I become altogether too serious for my age. I shall amend matters."

"We need not speak of it if you do not wish to, Elizabeth, but I might remind you that you have two very good examples of unequal matches in your immediate vicinity. Neither example is devoid of joy or contentment, although I think perhaps your parents might occasionally bewail the choice they made in their youth."

"Yes, that is certainly true. I suppose the other example is yourself?"

"As the youngest daughter of a poor curate, I was very grateful when your uncle wed me."

"Do you think me spoilt, then, Aunt? That I should deliberate so when it is so beneficial an offer?"

"Hardly. I admire the consideration that you are giving to a very important decision. Too many girls accept or dismiss a man based on frivolities, not thinking of either their future comfort or their happiness. Your circumstances are quite different from my own; I had to marry – I was a burden for my parents to feed from the moment I was weaned. It is the way of things, I fear; girls have so few ways of supporting themselves – marriage is the most palatable option unless the husband is a brute."

"I am sure that he is not that. Upon reflection he has nearly always been very gentlemanly around me. I do not think it a mask to hide a vicious character and lull me into a false sense of ease."

"Elizabeth!" exclaimed her aunt, "have you been reading novels?"

"Why, yes," laughed Elizabeth, turning a half skip into a sprightly turn to face her, "I crept into Papa's study at the dead of night and found them hidden between the good brandy and an old dusty tome containing a very dull treatise on the Battle of Hastings."

Mrs. Gardiner admitted defeat, for Elizabeth would not be drawn into a further discussion of Mr. Darcy, and they returned to the house in good spirits, with a great sense of harmony between them.

Mrs. Phillips, two days later, congratulated herself heartily on the veracity of her information. Being the first to bring accurate tidings of Mr. Bingley's return gave her a great sense of self-satisfaction when his carriage came into view on the main street of Meryton, just beneath the window of her front room.

It was two more days before those at Longbourn saw him, when he called upon them one morning with his sister Miss Bingley. They were all in readiness; Jane had schooled herself into a very convincing semblance of indifferent serenity, Kitty and Lydia were inclined to follow Jane's lead in all things at present, and Elizabeth had been mentally sharpening her wits in preparation to skewer the Bingley siblings verbally if they so much as made her sister frown.

They were received very cordially by Mrs. Bennet, who declared herself to be well pleased that they had called, and once each of the ladies had greeted the callers, asked leave to introduce her sister-in-law Mrs. Gardiner to them.

Mr. Bingley was very ready to make a new acquaintance and said so. He could not help but look often to Miss Bennet, for which no one present could fault him – Jane was entirely too lovely that morning in a pretty gown of cream sprigged muslin.

Seeing that Miss Bingley was nodding alongside her brother, apparently quite ready to forget that she had spent a quarter of an hour in her aunt's sitting room, Elizabeth lightly stepped into the introductions.

"Oh no, Mama – Mrs. Gardiner has already had the pleasure of meeting Miss Bingley, has she not? Oh yes indeed, for I recall reading Jane's letter from London that she had called at their house in Gracechurch Street. I do not believe Mr. Bingley called at the time though, did he, Aunt? Doubtless very occupied with important matters of business."

Mr. Bingley's look of blank astonishment was nearly as delicious to Elizabeth as the sour, uncomfortable expression that crossed Miss Bingley's face. Lydia, in a helpful mood, supported Elizabeth in searching her own vague memory.

"Yes, that is quite true, Lizzy, for I remember very clearly that we also received an account from dearest Jane of her first few weeks in London."

Kitty, being temporarily unable to speak for some reason, nodded vigorously.

Miss Bingley, quite outmanoeuvred, curtseyed to Mrs. Gardiner. " Of course, a pleasure to see you again, Madam," said she, her tone belying the courtesy of her words and determinedly ignoring her surprised brother.

Mrs. Bennet flapped her hands a little, not entirely following the machinations of her children. "Oh yes, how silly of me, Miss Bingley – I do tend to forget things that have been written in letters – I get so many, you know, especially now my dear Mary has married Mr. Collins and moved away to Kent. Yes. Well. Mrs. Gardiner, then, may I present our neighbour Mr. Bingley. Mrs. Gardiner is my sister-in-law, sir; dear Jane has been staying with them in London over the winter, but I daresay Miss Bingley and Mrs. Hurst have already told you of that; I am sure you must have been prodigiously busy elsewhere for I cannot recollect that Jane wrote of you at all."

Lizzy silently applauded her Mama, who was not, it seemed, a lost cause.

Reddening and sending his sister a pointed look that promised future discussion, Mr. Bingley bowed low to Mrs. Gardiner and, casting his sister to the lions, publicly disclaimed having had any knowledge of Miss Bennet being in town at all.

"I cannot account for it, Madam, for I should surely have called upon you all had I known of it." He looked at Miss Bennet again, who was attending with some concentration to the delicate stitches of her embroidery. "I cannot think of a happier time that I have spent than those months in Hertfordshire – we had such a jolly time, did we not? I do not believe I have seen any of you ladies since the twenty-sixth of November when we were all together at Netherfield."

Miss Bingley remained very quiet throughout the short call, responding only when asked a direct question – which was not often, given that no one really wished to speak to her. Jane also said very little, but when asked very tentatively by Mr. Bingley about her time in

London, opened up enough to take her part in the conversation and managed so well that by the time the Bingleys had gone, she was able to convince herself that the two of them had met as common and indifferent acquaintances.

She tried, unsuccessfully, to persuade Lizzy of the same, and turned nearly puce when her dearest but most treacherous sister had laughed heartily at the notion.

"Oh, Jane – *Jane!* I give the man one week," was all Elizabeth would say, between giggles, "*one* week."

Chapter Eighteen

Elizabeth was wrong. It took Mr. Bingley nine days altogether to summon the courage to formally visit Mr. Bennet to request his eldest daughter's hand in marriage.

Her prediction may have been rather more accurate had the skies not been rent for the space of two days together with the most terrific thunderstorm the county had ever seen. Trees had been blown down in the high winds, and the river that acted as a partial boundary to Netherfield had burst its banks so that those within were prevented from leaving the property until the flooding had decreased.

Mr. Bingley had called every single morning up until the storms began, each time without his sister. It appeared that some disagreement had taken place between them because it was whispered by the common folk in the town that the servants at Netherfield had been given orders from their master that Miss Bingley was confined to the house for the time being.

Mr. Bingley appeared to be in every way as he was when he had first come into Hertfordshire – lively and charming company and with a decided preference for Jane. He rather thought that she was just as glad to be in his company, even if there was a slight reserve about her now.

He was not an observant man, but even the dimmest fool in the kingdom would have been able to see that Miss Elizabeth Bennet's manners toward him had cooled significantly over the winter. Gone was the smiling cordiality of yesteryear, and in its place was a careful, frosty civility that was so daunting in its disapproval that had it not been for the great regard he had for the eldest Miss Bennet, Charles Bingley might have been frightened off.

He rallied, however, and, during the period in which he was unable to leave Netherfield, had quite made up his mind that as soon as the roads were again passable he would ride to Longbourn and humbly request the hand of Miss Bennet from her father.

He entered Mr. Bennet's study with a quick step and great confidence, finding that the master of the house was not quite alone. Miss Elizabeth was seated beside her father, their heads bent over the desk.

"Good morning, Mr. Bingley," said Mr. Bennet, closing his book and rising to bow slightly. "I gather that the roads are once again passable. That is excellent – I have been intending to go into town."

"Ah. Yes, sir. I was hoping that you might be able to spare me a few minutes of your time this morning."

Mr. Bennet nodded, fully intending to enjoy himself. "But certainly, Mr. Bingley. What is it that I may assist you with?"

The hopeful suitor looked alarmed and cast a significant glance at the man's daughter, who was looking at him with an unblinking, glacial stare. He shifted on his feet. "Er...I would...I mean that...you see I..." stammered Mr. Bingley, entirely unsure how one got rid of a female from within a room in her own home.

Mr. Bennet's eyebrow quirked up and he looked at Elizabeth. "Are you quite well, Mr. Bingley?"

"I am in excellent health, I thank you, sir. It is merely that...."

"Elizabeth, my love, fetch Mr. Bingley a glass of something. Do sit down, sir."

Lizzy rose, looking as though she would prefer to be making her way to the poison cabinet rather than her father's tray of porter, but she poured out a small glass for Mr. Bingley and offered it to him in silence.

Mr. Bingley swallowed it and was left awkwardly holding on to the empty glass when Miss Elizabeth omitted to offer to take it from him. He fiddled with the stem, feeling quite dreadfully uncomfortable. Things were not going at all how he had hoped that they might.

Mr. Bennet waited patiently for the space of five minutes, regarding his visitor over steepled fingers without much change in expression and then, at the chime of the little mantel clock, grew bored with this sport and ended the impasse.

"Thank you, Elizabeth – you may go."

Lizzy pouted slightly but rose without demur and left the room.

Relieved, Mr. Bingley rose to bow her out and did not receive so much as a look to acknowledge that he had done so. Evidently, Miss Elizabeth Bennet was fearfully displeased with him over some matter.

"How may I assist you, Mr. Bingley?" asked Mr. Bennet, mildly.

"Yes. Thank you, sir. I should like to apply for the hand of your daughter. In marriage I mean. Please."

"I see." Then Mr. Bennet waited.

Quite unable to bear the tense silence, Mr. Bingley began to ramble. "I...erm...I believe that I am well able to support a wife, I have some idea of purchasing Netherfield if Miss Bennet likes the notion of living there. If she accepts me, I mean. I do not at all wish to seem presumptuous but I had rather hoped that she might, you know." He fiddled with the stem of his glass once more. "I know that I ought have returned sooner, or called upon her when she was in London. I am afraid my sister...well, I was not informed that Miss Bennet was in town you see and...well, I have spoken to Caroline and...but that is not at all what I wished to speak of." He took a deep breath and looked away from the glass in his hands and into the satirical eyes of Jane's father. "I am deeply in love with Miss Bennet, sir; I think that she is the most...the most perfect angel I have ever met and this whole winter I thought of her every single day. I hope that you will permit me to ask her if she will have me."

"Very well, Mr. Bingley," said Mr. Bennet at last, after a considering pause so lengthy that Mr. Bingley began to squirm again. "You may pay your addresses to my eldest daughter. I will call her in." He rose to ring the bell and the butler appeared with great promptness and was dispatched to locate and summon Miss Bennet to her father's library.

Mr. Bennet regarded the man gravely. He was inclined to take a gentler view of him than was Elizabeth, but agreed that all of Jane's unhappiness over the winter ought not to go unpunished. He would leave that to Elizabeth – she might lack the gentler maternal instincts that Jane had in abundance but she more than made up for them with her ferocity when it came to protecting her sisters. He almost felt a little sorry for the tongue-lashing that Mr. Bingley was likely to receive. Poor fool.

Jane came shyly into the library. She did not at all look surprised at Mr. Bingley's presence for she had evidently been forewarned. Her fair hair was dressed simply that morning, but to the gentlemen in the library she lacked nothing by way of loveliness.

"Well now, my Jane. Mr. Bingley is apparently desirous of private speech with you. I shall take a turn to fetch a cup of tea, I think. This door will remain ajar. You have five minutes, sir. I suggest you make good use of them."

With that, he sent a stern look to the suitor and a reassuring one to his daughter and left the room.

Elizabeth had preempted him and was pouring out tea for him as soon as he entered the music room. She did not look happy.

"Do not be cast down, my love – I do believe Jane wants him after all. He will make her a good husband, I think."

"Yes, I suppose he will. Still, I do not at all like that she will leave us. Do insist on an odiously long courtship, Papa!"

He shook his head. "My Lizzy, only consider how much more money your mother will spend on wedding clothes if given more time to shop."

Elizabeth paced to the window and looked out.

"Life will not at all be the same without Jane here."

"No, my dear. It will not. Life is full of these little changes, I am afraid. At least this one will make her happy, we will get by, and I daresay that one day you will be in the same situation. Perhaps you will leave me for Mr. Darcy, perhaps not, but bear in mind your poor dear father, little Lizzy – I shall be left all alone in this house with naught but your Mama for company."

Lizzy glanced at the clock. "How long did you give him?"

"Five minutes. I'd have considered longer, but the man needed encouragement to come to his point. He is not at all concise. Do try to remember that you like the fellow, Elizabeth – he will be your new brother after all. Not," said her father dryly, "that anyone could ever take the place of Mr. Collins in your eyes, but if Jane cares for him she will be much more comfortable if you do not do irreversible damage to his self-esteem."

"I? I am far too mild a character to do any such thing, sir. You wound me with the suggestion."

He let out a bark of laughter and rose. "Well now, you had best warn your mother – I will go forth and deal with the tedious office of being stern."

He found the lovers hand in hand, Mr. Bingley looking relieved and beaming and Jane radiant with a quiet joy that set him at his ease. It was unnecessary for him to ask the outcome of the private interview for it was immediately apparent.

He nodded and took Jane's other hand. Her blue eyes were a little damp but her composure was mostly intact. "I wish you joy, my dear. You will be a very happy woman. Sir, you have the fairest of all of my daughters. I charge you straitly to treat her fairly and honestly from this day forward."

"Thank you, sir; I shall."

A merry time was had that day. Mr. Bingley was very cordially invited to dine with the family and so left Longbourn that evening as dusk was settling over the countryside. He was very satisfied with the outcome of the day and even found himself laughing at the hash he had made of things in the morning; he supposed that every suitor must do similarly – perhaps one day he might make his own prospective sons-in-law as anxiously garrulous as Mr. Bennet had made him.

He entered Netherfield with a cheery greeting to the footman at the door that left the man in little doubt of the day's doings. Miss Bingley, it was announced, had retired to her room with a tray and would likely see her brother at breakfast.

Unable to share his good tidings with Caroline, who, judging by the unpleasant things she had said of the Bennets when they had returned to Netherfield, would not be overwhelmed with joy, Mr. Bingley sauntered into the library and sought out a sheet of paper and pen. He would write to Darcy – his old friend would be glad to know that his advice to return had been successful. Having called on him in Grovesnor Square a fortnight ago, Darcy had confessed that he had recently had information that meant his advice to his friend had been entirely wrong regarding the eldest Miss Bennet.

Confused, relieved, and deeply curious, Bingley had requested clarification. "I cannot tell you exactly, Charles. There is a lady involved and I will not bandy her name about. Suffice it to say that someone who knows Miss Bennet, who is of unquestionable honesty and reliability, has indicated that the lady has been decidedly out of spirits since you departed from Hertfordshire."

"*Your source, my friend, was entirely correct,*" Bingley wrote. "*I have the privilege today of calling the sweetest angel on earth my fiancee. I was a veritable bundle of nerves when I went to find Mr. Bennet. Miss Elizabeth was there also and simply would not take the hint and leave. By the by, I am sure she heartily dislikes me for some reason – I **had** thought* *her very amiable in November but suspect her of being an archwife of the highest order after this last week. Do come into Hertfordshire and support me – I shall need someone to aid me in this last month of being a bachelor!"*

He spent a few blotted paragraphs rhapsodizing over his dear Jane's numerous perfections, and ended the letter with a scrawled adieu before sanding and sealing it ready to be sent off the next morning.

He briefly considered writing other letters, to Louisa for instance, and his aunt Bingley, but decided that today of all days he ought to be forgiven for taking the rest of the evening to enjoy himself – he did so dislike the task of writing letters.

So Mr. Bingley retired with a tumbler of brandy to the billiards room and remained there for an hour before taking himself, entirely pleased and content with his life, off to bed.

Chapter Nineteen

Meryton was humming with talk. Not only was the lovely Miss Jane Bennet to be married to Mr. Bingley, but such a delicious scandal had been unearthed by Sir William Lucas.

Mr. Wickham, whom everyone had praised to the skies as an amiable and gallant soldier, was by all accounts a wastrel and a gambler. It was rumoured that he had run up debts of honour as well as debts with the shopkeepers, and that he owed monies to the tune of almost two hundred pounds. What was more, it was beginning to be whispered that even while he was secretly engaged to Miss King (for it transpired that her uncle had not known a thing about the matter), he had been trifling with more than one young servant girl.

Colonel Forster was said to be enraged that the young man had called into disrepute the honour of the regiment, and had temporarily incarcerated him until matters could be sorted out through the official channels. Sir William was the hero of the hour as it had been he who had raised the alarm and written to Mr. King of his suspicions, and many a merchant in the town praised him for his quick actions.

Mary King had been whisked away to Newcastle and was unlikely to return to Hertfordshire at all; it was a pity, said wagging tongues, but she would likely recover. Even with her unfortunate face, her ten thousand pounds would mean that she would not end up a spinster – that much was certain.

Mr. Bingley, listening with half an ear to the gossip that had spread as far as Longbourn – Kitty and Lydia were agog with excitement at finding such goings on in their vicinity – had remarked that although he was sorry for anyone who had such a nice thing as an engagement broken off, he rather thought that Miss King had had a lucky escape if Mr. Wickham was half as bad as he had heard.

He had said as much at breakfast, for he was taking full advantage of his status as a betrothed man and calling at Longbourn at any hour of the day. Elizabeth rather suspected that Miss Bingley was more than usually sour-faced and he wished to escape her company as much as was possible; still, he could hardly be blamed for wishing to see Jane at as early an hour as he could. By all accounts, Miss Bingley had scarcely smiled since the engagement became public knowledge. She would have to think of a solution to that, thought Lizzy, or poor Jane would be stuck with the woman as a sister-in-law.

They walked out towards Oakham Mount one fine afternoon. Kitty, Lydia, and Elizabeth went on a little ahead and Bingley and Jane lagged behind.

Upon reaching the top of the hill – to call it a *Mount* was to stretch the truth rather further than it would go, Bingley remarked that it was a very pleasant view indeed, even though he had, only two years ago, climbed one of the highest peaks in Derbyshire with Mr. Darcy, while visiting Pemberley, but Oakham Mount certainly compared very favourably.

"Darcy is to come to visit us in a few days, you know – he wrote that he is eager to congratulate us in person. He is to bring his sister, which ought to delight Caroline for she is very partial to Miss Darcy."

All of the ladies turned to Elizabeth to judge how she reacted to this news, which was to raise her eyebrows a little and look politely disinterested.

Bingley, as he did so often around his future sister recently, shifted uncomfortably on his feet as he recollected the blistering scold Darcy had given him in response to his remarks on the second Miss Bennet and the generous instruction that he should be the one to make amends over whatever it was that he had done wrong. Miss Elizabeth was, after all, his future sister.

Why Darcy was so certain that it was he who had erred and thus earnt Miss Elizabeth's disdain, Bingley could not begin to fathom, but long habit of heeding his friend's opinions on various important subjects led him to offer his arm with a small smile to the lady as they turned from the summit.

She declined the arm, which disheartened him, but permitted him to walk with her down the path a little way, Jane walking by the younger girls. Bingley summoned his courage and plunged on ahead with begging her pardon.

"I say, Miss Elizabeth – I do believe that I must have occasioned you some grave offence and I should very much like to know what it is so that I may apologise for it and make things comfortable. Jane...er...well, I know she cares very dearly for you and I should not at all wish her to feel any awkwardness at all if things were...were strained between us."

Miss Elizabeth conceded his point with a nod, a little surprised that he had raised the subject so soon. She had thought that it might take him at least another week to notice her coolness – perhaps there was hope for him.

"I shall cut straight to the point then, Mr. Bingley. I am greatly troubled over your desertion of my sister in the autumn, and also by the fact that she – being quite dreadfully unhappy – travelled to London and was treated very shabbily by your sisters. I do not at all think she should marry into a family in which she is treated with such disrespect, but it is hardly my decision to make. She is a gentleman's daughter, sir; our ancestors have lived here for a hundred years. Do you indeed think that she should be so treated, sir?"

She felt, momentarily, a little guilty for this last insult. It was not, after all, his fault that his father had been in trade and she remembered how humiliating it had been when Mr. Darcy had made reference to her lesser lineage. It had the desired effect of wrong-footing him, however, and she watched as her words sank in.

Mr. Bingley, quite stunned, coughed and searched for the right thing to say. "I cannot say that I had thought of it, Miss Elizabeth. You are quite right when put in such terms – it is quite...oh dear." He bit his lip.

Softening slightly, Miss Elizabeth offered him a comforting smile. "As for your behaviour, sir, in leaving Jane open to the contempt of society, you having treated her with such distinction and then disappearing – well now, if she has accepted your explanation and forgiven you, then it has naught to do with me. What I am the most anxious about, sir," she said with steel, "is the possibility that whatever drove you away from her in the first place might do so once again when you are married."

Shocked, Mr. Bingley blurted out, "Miss Elizabeth! I would not. I could not do such a thing. You see...Caroline and...well...they persuaded me that Jane was indifferent and that all she wanted was...well...I mean...*well*."

Angered, Elizabeth gave him no quarter. "And you *believed* them? You, having spent weeks in my sister's company, you who ought to have *known* that there is no guile in her – she is entirely *incapable* of such deceit! I can only attribute it to an excess of modesty on your part, that you did not believe her to be genuine. What if Miss Bingley were to speak ill of Jane again, sir? I assume she will live in your house? I do not intend to slander your sister, sir, even as she has slandered mine, but the very thought of mischief being made, of you believing your sister over even your own knowledge of Jane's character – must she be made to suffer again or has the lesson been learnt?" Seeing that he looked offended, she gentled her tone. "Oh, I do not mean to scold you, Mr. Bingley; before Jane suffered so over the winter I was very inclined to think you the perfect man for her. I would still like to believe so. I...forgive me – I know my sister's good nature and the thought of trusting her to a man who may not defend her staunchly against hurt...it has been worrying me."

Mr. Bingley turned a little to look at Jane, who was assisting Kitty to pin back up a lock of hair that had become tangled in her bonnet ribbons. There was an ardent, shining love in his face that mingled with shame, and he spoke sincerely when he replied. "Miss Elizabeth, you need not fret. When a man has the honour to call Jane his wife, he then also has the privilege of being the first to defend her until the day he dies. My sister has deceived me, yes, and I am disappointed – both in *her* character *and* in my own for my blindness, but my eyes have been opened. I'll not make the same mistake again in a hurry." He saw the instant she dropped her anger against him; her eyes which had been hard when looking at him for the last week softened, and that old merry sparkle that his friend had so admired in the autumn had returned. He felt safe therefore to add, "Especially when considering that even under my care, Jane will still have a brave defender in her sister, eh? I should not dare to anger you, Miss Elizabeth, even if my heart allowed me to injure *her*."

Elizabeth, quick to forgive, took Mr. Bingley's arm. "I do think, my Almost Brother Mr. Bingley, that you had better start calling me Lizzy."

He laughed, relieved, and all was restored between them. They made their way further on.

"Thank you; I will count it a privilege, Lizzy. Tell me – did you truly threaten to poison Mr. Collins if you found his wife not entirely content with her life?"

Letting her head fall back with a peal of laughter, Elizabeth leant on the arm he had given her.

"Oh dear, Mr. Bingley! Is that what has been troubling you so? You almost had me convinced that my own cool displeasure was enough to unsettle you. Has my dearest, most silent sister indeed been telling such tales about me? I shall not incriminate myself, sir; you will have to wonder forevermore."

"No no," he said hastily, "Jane has not said a word – it was Miss Lydia that imparted that information. I was not sure if she was serious or not but Miss Kitty...well...."

Jane caught up with them, serenely delighted that the two people in the world dearest to her were getting along so famously.

Mr. Bingley's predictions regarding his sister's transports of delight upon hearing that both the Darcys were to come as house guests appeared to be fairly correct. In fact, she was so delighted that she entirely forgot that she was at outs with her brother over his engagement and swiftly reconciled herself so as to cajole an increase in housekeeping money from him.

The Darcys arrived from London in one of their own travelling coaches, a grand glossy black affair with a team of four sweating horses causing much staring as they drove through the main street of town. Elizabeth and Lydia were just stepping out of the cobbler's when they passed, and glimpsed Mr. Darcy through the glazed windows of the carriage.

He was not at that moment looking up so he did not notice her, and therefore Elizabeth did not think it necessary to drop a curtsey that would go unheeded. Lydia clutched painfully at her arm when she spotted him.

The moment did, however, give her the opportunity to gather her composure together for the call that would doubtless follow within the next few days. She supposed that he would first formally call upon her father, and then she would see him. Elizabeth was not so casual about this upcoming meeting as she gave her family to believe, who doubtfully applauded her coolness and wondered at it.

The sight of Mr. Darcy's admittedly handsome profile through the window had made her stomach clench for a moment. Elizabeth attributed it to nerves and scolded herself rigorously with dire internal threats of turning into her Mama.

Lydia, on her very best behaviour, did not mention to anyone that they had seen the Darcys arrive. Lizzy's favour was currently much to be desired, and, to the pleasant surprise of both young women, a certain affinity was found between them.

The youngest Miss Bennet, when not desirous of being the centre of envy and attention, was a sharp-witted girl with a decided talent for summing up a social situation accurately – when given the tools to do so. Given Elizabeth's judicious guidance and Jane's ladylike manners as a pattern to imitate, she caught on remarkably quickly. She did not lose the lively, confident manners that made up a great deal of her charm, but when reining herself in to pay attention and deduce likely feelings and motivations of others, she found that it made for as interesting a game as any their aunt and uncle sent from London.

The Bingleys and the Darcys called the very next morning, a fact that delighted Mrs. Bennet no end and made Elizabeth look vaguely anxious. The reason for her concern was twofold – not only was she nervous on her own account but also she worried that her mother's exuberance might overflow into vulgarity. She need not not have dwelt upon the matter for so long as she did, for Mrs. Gardiner, before departing Longbourn, had been at some pains to impress upon Mrs. Bennet the dignity of the Darcy name. As a result, Mr. Darcy's impending visit was regarded by the mistress of Longbourn with a certain amount of trepidation and awe.

Mr. Darcy had ridden on a little ahead of Mr. Bingley and the ladies who came by carriage, and therefore, once he and Mr. Bennet had emerged from the library, into which he had been instantly admitted, he was in time to hand down Miss Darcy, with very affecting solicitude, before Mr. Bingley could do so.

Miss Darcy was a tall young woman and quite as handsome as her brother. They were very much alike to look at, having the same colouring and striking features. In Miss Darcy the softness of youth remained, but it was quickly decided by the young ladies who watched from the windows that once fully grown she would doubtless be a true beauty.

Having introduced his sister to the room at large, and having offered congratulations and felicitations to the eldest Miss Bennet, Mr. Darcy led his sister over to the window where Elizabeth sat, embroidery cloth in hand, awaiting the inevitable.

"Miss Elizabeth," he said in his quietly commanding way, "I have been telling my sister that you are very fond of walking. Have you been out yet this morning?"

Chapter Twenty

Mr. Darcy, with a careful remark and a gentle hint here and there, succeeded in turning the whole party out of doors for a walk. Elizabeth reluctantly admitted to herself that he did so with a good deal of finesse. Even Miss Bingley, once having ascertained his wishes, lent her own support to a stroll and, desirous of demonstrating her great regard for dear Georgiana, latched on to her young friend, leaving Mr. Darcy entirely available to offer his own arm where he wished.

He swiftly led Elizabeth a little ahead of the others and bent his head to speak in a low voice.

"It is good to see you again, Miss Elizabeth. We may not have much time for private speech so I must be more direct than I would otherwise be. I spoke to your father briefly this morning and received his formal permission to call on you. I am only sorry that I have not done so until now – I certainly should have spoken to him from the first. May I now ask – are you still of a mind to allow me to court you? I did not speak well in Kent. I have scarcely been able to think of it without mortification, not least on account of how my thoughtlessness must have wounded you. I should like the opportunity to show you that I am not the arrogant, conceited fool that I was then."

Elizabeth, whilst trying to listen fairly, realised that a great deal of her anxiety regarding Mr. Darcy had been due to a fear of being bludgeoned into agreeing to all he demanded of her. She had imagined that he might not give so much as a sincere thought for her own feelings on the matter and so was immensely relieved by his evident concern.

"It is a good beginning, Mr. Darcy, that you thought to ask me. Yes, sir, I shall be interested to learn more about you. I said in November, did I not, that the differing accounts I have heard of you puzzle me. I hope I shall be able to reconcile them all."

His eyes were intent on her face and she could not avoid looking back at him. He was a serious man – there was little point in denying it; but when the hard lines of his mouth relaxed, as they did now upon hearing her words, he did not look quite so very grave as was his wont.

Impulsively, Lizzy added, "I must devise a means to make you smile more often, I think, Mr. Darcy. It suits you." She let out a little laugh when he quirked his eyebrow at her. "Oh, you need not fear that I shall tease you *constantly*. Tell me, how long shall you and your sister remain in Hertfordshire?"

They were to stay, he said, at least until Bingley's wedding, which was likely to be within a month's time. After that he would need to return to Pemberley for the summer – Miss Darcy's companion had been given the month to visit her relatives in Scotland and by the time Mr. Bingley was wed, Georgiana would need to be returned to her studies.

Latching on to the subject, Lizzy asked, "Has Miss Darcy a favoured subject? I shall attempt to engage her on it if so, unless it is something odiously stuffy like ancient Greek or Latin. I was a great disappointment to Papa, Mr. Darcy, for I have no head for a language that can be of no use to me. I tolerated French on account of the relative nearness of France and my desire to become involved in espionage, but alas, I heartily dislike the classics."

He would not be so very difficult to make smile after all, it seemed. Elizabeth, while still very conscious that it was not merely his eyes that rested on her so intently (Miss Bingley, a furtive glance told her, had barely looked away), found she rather liked the softness of his voice when he answered her.

"I daresay had you been a spy, Miss Elizabeth, the war on the continent would have been over rather more rapidly, however little I care for the thought of you hurling yourself into danger. My sister is very fond of music, but you may rest easy on that score for I know you will be able to speak at length without being anything other than delightful to her."

"Which is to say you have ordered her into friendliness. I suspected as much."

"I thought you said you would not tease me *constantly*, Miss Elizabeth."

How rapidly she had progressed to flirting with the man, thought she, a little alarmed at herself. She mentally reviewed their previous interactions, and, with a flash of insight, understood how he had thought she had been doing so for some time. Worse still, instead of the staid, stilted manners that she was used to seeing in him and misinterpreting as polite disdain, he appeared to be quite willing to flirt back.

The way he dragged out the syllables of her given name after the perfunctory 'Miss' was decidedly rattling to her ears, Elizabeth decided.

After a short while, Elizabeth permitted Miss Bingley to manoeuvre herself closer to Mr. Darcy and exchange companions. She did not mind, for she had a certain curiosity about Miss Darcy, particularly after Colonel Fitzwilliam's odd behaviour in Kent when she had discussed Miss Darcy in too sportive a manner.

"I must tell you, Miss Darcy, that I have recently been in Kent and met your aunt and two of your cousins. I enjoyed the countryside there but am quite willing to withhold judgment as to my favourite county until I have travelled them all."

Miss Darcy, who was studying Elizabeth with poorly disguised interest, shyly responded. "Yes, my brother wrote to me that he had enjoyed your company at Rosings. My cousin Anne drove out with you, did she not?"

Elizabeth repressed a shudder. "Yes indeed; it was most invigorating – I quite see why she should enjoy it so. I do prefer my own two feet, however. It is the one disadvantage of exploring the world, I feel, that we must spend so much time in a closed carriage. Were I able to walk to Scotland, I should pack my trunks and be off on the morrow."

Miss Darcy, glancing toward her brother who had been led further ahead by Miss Bingley, said, "Brother said that you liked to walk. Miss Bingley prefers to ride in general, I believe, but is not overly fond of the exercise. Do you ride, Miss Elizabeth? My brother enjoys it very much."

"I fear I am no horsewoman, Miss Darcy. Perhaps with proper instruction, I might overcome my irritation with horses; they do not listen well to polite requests, I have found. 'Tis vexatious for me to be so ignored by a dumb beast."

Surprised into forgetting her own awkwardness for a moment, Miss Darcy laughed. "Did you attempt such a civil approach for long?"

Elizabeth, eyes twinkling at her success, proceeded to relate a greatly exaggerated account of her last interview with a large farm horse and was pleased that, however elegantly dressed, however reticent her speech, Miss Darcy was as easily amused by the ridiculous as any other sixteen-year-old she knew.

The youngest Miss Bennets, apparently bored by Jane and Mr. Bingley making cow's eyes at each other, had come to join them.

"Lydia and Kitty are of a similar age to you, Miss Darcy."

Lydia, never lacking in confidence, launched into a barrage of questions regarding Miss Darcy's bonnet, which, though a little wary, she answered willingly enough.

"No, Miss Lydia, I did not alter it at all. Mrs. Hartwinkle, the milliner, made it this way for me. I do not believe I have ever trimmed a bonnet – is it not difficult to do?"

This was quite enough for the other girls to keep the conversation running smoothly with the occasional witticism interjected from Lizzy.

"Ah! Miss Darcy, beware – Lydia would quite have you believe she has never once erred in her taste and judgment but we know the truth, do we not, Kitty? Do you recollect the mustard yellow and black velvet creation of last winter?"

Graciously, Lydia admitted that that particular high poke bonnet had not been her finest moment of genius.

"For it did not look well on any of us, I fear. Not even Lizzy, who suits black rather well."

"Indeed, Miss Darcy, I did not dare to wear it outside for fear that the local hives should mistake me for their queen and follow me about."

The girls laughed together, and Kitty, in loyal defence of Lydia's talents, pointed out the pretty cap she was currently wearing and how well it matched her gloves.

"It looked very well before Lydia took it apart, Miss Darcy, but she has made it twice as pretty now."

Miss Darcy, caught into the spirit of the thing, asked if Miss Lydia was responsible for the eldest Miss Bennet's charming hat.

Lydia sighed wistfully and decided that Miss Darcy was an entirely worthy recipient of her great knowledge. "I finished that one last week, Miss Darcy, and presented it to her after she and Mr. Bingley became engaged. It is not at all difficult for Jane to look beautiful, but I do think I surpassed myself with that one. She was not even cross that I forgot to ask leave to make it over first."

Seeing that Miss Darcy looked a little shocked at Lydia's taking a bonnet that did not belong to her without permission, though she was too well bred to admit to it, Elizabeth intervened and led the talk to that of the upcoming wedding. Mr. Bingley and Jane, came to stand with the group and much frivolity and good humour made for a very pleasant twenty minutes.

Mr. Darcy, speaking civilly with Miss Bingley, looked over enviously once or twice and eventually found a plausible enough reason to wander back over to the others. Kitty and Lydia became more subdued in his immediate presence but remained part of the conversation and responded politely enough when addressed. Miss Darcy could barely bring herself to do more than answer in monosyllables in such a large group. Elizabeth was delighted by the kindness that Lydia showed both in noticing this and in shielding her rather skillfully from too many direct questions. To an unkind observer, it would have seemed that the youngest Miss Bennet was rather too fond of attention and directed it back to herself whenever possible. Lizzy smiled pointedly at Lydia in approval.

They eventually walked back to the house together. Mr. Bingley and his sister lagged behind and spoke in heated whispers. Miss Bingley appeared to be most put out about something, a frown creasing the skin between her eyes. Mr. Bingley seemed in turns conciliatory and irritated by her.

Elizabeth, once again on Mr. Darcy's arm, with Miss Darcy on his other side, watched them with interest until Mr. Darcy leant his head down to speak to her again.

"Will you be home tomorrow, Miss Elizabeth? May I bring my sister to call again?"

A little distracted by the Bingley siblings, Elizabeth agreed without really knowing what it was she said, and then, "Oh but I have promised Miss Lucas to visit the Browns after breakfast – I shall send her a note later on that I will be a little delayed."

"Who are the Browns? I do not recollect having been introduced to them last time we were in the neighbourhood."

"Well, no, you would not have been, sir. They do not frequent social gatherings. Mrs. Brown and her family have fallen upon hard times. Miss Lucas and I take up a basket when we can, that is all."

Mr. Darcy smiled slightly. "My own mother used to do the same when at home in Pemberley, Miss Elizabeth. The concept of charity is not entirely foreign to me."

"I did not think that it was, sir, merely that as a visitor to the area you could not have been aware of those who were in need during the short time that you were here."

"Then it is a good thing that Mr. Bingley is to marry Miss Bennet, is it not, brother?" said Miss Darcy, softly from the other side of him. "She will know how to go about things, being raised to it, as we have been."

A little amused by Miss Darcy's almost unconscious snobbery toward the relatively new wealth of the Bingleys, Elizabeth levelled Mr. Darcy with a challenging look. "I agree, Miss Darcy; the benefits of the match are not entirely on her side. But I am partial – I cannot think any man anything but utterly privileged to marry my sister."

Mr. Darcy, to Elizabeth's surprise, did not evade her prod but rather decisively spoke plainly of what Elizabeth was alluding to.

"I cry pardon, Miss Elizabeth – I was entirely wrong on that subject. You will note that matters are mended now?"

The young lady on his arm chided herself for being churlish and unforgiving when she had already decided that she should not be.

"You are quite determined to rob me of any victory in being right, Mr. Darcy. Very well, I do not intend to raise past mistakes, not when I have enough of my own that I would wish forgotten. I must put into practice some of my own philosophy, sir – to remember only that which gives me pleasure to dwell on. Shall we go into the house? The breeze is turning chillier and I do not think that Miss Bingley's pelisse looks at all warm."

Mr. Darcy looked down at his sister and slightly lifted his eyebrows.

"Oh! I shall go and ask her if she should like to go in with me. I do not at all like to be cold myself. Excuse me," said Miss Darcy, who

Elizabeth was fairly certain had been gifted with a great deal of tactful insight.

"Do you know, Mr. Darcy," considered Lizzy, when she had gone, "I do feel that Miss Darcy is quite five times as socially adept as other young ladies her age. I have been trying to teach the younger girls to take themselves off when glanced at sternly and it never seems to sink in. You are to be applauded, for did I not hear that you have been responsible for her upbringing? She is a very pleasant girl."

His other hand, which was now freed from supporting his sister, came to rest upon hers and she felt the warmth of it through her glove. She could not decide whether or not his actions were presumptuous, and so permitted them to go unchallenged and felt rather proud of her graciousness. She was so pleased with her fairness of mind that she nearly missed the wry humour in his voice when he answered her.

"I thank you for the compliment on her behalf, Miss Elizabeth. Georgiana *is* a delightful sister – may I recommend her as such to you?"

Miss Bingley, walking with her dearest Georgiana back towards the house, heard Elizabeth Bennet's musical laughter behind her and the fine lines of her displeased frown grew decidedly deeper.

Chapter Twenty-One

It was a curious thing, mused Elizabeth one bright afternoon when Mr. Darcy had returned to Netherfield, to have him as a suitor. He was ever courteous when addressed by an acquaintance, but always with a measure of reserve. That reserve appeared to vanish when he was in her company or with those select acquaintances with whom he was more familiar.

He liked to be outdoors, she had discovered, and she did not believe it was entirely on account of wishing to avoid her family, for, after one brief disagreement, his manners to them had improved and were now quite unexceptionable, even if his courtesy did not encourage over-familiarity.

She had not at all enjoyed calling him to account for being so dismissive of her younger sister one morning as Lydia had spoken with a little too much friendly enthusiasm on the subject of millinery, but upon reflection had found that it was a worthwhile exchange for it had demonstrated admirably that he was able to heed respectfully phrased criticism and to act on it. It was a good quality which she added to the once very short list that she was composing in her mind, entitled 'Mr. Darcy's virtues.'

She bided her time until they were on a favourite familiar path that she walked regularly. The air that day was cool and fresh, in that delightful way it always was after a short spell of heavy rain. The earth felt damp underfoot but the bright sunshine was rapidly drying up the puddles that had been left by the showers.

"I wonder, Mr. Darcy, if your sister finds my younger sisters' manners too lively for her comfort."

He held back a thorned branch that had grown across the path with his stick and waited for her to step past it before answering.

"She has never said anything of it. I believe she enjoys their company," he said, searching her face for some clue as to her meaning.

"Oh," said she, apparently made more cheerful at this new information, "I am glad of it, for it is so very awkward for young women if they are not entirely settled with each other. Lydia, of course, has a great talent for making friends with people, and Kitty is a sweet girl."

Mr. Darcy looked a little dubious and she pounced.

"Do you doubt me, sir?"

"I am trying to fathom what it is that you are aiming for, Miss Bennet. Your knowledge of your sisters is superior to mine, I am sure. One moment – let me move that briar for you."

"Thank you, sir," she said, primly, her expression not at all giving.

He looked at her eyes and, after a moment's consideration asked carefully, "Are you thanking me for moving a bramble for you, Miss Elizabeth, or is your meaning more oblique than that?"

It was decidedly difficult, trying to manage a man of his intellect, thought Elizabeth. Mr. Darcy was becoming more attuned to her tones and more often than not was swiftly grasping when she was deliberately keeping her implications vague. She tilted her head at him, considering. He was very handsome – she had to admit that even when she was irritated with him. She might not like to have her methods combated with the unflinching directness that he favoured but she admired its effectiveness.

"How clever you are, Mr. Darcy, at reading my character now. I daresay you are quite the most observant gentleman I know." He narrowed his eyes a little and she laughed, her irritation deserting her as quickly as it came. "I was thanking you for your kind permission in granting that I know my sisters rather better than you do."

"Is that all?"

"Not quite, sir," she said, ignoring his tone. "In knowing them so well, I am able to see very clearly when their feelings may be hurt by a gentleman dismissing them as you did this morning."

"I had no intention of doing any such thing, Miss Elizabeth. I am sure Miss Lydia's bonnets are very well but I stand by my words – such idle vanities are hardly something I want filling my sister's mind."

"How well you speak," marvelled Elizabeth. "Really, sir, in the event of your entire fortune being lost by some grave calamity, you ought to consider the church. My dear brother Mr. Collins would be proud of such a sentiment. If my sisters were attempting to engage your and Miss Darcy's interest in a subject that they are knowledgeable in...but I do not at all wish to lecture you. Oh, do look at that well-dressed rose – is it not beautiful?"

He did not look at the rose, merely continued to regard her steadily while she brought her thoughts into order, but with great wisdom, he said nothing.

"Consider, Mr. Darcy, how vexed you should be if I had spoken to your sister so slightingly of her music."

He frowned, "It is hardly the same, madam," he said, his tone clipped.

Elizabeth, looking up at him, wondered if he would be always immovable in his opinions and sighed.

"There now, if we take this path here it will lead us directly back to the house." Then she made to go in that direction but was stopped by the hand he laid on her shoulder. He did not exert force – merely laid it there. Had she wished to, she might have brushed him off with little difficulty. She elected to remain and listen.

"It is not at all necessary to run away from me, merely because we are in a disagreement, Miss Elizabeth. You are not at all frightened of me, nor of my displeasure, so we may dispense with such a supposition."

"I was not running away," she replied, lifting her chin and rather resenting any implication that she was a coward, "but if there is no helpful discourse between us then it does no good to stay. If *you* will not deign to be kind to my sisters, however silly their conversation may seem to you, and I will not bend in thinking they deserve respect, then what good is it to remain in each other's company?"

"May I not enjoy your company, even if you are irritated by me?"

Feeling pleased despite herself, Elizabeth fiddled with her bonnet ribbons and averted her face. His hand was still on her shoulder, as though he feared she might run from him if he removed it.

"Your point is sound – if I wish your sisters to be as my sister, then I ought to treat them the same. I will do so." A more contrary man had surely never existed. Just when she thought she had established that he was a stern, unmoving rock, he surprised her with his gracious capitulation. "I have not made so good a new beginning with you as I had hoped. I had rather wished that by now you might think better of me than my previous behaviour had merited." Still he did not move his hand.

"I think you might be surprised, Mr. Darcy. You have a host of advocates, you know. Whatever it was you wrote in your letter to Papa caused him to argue most convincingly that you ought to be treated fairly, and Lydia and Kitty seem to think that accepting you must mean that great and bountiful amusement will come to them. Much was said in your favour in the time between Kent and your return to Hertfordshire."

"I am glad that my letter persuaded your father that I should not be barred from seeing you. I hoped that it might. Your sisters...well, if they have been directing your attention to the benefits of an alliance between us, then they have my gratitude. However much," he added with a slight grimace, "I would have wished that you needed no convincing."

"I suppose you would have preferred me to flutter my eyelashes at you and laugh at all of your jokes," said Elizabeth, feeling a little guilty for her obvious hesitancy and trying to make him smile. Such clear reluctance on her part would probably be quite a blow to his pride.

"The idea has merit." The corner of his mouth lifted infinitesimally.

Elizabeth laughed and, at last, he smiled on her again, "I do not believe I have ever fluttered my eyelashes at a man in my life."

"I am very glad to hear it," said he, firmly and raised his other hand to brush off a leaf that had blown onto her other shoulder.

It was then that two things occurred to Elizabeth – the first being that she was standing closer than she had ever done to a fully grown man who was not her father, in a secluded part of a wood no less, and the second being that although now extremely embarrassed, she did not mind.

She did, however, mind very much when Miss Charlotte Lucas emerged further down the path and coming within view, exclaimed in shocked tones, "Elizabeth Bennet!"

Guiltily, Elizabeth jumped away and Charlotte approached.

"Charlotte! What do you do here?" she asked, knowing that she sounded as though she had been caught in some dreadful impropriety. Mr. Darcy was looking at her, clearly concerned by her agitation.

"Good day to you, Mr. Darcy," said Miss Lucas very properly, and curtseyed.

He bowed elegantly, "How do you do, Miss Lucas."

Satisfied that the formalities had been dealt with, Charlotte rounded on Elizabeth. "My dear, you should be *very* grateful that it was I who came to call on you today and not my father as he had intended. If Sir William had turned that last corner to receive such a shock, you would be on your way to Longbourn, having forfeited any choice in your marriage partner."

"It was not at all how it looked, Charlotte!" protested her friend.

"What does that matter, Lizzy? Veracity is not so very important when there is the possibility of a scandal to be spread abroad."

"Miss Lucas, you ought to know that my intentions toward Miss Elizabeth are of the most honourable."

"Then perhaps your behaviour ought to come a little more in line with your intentions, sir," said Elizabeth's friend tartly. "It matters not at all to you if Elizabeth is marched to the altar but it would matter a good deal to *her*. I should have hoped that any man wishing to earn her acceptance might realise that."

"Charlotte, you are in every way wonderful for wishing to defend me so but Mr. Darcy was merely removing a leaf from my shoulder – it was nothing so terribly shocking!"

Charlotte raised an eyebrow and responded witheringly, "Eliza, I may not have quite the same level of intellect that you enjoy, but do you think you might do me the courtesy of pretending that you do *not* think me a complete dolt? A leaf? From both of your shoulders at once no doubt. A leaf so large and unwieldy that both hands were required? In the middle of a deserted wood, with no chaperone on hand to assist?"

Mr. Darcy intervened. "Thank you, Miss Lucas; your point is made. That will do. Shall we walk back to Longbourn together?"

Charlotte, responding to the quiet authority in his manner, nodded.

"I came to speak to you about the goings on with Mr. Wickham."

"Mr. Wickham!" exclaimed Mr. Darcy, looking stern. Elizabeth supplied him with the necessary news that he had missed.

"Charlotte's father heard a report that Mr. Wickham is not an honest man and investigated the matter. It turns out that he had run up debts and did not have Miss King's uncle's permission to marry her after all. What has happened now, Charlotte?"

"Well, Colonel Forster is not at all pleased and wants to disgrace Mr. Wickham publicly for conduct that does not befit an officer in the militia, but Miss King will not say a word against him. Mr. King wrote to my father, since it was he who wrote to him in the first place, saying that the poor silly girl is adamant that some mistake has been made and that Mr. Wickham would have applied properly for her hand *eventually*."

"What of the debts?" asked Lizzy, sending Mr. Darcy a curious look. He looked a little pale, and his eyes that had held such softness in them but moments ago were hard.

"Well, more merchants are coming forward and there have been some rumours of debts of honour between the officers. People are beginning to worry that they won't be settled."

"It will have to be the debts, then," said Elizabeth, "at least if Miss King won't speak."

"I do not know if there will be sufficient time for that – the regiment is to move to Brighton next week."

"I suppose it is out of our hands," sighed Lizzy, annoyed. "At least Colonel Forster has heard enough about the man to cause sufficient alarm."

Mr. Darcy had been deep in thought and now spoke. "If the debt was a larger one, against a single party, he could be brought to justice sooner. The debts owed to the merchants and to the officers ought to be purchased, and once it is proven that they cannot be redeemed, removing him would be both simpler and swifter."

Such practical advice pleased Elizabeth just as much as the fact that he had not metaphorically patted her on the head and told her not to fret. "A good idea. I will speak to Papa about it when we return home."

"It is likely to be a sizeable sum, Lizzy," warned Charlotte.

"Well, if Papa cannot stand it I daresay we will have to think of something else." She said this glumly, as they had reached the outer porch of Longbourn.

"Maria has charged me with a message for Kitty that I must deliver. I will find her while you speak to your father. Mr. Darcy, is your sister within? Shall you come with me?"

"No, Miss Darcy remained at Netherfield this morning. However, I wish to have a word with Mr. Bennet – shall we go in, Miss Elizabeth?"

Mr. Bennet's eyebrows rose when the two of them entered his study, Elizabeth ducking under the long arm that Mr. Darcy had opened the door with. Lizzy thought it best to dispel the obvious conclusion quickly.

"I am come to speak to you of Mr. Wickham, Papa."

"*Again*, Lizzy? Have you not already set the hounds on him with your innocent conversation with Sir William?"

Mr. Darcy chuckled as she attempted to disclaim involvement. "Do not dissimulate on my account, Miss Elizabeth; I am well aware of your talent for persuasion."

Elizabeth looked uncomfortable and Mr. Darcy took the opportunity to take control of the situation.

"Miss Elizabeth and her friend have expressed a desire to be rid of the company of Mr. Wickham. I wish to facilitate matters."

"Mr. Darcy, there is really no need...."

"If I were to have my secretary compose a list of all of Mr. Wickham's debtors in Meryton and supplied the funds, would you be willing – as a respected member of the town here – to act as a face for the scheme and call in the debts? I have good reasons for wishing my name to remain entirely unconnected with the matter."

Mr. Bennet smiled. "Well, well, I now see why you find my daughter's antics amusing, Mr. Darcy. That is a quite delightfully presented proposal – you must have a fairly accurate notion of my character. A scheme that gives me all of the credit and little of the work or expense – certainly I should be quite *enchanted* to be of use. Mrs. Bennet will think me quite the knight in shining armour, I daresay."

Having secured Mr. Bennet's promised assistance with such remarkable ease, Mr. Darcy took Lizzy from the library with a polite wish that Mr. Bennet should return to Euclid once more.

Elizabeth looked at Mr. Darcy with a bright smile once they were the other side of the door. "Mr. Darcy, I do believe you are a very useful man. I have rarely brought my father around to my wishes with such little effort. I am all admiration." She presented him with her hand, thinking he might shake it.

Mr. Darcy smiled enigmatically and slowly bringing her hand to his mouth, lightly kissed it.

Chapter Twenty-Two

"Miss Elizabeth," said Miss Darcy one evening, when they had all been dining at Netherfield and Miss Bingley was safely on the other side of the room, "my brother and I would be greatly honoured if you would consent to joining us at Pemberley for the summer after Mr. Bingley and Miss Bennet are wed. Mr. Bennet has said that he would consent to your travelling with us and remaining for a month or so – that is, if you would like to. Derbyshire has many beauties to be enjoyed and I am sure we could entertain you very tolerably while the Bingleys are on their honeymoon."

Elizabeth, recognising the effort such a long speech must have cost the young woman, smiled brightly at her and thanked her for such a kind invitation. "I am always quite delighted to travel, Miss Darcy, and I have heard enough of Derbyshire to have a great curiosity to see it. My aunt Gardiner thinks it the dearest place in all the world and I am inclined to seek evidence of such an opinion." She kindly refrained from teasing Miss Darcy about being such a willing mouthpiece for Mr. Darcy, who showed his hand rather obviously by his quick glance to the two of them once the gentlemen had come in from their port.

"Well, my dear, are we to have Miss Elizabeth's company for the summer?"

"She has agreed, brother. I am sure we will do delightfully. There is no place like Pemberley in the summer, Miss Elizabeth."

"I shall look forward to it, Miss Darcy. It will be good for me, I think, to have some distraction after the wedding. I do think it a little melancholy to lose a sister to a man, regardless of the excellence of the match and the certain happiness of the couple."

"I thought to invite them to join us there after they have finished exploring the lakes and have done with staying in Scarborough. If you wished to, you could travel back to Longbourn in their company."

Unspoken was the knowledge that things must be settled between Mr. Darcy and Elizabeth before the summer was over. Mr. Darcy did not shy away from the topic if it was raised but neither did he continually burden her with the subject of his regard for her.

Elizabeth found, with more time spent in his company and misunderstandings mostly dispelled between them, that she liked him. There was much good in him, and her accusations at Hunsford troubled her. The extreme care he took for his sister's wellbeing and happiness convinced her that should she marry him, he would not neglect her; neither would she be made unhappy if he could do anything about it.

He had kept his word in regards to dealing with Mr. Wickham, who, when faced by the most senior gentlemen of the village armed with the evidence of his extravagance, had bribed the watching soldier assigned to him and fled the area. No sign had been seen of him since and Colonel Forster obtained from higher authorities a warrant for his arrest on the grounds of desertion. Meryton by this time was not at all sorry to see him go, and his fellow officers were overcome with gratitude to Mr. Bennet of Longbourn for having ensured that they did not feel the lack of the funds that they had been robbed of. Mr. Darcy, having dealt as fairly as he felt he could, was content to have his name left out of it. He wanted no gratitude, he told Elizabeth – if she thought the better of him for doing his minimal duty to society, so much the better, but he did not want adulation. He was content to have George Wickham gone and that was that.

He was not a lazy master either; that much was clear in the number of letters that went to and from Derbyshire and Netherfield. He had confessed to her that as a young man succeeding to the responsibilities his father had bequeathed him, he had been burdened with the fear that he might fail in some way, that the Darcy name should be less respected on account of him.

She had liked him then, better than she had ever done, and softened yet further with the evidence of his conscientious approach to the privileged life he led. He was not a young man who squandered all his wealth on riotous living, as though he were entitled to be rolling in luxury while the workers on his estate well nigh starved.

All that she could fault him with, by the time the eve of Mr. Bingley and Jane's wedding arrived, was an excess of reserve and dignity in his manners. She supposed that a wife might soften his harder edges with gentle direction, and decided that, really, she was quite equal to the task. The list of reasons in favour of marrying him continued to grow, all the while outweighed by her own doubt as to whether she liked him enough to spend the rest of her days with him.

It was not until she had walked over to Netherfield that morning to call upon Miss Darcy that she decided with certainty that she actually wanted to be Mrs. Darcy.

The fields had not been excessively muddy, and so by the time Netherfield came into view, she was not so very dishevelled, and was pleased with herself that, should she accidentally encounter Mr. Darcy, she would not show to dreadful disadvantage. She could not precisely say why it mattered that he think well of her – just that she would not like that stern, steady gaze to be coloured with disdain rather than admiration. Perhaps she had not cured herself of vanity after all.

She came across him sooner than she expected, and stopped short. Miss Bingley and he, dressed for walking out, were moving across the lawn. She watched the two of them, both tall and handsome figures. Miss Bingley, whatever her defects of character, dressed very well, and, as she was probably well aware, did him credit with her appearance. They might have been taking the air in a London park or strolling through a museum, so charming a couple did they make.

Elizabeth felt a roiling in her stomach, and her temper, ordinarily bright after a long walk, turned decidedly sour. Her step slowed and she became deeply conscious of the trace of dust on her simple muslin skirts.

As she drew nearer to the house, feeling by now sick and unhappy with herself, Mr. Darcy spotted and hailed her, leading Miss Bingley across to her.

"Miss Elizabeth! I had not expected to see you this morning. Your mother said yesterday that the ladies of Longbourn would be quite well occupied in last-minute arrangements."

He bowed to her as well as he could with Miss Bingley still attached to him.

"Why, Miss Elizabeth, can you have walked here all alone again? I should be positively terrified for my safety," said Miss Bingley, a cool assessing glance at once taking in the countryish dress her rival was wearing.

It did not at all help the unpleasant feeling in her stomach to see Mr. Darcy's jaw clench a little and his mouth set hard.

She quailed for a moment before anger encompassed her. Why should she apologise to him for her dress, or for her solitary habits? She had walked these fields and woods since she was a girl and no harm had ever come to her, nor had anyone save him ever so much as commented on it.

"Yes, Miss Bingley," said Elizabeth steadily, "all alone. I encountered no greater difficulty than my boot laces undoing themselves. I recommend a good walk – it does much to restore me if I am feeling in an unpleasant mood."

Her implication was clear, and Miss Bingley lifted her chin a little so that she could look down her nose at the upstart who dared to insult her disposition without allowing her room to retort. If she were to take exception, it would be tantamount to admitting that she was not a cheerful sort of person and she did not want to appear less than perfect when walking beside Mr. Darcy of Pemberley.

Mr. Darcy very politely invited Miss Elizabeth to walk with them but she declined.

"I am come to see your sister, sir. When she came last evening she forgot her gloves. At least three claimants tried to commandeer them before realising that they were not at all the right size, and so, like Cendrillon, they must be returned to their rightful owner. Do stay and finish your walk together. I was very much admiring the charming picturesque you both make when I came about the corner," lied Elizabeth. "I shall see you tomorrow at the wedding if you are not returned to the house before I have finished visiting Miss Darcy."

And with that, she made her way to the house with deliberately measured pace, presenting not the least outward appearance of running away.

Miss Darcy was pleased to see her friend and thanked her prettily for coming such a way to return her gloves.

"I have other pairs, of course, but I do not know how it is but these are my favourites. They fit so much better than any of the rest."

"Oh, I know exactly what it is you mean. I have a favourite pair of boots – no others seem half so well suited to me, however shabby they look now. I have had them these three years together. I wonder if the cobbler is wearied of mending them yet."

"I am so glad you are come this morning, Miss Elizabeth. The Hursts have arrived, you know, and I am never entirely comfortable in close quarters if I do not know people well. I envy Miss Lydia her fearlessness."

Elizabeth laughed, "Oh, Lydia is Lydia. A very dear sister to me but I do think she has never felt anxiety since the moment she was permitted to put her hair up and wear long skirts. It might not do her any harm to feel self-doubt every now and then."

"I am devoted to my brother, Miss Bennet – there is not a dearer one in all the world – but I have often longed for a sister."

"Well, I daresay Mr. Darcy will provide you with one by and by – he does so like to grant your wishes. He was telling me a very great secret concerning your upcoming birthday and I have been quite fearful of accidentally blurting it out ever since. Suffice it to say he has done splendidly this year."

Miss Darcy, having grown a little more used to Elizabeth's teasing, smiled and peppered her with questions. She saw her friend to the door some ten minutes later and they saw Mr. Darcy waiting at the step.

"Ah, Miss Bennet. I wish to offer my escort home."

"I do not know that I ought to accept, Mr. Darcy – you look to be in a fearful temper. I almost think I prefer to face the likelihood of a stray boar."

He sent her a level look and told his sister, who looked a little alarmed, that Miss Bennet was teasing. "Depend upon it, Georgiana, I shall see your friend home safely. I do not think Miss Elizabeth would wish you to feel a moment's anxiety."

Upon it being hinted that she should feel concerned, Georgiana willingly obliged by expressing a great sense of worry that some accident might befall Miss Elizabeth on the journey home.

Outmanoeuvred, Elizabeth accepted Mr. Darcy's escort without any noticeable sign of the deep gratitude she must surely be feeling towards him for such noble consideration.

They set off across the fields, Mr. Darcy matching her paces without any difficulty. Lizzy was content with silence between them as they walked; she was much occupied by the shifting and sorting out of her feelings.

She had seen Miss Bingley walking on the arm of Mr. Darcy many a time and had done so without feeling the revulsion of this morning, so it stood to reason that something had altered within her. She pondered the subject.

It was not until they left the boundary of the Netherfield estate and Mr. Darcy offered Elizabeth his hand to step up to a stile that she realised the cause.

Clearly, without being very much aware of it, she had started to regard Mr. Darcy as her own rightful property, and had disliked very much having her claim to him seemingly usurped by Caroline Bingley.

It was a new, strange feeling, this jealousy, but she rationalised within herself, as they entered the wood and the path widened enough for them to walk two abreast, that it was not so very odd for her to feel a little possessive of him. She had unconsciously attracted the regard of a very eligible man – was it any wonder that having become aware of it she should also realise that it wasn't just she who wanted to marry him?

She stopped short on the path, a little shocked.

Mr. Darcy, blessedly silent while she had been lost in her thoughts, stopped also.

"Are you unwell, madam?"

She looked at him, in the new strange knowledge that she wanted him to be her husband. She needed no more evidence. He was a good, honourable man with both the means and desire to support her well in life – why on earth had she hesitated for so long?

"Miss Elizabeth?"

"Oh! I beg your pardon, sir – I have been woolgathering."

"I had noticed."

She smiled, a little hesitantly, "I have been a shockingly bad walking companion. I shall amend matters and you will forgive me for my inattention. I am at your disposal; if you wish to choose the subject, I will exert myself to be as entertaining as I am able."

"You need not feel obliged to amuse me, Miss Elizabeth. I am quite content just to walk with you, but if you are done with your musings, I do have something I wish to speak to you about."

Her heart beat a little faster and she looked expectant.

"You are to come with us to Pemberley tomorrow. I am glad of it, for I have wanted you to see it for some time. There are many beautiful walks to be enjoyed there, but not…" and here he paused to ensure he had her full attention, "but not alone."

Well, if she was not to become an engaged woman by the end of this walk, she might as well enjoy a lively battle of wits.

"Mr. Darcy, I was well aware by the black frown upon your otherwise very handsome brow that I had incurred your displeasure. I was most put out that you did not seem at all pleased to see me." She pouted a little. Mr. Darcy blinked and then looked severe.

"Miss Elizabeth, you are a little too fearless sometimes," he said mildly, still frowning.

"What have I to be afraid of in this country? I have walked it many times and not once encountered harm. My father is aware of my habits and has no objection. I do not quite see why you are so set upon my having an escort when I have managed quite admirably without one for years."

"That is not the kind of fearlessness I was referring to, madam."

"Sir?"

"I would have rather thought that your friend, Miss Lucas, might have read you a lecture about the dangers and consequences of flirting with a man in a secluded wood." So bland was his tone that it took Elizabeth a moment to register the warning.

Elizabeth gaped, blushed hotly, and started walking again. At length, she said, "I do not believe that you would do harm to any woman, Mr. Darcy. I am quite safe, I think."

"If I recall correctly, one of your objections to marrying me was that you could not trust yourself to my care. How those words have haunted me! I have tried to act to counter each of your other reservations, but this one has been the hardest – only time and your own feelings could overcome it. Alas, I am not in control of either. It has been a hard-learned lesson in patience."

"I beg your pardon. I did not know you then and had not thought that my words were so offensive. I see now, of course, since meeting Miss Darcy, that you take your responsibilities very seriously. I think...I think that any woman under your care would count herself fortunate."

She spoke this last part quickly, quite embarrassed and further flustered by the suddenly intent look in his eyes. She was unable to say more, but she stopped walking when he did and listened.

"You are too generous to trifle with me, Miss Elizabeth. Nothing could have been kinder or more civil than your response to my abysmal proposal in Kent – your generosity of spirit and good manners shamed me deeply in contrast to my own. I had no cause for pride that day – my arrogance was very ill placed. Regardless of your answer to me now, I remain grateful for the lesson. Do you think you might be persuaded to marry me, Miss Elizabeth? I do not think that I can comfortably live my life without you in it."

"Oh," she said, touched by the simple honesty of the sentiment. "Yes. Thank you. I would like that, I think."

Visibly relieved, Mr. Darcy took her hand and bowed over it. "I shall endeavour to ensure that you never regret your choice, Miss Elizabeth."

Somehow, Elizabeth was sure that she would not.

Chapter Twenty-Three

Mr. Bennet was subsequently applied to, permission was granted with a dry comment on the conveniently timed resolution, and only the good wishes from him and Jane were sought. Elizabeth persuaded Mr. Darcy that Jane deserved to be the only bride spoken of on the morrow and so it was decided between them that Mrs. Bennet and the two youngest sisters should be told once all the wedding guests had departed.

"You are a very devoted sister, Miss Elizabeth," said her betrothed, smiling tenderly at her and entirely inclined to give her whatever she wished for. "Very well, we will delay our departure for Pemberley until the afternoon the day after next. We will need to make an extra stop en route but it ought not create any difficulty. You will be able to tell your friends and acquaintances in person. I daresay Miss Lucas will be relieved that I have lived up to my promises in the woods."

"Oh indeed, I cannot at all think what possessed her, so very unwilling to take my word for it that naught untoward occurred. Thank you, sir; I would like to visit some of my friends."

"By the by, would you furnish me with the direction of the Browns?"

"Certainly, although I cannot at all see why you should want it. You are not at all known to them, are you?

"Not at present, no."

"Ah well, 'tis a wretched beginning if you are intent on keeping secrets so soon after Papa has given his blessing."

"Quite so. I daresay it will do you a great deal of good to not always have things your own way. The address, Miss Bennet?"

"Fie, sir! Such a pretty opinion you have of me – I am surprised you should wish to marry me at all!" High spirits suited Elizabeth; having reached a resolution, her merriment would not be contained and she was rather well pleased with herself.

"Are you angling for a compliment? I am quite at your disposal. Would you like me to compose a sonnet to your eyes or do you feel my regard too weak to withstand the test of it?"

"Could you do it, I wonder?"

"I doubt even Wordsworth could do you justice, my...Miss Elizabeth."

She caught the slip and to his satisfaction turned red to her forehead. "The Browns live on the farther side of Meryton from Lucas Lodge. Walk up the main street as far as the post office and turn left. They live in the little cottage with the well in the front garden. Shall I write it for you?"

"Despite my advanced years, my memory is excellent; thank you, madam."

"I am pleased to hear it, although I am entirely used to living with a man stricken with senility so it would not trouble me overly much if your mind *occasionally* failed you."

His shoulders shook in silent laughter. "Miss Bennet, when we are married I shall find a method to control that acid tongue of yours."

She laughed gaily and wished him well in such an endeavour.

He sobered. "I ought to leave you. I wish that I might remain but I know you have much to do and Georgiana does not do well in a house full of people. I promised her that I should not abandon her for long once the Hursts came. I am sorry for it but I must keep my word."

"I am glad of it, sir. It bodes very well, I think, that you do your duty even when your inclination bids otherwise. I will not dissuade you from it. I shall see you tomorrow. I will be the one in the pink dress with the eyes red from weeping."

He looked into those eyes and gently ran a finger down her cheek. "I will bring my largest handkerchief to offer you, then." His finger ever so lightly traced her bottom lip and Elizabeth couldn't breathe. "You have made me very happy this day, Miss Elizabeth. I shall not cease to be grateful for the justice in you that permitted me a second opportunity. I'll not waste it. Good day and God bless you."

With that he left her, feeling odiously missish, weak in the knees, and unable for the entire day to think of anything other than him. Jane had to call her to attention many times when her mind wandered from the tasks they had set themselves to accomplish.

She did not live up to her promise of red eyes at the wedding. Jane's radiance was readily apparent to all in attendance. Mrs. Bennet declared loudly that indeed there could not be a prettier bride in the whole of England, and if some shook their heads at her, she was largely considered to be right.

Mr. Darcy discreetly made his way over to Elizabeth in the churchyard as she stood a little apart from the others, watching the children of the village eagerly hunt for the pennies that Mr. Bingley had thrown. She laughed at a small girl who successfully warned off a much older boy with a well-placed elbow and clutched her prize gleefully.

"I cannot at all reconcile with myself how I could have misjudged your sister so sorely, Miss Bennet. It is as plain as the nose on my face that she is very attached to him. I am glad for them both – I daresay that they will do very well together." He saw the slight tightening in her eyes and casually remarked, "I am good friends with Bingley – I usually see him often."

Lizzy, who had indeed been on the cusp of tears, recovered herself with aplomb. "I do not think the nose on your face is at all plain, Mr.

Darcy." She peeped up at him through damp lashes. "It is in perfect keeping with the rest of your face, sir."

Mr. Darcy coloured and leant down to murmur in her ear, "Shall we go and see if the good reverend within is inclined to wed another couple today, Miss Bennet? Or would you like to stop flirting with me?"

Glibly she returned, "Oh, neither, thank you, sir – I shall enjoy our engagement period. It will be interesting to see how you alter your behaviour now that you have hunted down the hare."

"I do not at all think of you in such terms, Miss Bennet," he said primly.

"Very proper, sir. I do not think you should think of your affianced wife as a docile little rabbit."

"It is not a comparison I am likely to make. I should think a vixen would be more apt."

Seeing they had drawn the notice of a few onlookers by her laughter and his own smile, he bowed and said, "I shall go and defend Georgiana, Miss Bennet – she looks quite alarmed."

"Yes, I see that young Mr. Goulding has decided to approach her. Poor boy, he is very pleasant but has not the least idea of how to talk to a female. I daresay Miss Darcy will be clapped on the back and declared to be a good fellow."

Mr. Darcy frowned and left her side, and Elizabeth could not quite contain her grin.

He was replaced by Mr. Bennet, who offered his daughter his arm.

"Well now, my little Lizzy, you made it through the ceremony without a single tear shed. I cannot blame you – it is hard to be sad for two people so very satisfied with their lot in life."

"Quite so, Father. If I had succumbed I should rather account it to an excess of joy."

"Shall you weep at your wedding, I wonder?"

Elizabeth was watching Mr. Darcy bid Mr. Goulding a distinctly chilly good morning and trying to concentrate on her father while admiring how handsome her affianced looked in his blue coat, and how very becoming his haughty manners were on such a noble countenance. Her father looked amused.

"How soon our daughters forget us when a young man comes along. Can't take your eyes off him, I see. I am almost concerned that I am sending you off to Derbyshire in his company, given how you look at him."

Elizabeth blushed and gave him her attention, which had been Mr. Bennet's aim after all. "I assure you, sir, Mr. Darcy is a very proper gentleman. I have no fear that he would take any advantage of the necessary closeness that travelling together entails. Miss Darcy will be there with her maid, too. I understand Mrs. Annesley is to be at Pemberley when we arrive."

Mr. Bennet smirked. "I wasn't concerned about you, Elizabeth – I am fearful that you will quite embarrass the fellow with your blatant admiration. Do rein yourself in a little, my love. Your mother was the same with me – it is quite irresistible to a man, I assure you. We had better make our way to the house. Indulge an old man, my dear, and take a walk with me."

There was a bittersweet contentment between them as they walked together arm in arm. Her Papa was not so young as he once was but he did not require the support of the stick he carried. Elizabeth reflected that it would not always be so – he would grow older and frailer and she would soon marry and go far away.

She had always known that it must be so; she could not always dwell at Longbourn, the favoured daughter of an indulgent father. Elizabeth thought, though, that had the necessity of marriage not been so certain, she would have chosen to remain at home rather than marry anyone that she was not desperately in love with. It was a hard thing, to know that their lives must change so. Friends and neighbours she had grown up with rode past in their carriages; others walked behind them. The lanes that she was so familiar with looked as they ever did, and she wondered when her last walk there would be so that she might bid even the wayside flowers a fond farewell.

"Chin up, my love. Don't let your Mama see you look so downcast on her day of triumph. Ah, Lydia, do cheer Elizabeth up, will you? I must needs brave the masses and greet the newlyweds."

Lydia, who had seen Elizabeth's sombre face, had wandered over, concerned. "She will not be so very far away, Lizzy – you have walked to Netherfield often – it need not alter so very much and I do think she will be happy."

Lizzy returned the embrace from her youngest sister and was surprised by how much taller she was now. "Ah, do not mind me, Lydia. I am resisting the inevitable and it does naught but make me feel low. You are quite right – she will be very, very happy. If she is not, we shall both of us conspire to take dire revenge on Mr. Bingley."

"Oh yes! I should enjoy that!" laughed Lydia, betraying her youth with her undue enthusiasm, then, recollecting herself, added, "Of course I hope that it is not at all necessary."

There were no great dramatic scenes for the whole day of the wedding. Speeches were made and the newlyweds were toasted. Lydia and Kitty behaved with great propriety, still holding fast to the hope of a season in London if they comported themselves well. If Mrs. Bennet drank a little too much wine and boasted a little too freely of their good fortune, those who assembled were mostly fond enough of the bride to pay her mother little heed.

Miss Bingley smirked and looked superior but was swiftly abashed when Mr. Darcy scowled at her rudeness. When she attempted to speak of the inferiority of the Bennets in his ear, he coldly bowed and excused himself. Elizabeth restrained herself as best she could but was forced to speak to Miss Bingley when the lady intercepted her on her way across the room.

"Why, how charming you look, Miss Eliza! I do not believe I have ever seen you dressed so. I do not dare wear that particular shade of pink myself, though – it is so difficult to wear well."

"Thank you, Miss Bingley. Jane must take the credit for choosing this particular dress. You will find your new sister has a very good eye for such things if you care to make use of it. Lydia is the same – such a talent for selecting fabrics! I am doubly blessed. I daresay you are able to wear most shades fairly adequately, Miss Bingley, but you are very wise to know the limit of what will look well on you. Oh, I do beg your pardon, I have been wishing to speak to Mrs. Bingley before they depart for Netherfield."

She made her way over to the bride and embraced her tightly. "Mrs. Bingley, I hereby volunteer myself and Lydia to find a gentleman who will quickly wed Miss Bingley if she becomes unendurable. Do you suppose she would *strongly* object to a widower?"

Jane tried to look stern. "Lizzy, do not be unkind…."

Her sister had a mischievous glint in her eye. "I am duly chastened. You are quite right, I know – the poor man deserves our compassion, whoever he may be!"

Chapter Twenty-Four

The delight with which Mrs. Bennet later looked back on the day of dear Mrs. Bingley's wedding was the main source of her discourse for some weeks after the Event. Not only had her eldest daughter never looked in greater beauty, but the entire day had passed by with great success. The neighbours were entirely amicable, the food sumptuous, and the crowning triumph of the day had been that evening when Elizabeth had entered her sitting room and perched upon the arm of her chair.

"The day went well, did it not, Lizzy?" she said, weary but well content. There was an ache in her heart to be sure, but it was mostly surpassed by the enormity of her satisfaction.

"Aye, Mama, it did. Jane made a very beautiful bride. I do not believe anyone could dream up a handsomer one."

"No, you are quite right, my love. Although I will say that the rest of you girls did me great credit. I do not suppose you were able to speak much with Mr. Darcy today?"

"Not a great deal, no, Mama."

"Well, that is a pity, but you will have ample opportunity from tomorrow, will you not?" She gave a delighted crow. "To think you will be at Pemberley for the whole summer in company with so fine a family as the Darcys. Perhaps you will meet Mr. Darcy's uncle, the earl!"

"I daresay I will do so at some point in the future, ma'am. I accepted Mr. Darcy's proposal yesterday so it may well be that some of his family attends the wedding."

Mrs. Bennet let out a startled shriek, which drew the attention of Mrs. Hill from the dressing room and she came in.

"All is well, Hill – Mama is merely pleased."

"Very good, Miss Bennet," said the faithful servant, quite used to an excess of noise from her mistress.

"Pleased! *Pleased*, Elizabeth! Oh, Lizzy, I shall go quite distracted." Mrs. Bennet clutched at her daughter. "Mrs. Darcy! You will have such fine things, my love – depend on it, I should think he will be a very generous husband. Oh!"

After that, she could barely speak, such was her excitement. Her only regret was that she could not boast that very moment to the other matrons of the neighbourhood. She had to content herself with her maid and then, summoning her younger daughters, bade them congratulate their sister.

Kitty squealed. "Lizzy! How could you possibly keep such a thing to yourself all day? I should have wanted to tell everyone immediately."

Lizzy smiled knowingly. "I am not at all surprised to hear it, sister. I suggest you learn some discretion whilst I am in Derbyshire if I am to keep to my bargain."

Lydia surprised them all. "Lizzy, you will be happy, won't you? Jane and Mr. Bingley are a different matter altogether – they are so obviously...well, what I mean is that even if it means not going to parties and balls and such, we would not want you to marry such a stern man if you did not truly wish to."

Lizzy's eyebrows shot up. "Lydia, my dear, are you quite well? Perhaps you are over-fatigued by the day. Shall I fetch you a draught from the stillroom?"

"Very amusing, Lizzy. If you are content, then of course I wish you joy. It is just that he is so very severe."

"Thank you. I do not believe we shall encounter any great bar to our happiness; he assures me he means to be a good husband and I am inclined to believe it. I am not at all inclined to be morose either, so I am certain we shall deal together well enough. Marriages have succeeded on less."

Lydia frowned a little and Kitty overrode her. "No, no, Lydia. We are very happy for you, Lizzy. We shall miss you, of course, but if you invite us to stay with you we will feel the want of your company much less. Do write to us as soon as you get to Pemberley tomorrow – Miss Darcy would only say that she could not do it enough justice and that doesn't help us picture it at all."

Mrs. Bennet, who had been smiling benignly, only half listening, said, "Oh yes, my love, do write to us of all that you see. We all want to hear in great detail about your future home."

Lizzy promised and saw that Kitty was smothering a yawn. "Ah, but if I am to leave first thing in the morning I must hasten my steps to bed. On no account must you two rise before times to see me off; I shall do very nicely with Hill to give me some breakfast. We have all had a long day – you are doubtless exhausted." With that, the three daughters kissed their mother on the cheek and left her to her happy thoughts.

Once in the hallway, Lydia whispered to Kitty that she should be in shortly, and followed Elizabeth into her room.

Lizzy was glad of it, for the bedchamber which she had often shared with Jane suddenly seemed so very empty. There would be no more bedtime confidences and muffled giggles with so grand a person as Mrs. Bingley. How strange it would all be. She supposed that Mr. Darcy would become her main confidant, as was proper between a husband and wife, but she could not at all envision them side by side shaking with restrained laughter as Jane and she had done too many times to count. Lydia broke into her thoughts.

"Lizzy, I overheard Mr. Bingley and Mr. Darcy speaking today outside Papa's study. They did not know I was there – I was avoiding Miss Bingley, you know, so could not be easily seen."

Her elder sister laughed at Lydia's artless honesty. "Yes, I know. What grave matter did you overhear? I know from experience that nothing good comes from eavesdropping on those two gentlemen."

"I do not know that I ought to tell you really – if you are well content ought I leave things be?"

"Goodness, Lydia – how you do provoke my curiosity. One might suppose that Mr. Darcy has some nefarious plan to murder me – how very gothic! Have you been reading novels, Miss Lydia?"

Lydia was dismissive but still serious. "Oh, Lizzy, you know I never read anything if I can help it – I have so many more important things to do. It was nothing like that, not really. If it were, I should, of course, have spoken to Papa."

"I am glad of it!"

"Yes, but Lizzy, this is *serious*. Mr. Darcy was saying to Mr. Bingley that he could not at all understand why he had made such a handsome settlement on Jane!"

All amusement vanished. "Truly?

"Yes, and when Mr. Bingley said that it was befitting his wife, Mr. Darcy said that he should bestow only half so much. Mr. Bingley was very uncomfortable and muttered something about Miss Bingley's allowance but Mr. Darcy replied that a wife – *any wife* – did not need so much."

Sourly, Elizabeth said, "Do tell me that next Mr. Bingley told Mr. Darcy to mind his own affairs and planted him a facer."

Lydia looked anxious. "*No*, Miss Bingley walked past then. She was prodigiously annoyed about something – perhaps she did not like the quality of the ham. Anyway, they dropped the conversation and I couldn't hear any more; besides, Papa found me and told me that I should come out from my hiding place. Ought I not have told you, Lizzy?"

Elizabeth grimaced. "It is good that you did, dearest. I will speak to Papa in the morning and possibly to Mr. Darcy before we set off. We shall see if there is a reasonable explanation and if there is not...well now, if there is *not* then you are a very good sister to me."

Lydia embraced her. "I will try to be up when you are, Lizzy. That way I can tell your grim-faced Mr. Darcy off for being so close-fisted if it is necessary."

Elizabeth trusted that it would not be at all necessary but kissed her sister fondly. "You know, Lydia, I should like a letter or two from you while I am away – if I go. Do keep me abreast of the goings-on in Meryton, will you?"

"Oh...very well then," said Lydia, with evident reluctance. It was well known that she much preferred receiving letters to writing them. "Good night, Lizzy. I am sorry if I have said what I ought not."

Elizabeth laid her head down that night quite unable to account for what Lydia had overheard. Mr. Darcy, according to his sister, was all that was generous – she was not so vulgar to disclose what funding was available to her, of course, but had often said very sweetly that her brother was often too kind to her, that she did not deserve half of the things he did for her. It was a puzzlement. The only reasonable explanation for Mr. Darcy's attitude was that he had not actually changed his opinions about the unworthiness of the Bennets, and yet, Elizabeth could not at all see that he was capable of deceit. Everything she had seen of him showed him to be a good, honest man.

She fell asleep trying to make it all out.

The next morning, the Darcy carriage arrived promptly at Longbourn and Mr. Darcy handed his sister down once the footman had put down the steps. Elizabeth, tired and a little pale, stood slightly out of sight while her father greeted him. She was able, therefore, to observe him as his eyes searched for her and to see the clear delight in his face once she stepped forward. It did much to reassure her, and her greeting, although subdued, was decidedly less cool than it would otherwise have been.

Miss Darcy was all enthusiasm for Miss Bennet to accompany them. Her brother, she said, had imparted the good news to her last evening and she was beside herself with joy. She could not, she said, have chosen a better sister for herself than the one he had found her.

Mr. Darcy, speaking quietly with Mr. Bennet in a more sedate, dignified fashion, was watching them, fondness and affection readily apparent in his eyes as the two ladies he loved most in all the world spoke rapidly of their pleasure in each other's company.

Lydia came well-nigh bounding down the stairs as they were walking into the sitting room together.

"Oh, good, Lizzy; I was so fearful I had overslept – I had meant to be earlier. Good morning, Mr. Darcy," she said coolly. "Miss Darcy, how do you do."

Knowing her own difficulty in rising early, Elizabeth thought this sisterly display of affection and loyalty to be quite outstanding and that Lydia almost certainly deserved a great success when she came to town for her season.

"No, I am not gone yet, Lydia. I wanted to have a quick word with Mr. Darcy before we depart, if you would not mind, sir."

"I am entirely at your disposal, madam," said he courteously.

Lydia looked as though she would like to dispose of him herself but thought her sister deserved the pleasure.

The couple walked to the further side of the room and looked out the window together. Lydia heroically attempted to cover their quiet voices by drawing Miss Darcy out.

Mr. Darcy had by this time noted Elizabeth's pallor, and a small crease appeared between his brows. "What is amiss, Miss Bennet? Are you longing for Mrs. Bingley? We can drive back to Netherfield for a quarter of an hour if you wish."

Such solicitude softened Elizabeth further.

"It is naught that an explanation will not cure, Mr. Darcy. I do not deal well with unsatisfied curiosity, I fear. My sister Lydia overheard a conversation between you and Mr. Bingley yesterday that has caused her great uneasiness."

It took but a moment for understanding to dawn and then he began to look decidedly amused.

"Ah. That explains why Miss Lydia is looking as though you will throw something at my head. I do hope you will disappoint her."

"That will likely depend on the level of my own disappointment."

"I shall be swift then. Miss Lydia overheard your brother and me speaking of financial matters that we had no business talking of in a public space. Furthermore, Miss Lydia is gravely worried that I will turn parsimonious once we are married and there will be no more bonnets nor ribbons nor books to give you any joy ever again. Am I quite correct?"

"She does not wish either Jane or me to be treated unfairly. She is not unreasonable, I do not think."

"Not unreasonable at all, Miss Bennet. I quite admire her resourcefulness – I did not see her at all and I had cause to be looking about me. That speech she overheard was entirely for Miss Bingley's benefit – she has been rather insistent that I should make a delightful husband, which I fully intend to be, by the way, just not to her."

Elizabeth watched the men load her trunks onto the back of the carriage. "So you found it necessary to persuade her that you will be the epitome of austerity as a husband."

"Yes. I do not at all like the disguise necessary but I thought it intolerable that she should feel a right to be envious of you, and although Bingley has attempted in the past to be direct, the lady in question has a good deal of...er...self confidence and would not be dissuaded."

Lizzy let out a breath. The relief she felt was palpable and she did not care to examine with any great detail why it was she had felt so unhappy since last night. "I suppose I had better warn you then that you should not accept any drink from Lydia. Thank you for explaining matters so plainly. I could not at all comprehend how such doings could at all fit in with my knowledge of your character. I had quite decided that I should be doted on as a wife, you see."

Mr. Darcy smiled. "It is a good sign, my dear, that you asked me first before administering poison. I foresee a happy marriage if we continue so."

Elizabeth's fingers trembled a little and she clutched them behind her back. It was decidedly unfair how well such a fond smile suited him.

"For sure, sir, if you always have such reasonable explanations, I shall be forced to dispense with all of my more fatal substances and keep only the ones that cause unpleasantness such as severe itching and the like. Shall we be off? I am ready to go with you – I need only to put on my bonnet and gloves."

"One moment, Miss Bennet."

She paused expectantly. He darted a quick look to the other occupants of the room to ensure that they were not attending them. They were all very carefully engaged elsewhere.

"I had considered a dashing, sweeping declaration of my love for you. I do not think that will do, though. I know that...that there must be a disparity of affection between us and I would not have you feel in any way as though you must make yourself feel more for me than you do. I count myself fortunate merely to have won your hand and that you are as fair in mind as you are in face. I wish you to know, with certainty, that I will not burden you with my affections and that first and foremost throughout our engagement period I will treat you with all the respect you deserve." He swallowed. "That is all. You need not fear me, Miss Bennet." Concerned by the tears that had sprung, yet again, to her eyes, he took her hand and pressed it earnestly before softly repeating the sentiment, anxious that she should believe him, "I would not have you fear me."

Chapter Twenty-Five

Pemberley, 25th May 1813

*D*ear Miss De Bourgh,

Since writing my last, I find myself in altogether different circumstances to pen you an epistle. Letter-writing at home involves finding a private space, a pen, and a flat surface, and making the best of things. Papa, you will understand from my masterful descriptions, does not at all care to share his library for prolonged periods. I have been hinting to him for several years that I should be deeply grateful for a portable lady's desk set such as I saw in London once upon a time, but he declares that I would doubtless turn my hand to novel-writing like Mrs. Burney or – perish the thought – some other anonymous female. You may imagine my delight to arrive at Pemberley and being shown to my room and seeing that a little writing desk has been set up with pen and paper for my own private use.

Alas, it has hindered my letter-writing quite dreadfully, for every time I sit down, determined to be a superb correspondent, I look up and see such a view that I spend many minutes deciding which paths to wander when next I go out.

And now, Madam, prepare yourself for a not very severe shock. Before we left Hertfordshire, Mr. Darcy and I came to an Understanding and are likely to wed in Meryton Church at the end of the summer! I do not doubt that you will enjoy imparting such *news to Her Ladyship; it is so pleasant to be the bringer of news rather than the receiver sometimes. I requested that Mr. Darcy should not send his letter to your Mama until mine had been a full day in the post to be sure that you would know something before she did. I do hope he will be so obliging once we are married.*

I am entirely charmed with Derbyshire thus far. I have been given a grand tour by Mr. and Miss Darcy and am now convinced that the very best travel companions are local ones, who can relate such interesting tidbits of information that will quite enrapture the listeners. I do not know that it is quite proper but Mr. Darcy told me, while we were visiting some ancient caverns near Buxton, the most harrowing tale of Old Jack Parr the inebriate who wandered from his companions one evening and was never seen again, but his ghost can be seen and heard in the echoes if one does not stay very close to one's companions. I declare, Miss de Bourgh, that the hairs on the back of my neck stood on their ends and I was not at all easy until we returned to the light.

I am no longer at all astonished that Miss Darcy is the very pattern of perfect obedience to her brother, if those are the methods he employs to ensure that she does not go exploring. I am content that I quite robbed him of any self-satisfaction, however, by pretending a great interest in visiting the caves again after dark to prove that nothing could lurk in such a way as he described, and I do think I have cured him of such underhanded tactics for the present. I had such horrid dreams that night, though – I trust I convinced him rather better than I did myself that I was entirely fearless.

"Miss Bennet?" inquired her maid, interrupting her composition. "I beg your pardon, madam – I did knock but assumed you were without."

"It doesn't matter, Harding. I was entirely too caught up in my letter; that is all."

"Mr. Darcy has given me orders to get you into your outdoor wear and requests that you meet him on the southern terrace."

Elizabeth sighed happily. She had been at Pemberley for nearly five complete days and Mr. Darcy had shown her every attention and civility.

"Very well then, Harding. I suppose Miss de Bourgh's letter shall have to wait yet again. Shall Mrs. Brown like to come or is she to remain indoors? Oh, and is it windy out, do you know? I wonder if I ought to risk my new straw bonnet."

"There's a slight breeze, Miss Bennet, not too gusty though. Mrs. Brown has walked to the Post Office at Lambton."

Lizzy grinned. Mr. Darcy had greatly impressed her parents with his extraordinary sense of propriety by employing Mrs. Brown of Meryton to act as a chaperone for the duration of Elizabeth's stay. That lady had been quite overcome with gratitude to him for offering her paid work. Her children were to be taken care of by the eldest Brown son, to whom Mr. Bingley had promised work at Netherfield when he returned from his honeymoon to take up residence. To all outward appearances, Mr. Darcy had ensured that not a murmur of scandal could be raised by anyone. The lady did a fine job of accompanying her charge wheresoever Miss Bennet wished to go, and although very quiet, was pleasant enough company. If only she had not been quite so easily directed by Mr. Darcy's hints to occasionally take herself off, she should have made a perfect chaperone. Doubtless, Mr. Darcy had been well aware that the good woman was to go to the village and took full advantage of her absence.

"Very well, I shall wear my straw and my half boots, and take a shawl with me – yes, the cream one with flowers will do nicely, thank you."

She was met on the terrace by Mr. Darcy, who was leaning against the balustrade in as casual an attitude as she had ever seen him in. He had removed his hat and was surveying the roof of the house, his eyes squinting against the bright sunlight.

She was struck once again by how handsome he was. It was not at all fair to the rest of mankind that Mr. Darcy should be blessed with wealth, intelligence, high morals, and a handsome face. She felt a glee that threatened to burst forth in a giddy laugh, that she would be married to him and see such a model of gentlemanly perfection every day at breakfast for all her days.

"Oh, good – your maid was not sure if you would be resting or not. I had expected to wait at least a quarter of an hour. I am going to abduct you, Miss Bennet."

"If you wanted to take me to Gretna Green, sir, I suggest you should have ordered Harding to bundle me into a coat." She was a little distracted by the thick hair that brushed his collar.

"No need. I have already bribed her to pack you a trunk – there will be a coat in there."

"I have not," said Elizabeth, "given a great deal of thought to the mechanics necessary in an abduction, but I do rather think that Mrs. Radcliffe might prefer a little less forethought and more impulse."

He bowed to her logic and abandoned the whimsical line of conversation. "I am taking you only so far as the folly, madam. I thought you might like to admire the view – it is the easiest high point to access."

"Oh, the little white one I can see from my room? Yes, I should like that. I have been attempting to write your cousin a nice cheerful letter but my concentration has been sadly errant."

They set off together. Elizabeth was still new enough to the grounds to be looking all about her and asking whatever questions sprang to mind. Mr. Darcy, well-nigh garrulous when it came to his home, answered them thoroughly enough to satisfy her. It reminded her of the old abbey at Rosings, when the good colonel had told her that Mr. Darcy was the man to answer factual questions regarding family history.

"How is your cousin, Mr. Darcy?" she asked him. "The colonel, I mean, not Miss de Bourgh."

"Well enough, judging by his last letter. He is in London presently, which is well, for my aunt Fitzwilliam is never so pleased as when she has all her sons together."

"I am glad of it – I enjoyed his company in Kent."

"I daresay he will wish to be at the wedding when he eventually hears of it."

"How strange it is to hear talk of a wedding and know that it will be my own!"

He smiled. "Do you regret being away from Hertfordshire for the planning? Letters are not always the same."

"Mama will be quite delighted by the freedom of choice, sir. I have always been the most opinionated of her daughters but Lydia has excellent taste in general. I will have a week or so to undo any disastrous decisions she has made so you need not fear that I will turn up in my boots and favourite walking dress."

Mr. Darcy laughed quietly, almost rueful. "If you only knew, Miss Bennet, how much ruin you made upon my composure when you arrived so attired at Netherfield last year, ready to do battle with your sister's illness – and with me, if memory serves correctly."

"I suppose I ought to apologise for antagonising you or some such thing. I daresay that once I summon up sufficient regret I will do so."

"Which is to say that I fully deserved every impertinent remark you threw at my head. I am sure you are right. Are you full of energy, my dear? We must ascend the hill. There used to be steps but Mama thought that they were ugly and ruined the natural beauties of the landscape and so had them removed. I am inclined to agree with her but it does make for a more arduous climb."

"Energetic! Mr. Darcy, I shall see you at the top once you arrive behind me. I shall not at all mind waiting."

She released his arm and scampered on ahead. He kept pace with her easily enough, and although Elizabeth fought to conceal her heavy breathing once she gained the top, she readily admitted that Derbyshire had decidedly steeper hills than Hertfordshire.

"This makes Oakham Mount, the pride of Hertfordshire, look like a mere hillock. Has this mountain I have just climbed a name, sir?"

"I am afraid that it is not deemed a worthy enough slope for anything so formal, Miss Bennet. I propose that we name it after you."

"How charming! I now have claimed for myself a woodland in Kent and a mountain in Derbyshire. Miss Bennet's Mount – yes, I do think it suits." She was still hot and pink in the face from the exertion of the climb, and discreetly attempted to cool herself by waving her hand a little for breeze.

Mr. Darcy watched her with fondness. "I think that Mrs. Darcy's Hill would be more even more suited. If you care to turn around you will have an excellent view of the house."

Elizabeth did so and her laughing retort died on her lips. Pemberley lay below them, spread out and gleaming in the sunshine like a jewel in a crown. The lake shone blue and clear and the carefully laid out patterns of the lush green formal gardens only added to the magnificence. Mr. Darcy approached her and murmured low in her ear.

"Well? Are you pleased with Pemberley?"

She felt his warm breath tickle the lobe of her ear and could think of little else but that.

"What?" she said, distracted, "Oh! Yes. It is very – nice."

"Nice!" exclaimed her betrothed, sounding extremely shaken. "The very best thing I have to offer, the most lauded thing about me, and she calls it 'nice.'" He saw her begin to smile and said severely, "Miss Bennet, I shall compose for you a list of appropriate and acceptable words to describe your future home when we return and you must study it at great length."

Seeing him thus, relaxed and playfully scolding her, Elizabeth was hit with a bolt of realisation. Here with her, on this hill, he was able to forget every other responsibility and duty that he had. He was not the staid Master of Pemberley that she had seen much of in recent days, nor was he the proud Mr. Darcy that she had seen too much of in Hertfordshire and Kent, but rather he was quite simply Fitzwilliam Darcy and she loved him.

Her lips parted in surprise and she swayed a little on her feet. How could such a feeling have come upon her so gradually that she had not realised it until just at this moment in time?

She could not tell him, not just yet when the knowledge was so new to her, too precious a feeling to share, even with him. After all, she had never been in love until now. She felt unaccountably shy and a little vulnerable. This man before her held her heart – it was uncomfortable to know that he could either guard it well or bruise it dreadfully.

He had stopped speaking now and was watching her carefully. His hand came securely beneath her elbow in a firm clasp.

"Miss Bennet? Are you feeling unwell? You have gone quite pale. I am sorry if the walk has worn you out; we do not at all need to continue on to the folly – let us turn back in a moment."

The euphoric, foggy feeling of love dissipated, leaving only a delightful warmth in her heart, and she shook her head as though to clear it, but her gentle smile would not at all be removed from her mouth despite her efforts at appearing normal.

"Mr. Darcy! I am not such a weakling. You have promised to show me your folly and I should like to see it very much. I am quite well, I assure you." She shook off his hand from her elbow so that she could clasp his fingers in hers. She had never done so before, but it felt so right and natural to her that she did not feel overmuch embarrassment. "If you are feeling weary, sir, you must not try to gain resting time by accusing me of such weakness."

They walked on a little way, Mr. Darcy not entirely convinced of her good health – she had looked very odd a moment ago, but was now as vivacious and teasing as ever. Lizzy determined to hide the contents of her thoughts, if for only a little while longer.

"By the by, Mr. Darcy – I think that you are very nice as well as Pemberley. Do you think you might consider calling me 'Elizabeth'?"

Chapter Twenty-Six

Three weeks later, Elizabeth still had not told Mr. Darcy of the alteration in her feelings for him. Of course, she thought, from his point of view, he had never realised that she had once heartily disliked him, and even if he suspected a lukewarm regard on her part now, he could not possibly guess that she had fallen headlong into love with him.

They had received word from the Bingleys that they had concluded their honeymoon and would arrive at Pemberley shortly. Mr. Darcy, upon reading the elegantly written note, had exhaled in relief and remarked, with a warmth that he did not often express, that it was a truly wonderful thing that Mrs. Bingley had accepted his friend.

Elizabeth, although agreeing heartily, looked up from her book with a quizzical expression and sent him a look of enquiry. Georgiana, who had been frowning with some ferocity at her sheet music, giggled.

"Fitzwilliam does not at all get on with Mr. Bingley's hand – it is not very legible. I know for I have seen it."

Enlightenment and amusement dawned. "Ah! Jane is very particular about neatness, and her hand is very clear. When we were growing up she always took an age to copy out her letters, but never had to do them twice over as I often did."

Mr. Darcy, who had told Elizabeth that he greatly enjoyed hearing the anecdotes of her younger self, smoothly remarked that if the new Mrs. Bingley would engage to write all important correspondence he would be forever in her debt. "I imagine I might feel much more kindly toward Bingley if he did not give me a headache with each paragraph he adds. We had a professor in Cambridge who grew so tired of Bingley's disorderliness that he eventually gave up attempting to decipher his papers. He simply assigned whatever merit he had given the last fellow he graded."

"If that is the standard by which young men are deemed educated, I wonder your comments at Rosings that a woman could not manage it," exclaimed Elizabeth, who in truth still felt indignant at his remarks that evening, despite the fact that she had disposed of such ridiculous arguments satisfactorily.

Georgiana played a discord and drew the attention of Mrs. Brown, who had been sewing in the corner of the window where the light was better. "Did you really say that, brother? I suppose you have not mentioned to Lizzy that you spent weeks persuading Uncle Fitzwilliam that he must open a school for girls on his estate."

Mr. Darcy, who had risen from his chair by the fire to sit beside his future bride, stretched out his tall frame more comfortably. "No, I don't believe I had got around to speaking of it," he said casually. The fringe of Elizabeth's shawl was within his reach and he smoothed out the tassels before crossing them over each other absentmindedly.

Elizabeth lowered her book, concentration quite dispelled. "Mr. Darcy, I profess myself to be most confused. You cannot possibly believe in the futility of educating the female mind and simultaneously be the same man who does such a progressive thing as Georgiana declares. I do hope you mean to clarify."

"I did not say that I thought women were unable to learn, Elizabeth, merely that their boundaries are so confined that it seems useless to teach a woman if she is not permitted to make use of her brain. You are the one who wilfully misunderstood me and supposed I believed that all women should be kept ignorant."

"Confess, sir! You deliberately misled both me and the entire table. I think Mrs. Collins and Lady Catherine would have argued with you if I had not."

He smiled slightly, tangling her shawl ends quite dreadfully. She looked down, and once noticing, lowered her hand to thread her fingers through his lest she never restore the fringe to order. His hand ceased its destruction of her favourite paisley and instead occupied itself in becoming acquainted with her fingers.

"Perhaps," was all he would allow.

Georgiana, unable to see from her position at the pianoforte that her brother was playing with both Miss Bennet's hand and her composure, felt that his modesty was a little overdone. "Brother has always said to me that he finds ignorance in women deplorable."

"I find ignorance in anybody deplorable, Georgiana," said her stern brother, "which is why I harangue you over your abuse of punctuation so often."

Seeing the poor girl looking chastened, Elizabeth intervened, "Mr. Darcy, I do think you might be accused of being quite modern in your views. Next thing I hear, you will have set up a schoolhouse for the illiterate farmhands in Derbyshire and will sally forth on a weekly basis to bully them into a perfect understanding of Latin declensions."

He raised her squirming fingers to his lips. "Certainly not;" he murmured provocatively, having kissed the hand and lowered it back down out of the others' line of sight, "that must be a duty Mrs. Darcy must undertake."

"I hope you mean to offer the job to someone else then, for I absolutely detested Latin and would only encourage them to revolt."

"It isn't possible now, my dear. Even if it I wished it, all papers are signed and sealed. Mr. Bennet sent the correct copies to me yesterday. The banns have been read and all that remains is for us to travel to Hertfordshire within the fortnight. Then I can bring you back here and keep you forever. I am afraid that if you want to be rid of me, my love, you will have to prepare yourself to be labelled a jilt."

He sounded satisfied with the prospect, and Elizabeth, remembering with a little guilt that she had once toyed with the idea of rejecting him at the end of their courtship, allowed the matter to rest.

Mr. and Mrs. Bingley arrived the following afternoon. If it was possible, Jane had grown even more beautiful in the weeks since her sister had seen her.

"Goodness, Lizzy!" was all she could say as she stepped down from the carriage with her proud husband's assistance and looked up at the grandeur and size of the house in which her sister would reign as mistress.

Elizabeth sent Mr. Darcy a mischievous look, her eyes dancing with merriment. "Yes, it's very nice, isn't it?"

"It is entirely delightful!" responded Jane bluntly, and pulled her younger sister into a tight embrace.

Mr. Darcy very correctly bowed over Mrs. Bingley's hand and welcomed her into Derbyshire. Mrs. Reynolds gestured a maid forward to assist with hats and gloves.

Once Mr. and Mrs. Bingley had refreshed themselves in their rooms, the party reconvened on the terrace. The servants brought out fresh fruits and delicate little pastries for them to enjoy. Jane and Elizabeth wandered over to admire the rose gardens that stretched out below.

"Oh, Lizzy, I am so happy! If only I could see you as happy."

"Can you really doubt that I will be, dearest?"

"You will understand once you are married, I think."

Elizabeth laughed. "Ah, Jane, but a few months ahead of me into matrimony and already you are tormenting me with that which I cannot know. You need not fear – I am as certain as I can be that I will be absolutely happy to be here and married to Mr. Darcy."

"Well, if you are so sure, then I am very glad of it. I do not think I have quite accustomed myself to the notion that you will be the mistress of such an estate as this. It is immense!" Mr. Darcy walked over to join them, handing Elizabeth a little plate with a pastry on it. She did not need to glance at it to know that it is was a flavour that she favoured, and she smiled at him affectionately. Jane raised her brows at the obvious regard between them and spoke to her future brother-in-law. "I wonder, Mr. Darcy, that you have managed to keep Lizzy within doors at all since she has been here. I suppose you have not wandered off and gotten lost very often, Lizzy?"

Elizabeth sighed. "I have an excellent sense of direction, I thank you, sister, but it is all entirely beside the point as Mr. Darcy has been a veritable ogre with regards to my always having a servant to escort me."

Mr. Darcy bowed, accepting a compliment that had not been intended, "I am not always available to walk with you, Elizabeth, as much as I would wish to be."

She lightly rested a hand on his forearm and leaned a little into him. "I have no objection to your company, sir."

"Thank you," he said very politely before turning with a smile to walk back to the others.

Lizzy laughingly remarked to Jane, "I shall redouble my efforts next time I wish to walk and persuade him that there is no duty so rewarding as being at my disposal." He heard her, as she had intended him to, and raised an eyebrow at the deliberate provocation.

She was true to her word, and entered the sanctuary of his study the next morning with her walking boots already on and a spring in her step.

"Jane and Mr. Bingley are being decidedly tiresome making eyes at one another, Mr. Darcy, and Georgiana is doing battle with Herr Beethoven. Dear Mrs. Brown has the headache and has retired to her room, so I must either plague you for my entertainment or walk out so far as the west lake."

Mr. Darcy was writing steadily and did not look up, "Enjoy your walk, my dear. Take Holden with you."

Elizabeth breezily replied, "Oh, I am not going so far as that, sir – I shall practically have the house always in sight. I do not see the need to disturb Holden from his other duties."

Mr. Darcy very carefully laid down his pen and at last gave her his full attention. She rather pitied any errant dependents of his that were summoned to face his displeasure when he looked thus. He did not look angry, neither did he look cross, but regarded her steadily from across his desk.

"Elizabeth," he said with great patience, "would you prefer it if I were to walk with you?"

Delighted by his speed at catching on to her aim, Elizabeth was instantly wreathed in smiles. "What a charming idea, Mr. Darcy. I should not at all wish to inconvenience you but if you are certain that you can spare me the time I should be very happy with your company."

The master of Pemberley frowned at a letter in his hand. "Miss Bennet, I find it quite entertaining when you manage others – amusing, even. Your efforts may be a little amateurish but they are surprisingly effective."

Elizabeth frowned too and opened her mouth but was forestalled by his raised finger. It spoke much for her honesty that she was more insulted by the suggestion that she was an amateur than she was that he thought her manipulative.

"I feel that, in the spirit of friendliness and in the interests of our future marital harmony, you should cease any future attempts to manipulate me into complying with your wishes. I am in every way at your service but only," he said firmly, "if you tell me directly what it is that you want." He dragged his attention away from whatever correspondence so fascinated him and noted her furrowed brow and pout. "I tell you, madam, that if I suspect you are attempting such manoeuvres with me as I have seen you inflict on other people, I will do the absolute opposite of whatever it is that I think you want. Starting from now. I myself will inform Holden that there is no duty more important for him than ensuring your safety."

Elizabeth, irked beyond measure, watched him pick up his pen and dip it in the inkwell with the efficiency of long practice.

She waited until he had begun to write again and, with a cunning gleam in her eye, said in the mildest of tones, "As you wish, Mr. Darcy. I shall leave you to your work, sir. Do have a good morning's work."

She walked steadily towards the door but turned at the last minute. He did not look up from his neat even pen strokes.

"By the by, you were quite correct. I did not wish to go for a walk alone – I had quite decided that I should prefer to sit with you in your study and kiss you instead." She laughed when his head shot up from his letter and deep shock was in his eyes. "It is a pity that you have promised so faithfully to disoblige me. Good day, sir – I shall see you at luncheon, I daresay." With that, she stepped nearer to the door and prepared to make a grand exit.

She had successfully twisted the doorknob and opened the door an inch when two hands were set on the door, one on each side of her head, and the door closed again. Elizabeth, surprised by both the speed and the quietness with which Mr. Darcy had rounded the desk and crossed the room, slowly turned in the circle of his arms and looked up at him.

His voice, when he spoke, was very quiet and very deep.

"I propose a counter suggestion then, since you have pointed out the obvious error in my last edict. Behave as you wish, speak as you please, but be aware that each and every time you look at me with that particular gleam of victory in your eyes, you will deserve what will inevitably come your way."

Elizabeth wondered how he could speak so calmly, so clearly, when she could hardly think with any coherence at all. She thought that she had better surrender gracefully and leave. She drew breath to say something suitably docile when he bent his head and she, quite forgetting that she had intended to speak at all, raised her face instinctively.

There was a firm knock on the other side of the door that reverberated through the wood and sounded directly between her shoulders.

Elizabeth jumped guiltily and would have squeaked with surprise except that Mr. Darcy raised his hand and, with great presence of mind, covered her mouth.

"Who is it?" he called out, sounding entirely unaffected. Elizabeth found this so inexplicably irritating that she had to remind severely herself that young ladies did not bite hands, even ones that rudely covered their mouths.

"Reynolds, sir. An express has just this minute arrived from Rosings. I thought you would wish to be informed directly."

Elizabeth having by now realised that Mr. Darcy had clearly been intending to kiss her, decided that Mrs. Reynolds, however exemplary her years of service, needed to be replaced immediately.

The hand was removed from her mouth and she was gently pulled away from the door so that it could be opened and the letter received. Mr. Darcy opened it and read it quickly.

"Tell the man who brought it that I will be with them there within a few days. Alert the stables that I will want the travelling coach made ready and the roan horse saddled. Tell Fareham that I require a travel bag to be packed and that he had better ready himself for a journey. Fetch Mr. Bingley too, if you please, Mrs. Reynolds."

Mrs. Reynolds, unseen on the other side of the door, did not appear to find this flurry of succinct orders in the least bit surprising.

"Very good, Mr. Darcy," she said calmly, and scurried off to do his bidding.

Their eyes met, both aware of what had almost happened but knowing that it could not be spoken of, not just now. Mr. Darcy raised a trembling hand to Elizabeth's cheek and she, feeling a great rush of love for him, kissed it quickly before she could think of whether or not she ought to.

"Bad news, Mr. Darcy?"

He nodded, dragging his eyes away from her and looking down once again at the note. "From Lady Catherine. Anne will not last the fortnight, according to the doctor."

"I am sorry for it," she said simply and meant every word.

Chapter Twenty-Seven

I t was swiftly decided between them that their time at Pemberley had come to an end for the present. Lady Catherine needed her nephew at Rosings and his strong sense of family duty forbade him to do anything other than comply.

They all of them spoke together that evening, trying to decide what must be done and in what order. The difficulty lay in the awkwardness of the timing. Should Miss de Bourgh pass away within a few days, Mr. Darcy would be able to go into black gloves for two weeks and feel perfectly ready to marry knowing that he had observed the requirements of mourning. Should Miss de Bourgh cling to life for more than a week, their wedding must be necessarily delayed.

Elizabeth tentatively suggested that she was perfectly ready and willing to marry him straight away once they returned to Hertfordshire if it aided him in matters of conscience. His eyes warmed at this and he agreed that it was very likely that such a course of action would cause the least amount of difficulty in terms of propriety.

Eventually, a course of action was laid out. Mr. Darcy would travel with the others so far as Hertfordshire, speak with Mr. Bennet to make any necessary arrangements, ride on to Kent for a day or so, and then return to stay at Netherfield until they could be married. Georgiana was extended a very pretty invitation by Jane to remain with them at Netherfield so that she might attend her brother's wedding. Knowing that the lovely Mrs. Bingley was quite the least frightening person in the world, this was accepted with less trepidation in the young girl than she might have felt if it had been Miss Bingley offering to host her.

Elizabeth went to bed that evening quite distressed over her own silliness. She would be wed within the week if all went to plan, and still had not told Fitzwilliam Darcy that she was not merely pleased that she would marry him but that there was nothing on this earth that could make her heart gladder than the prospect of spending every day with him until the Lord in heaven took one of them from the earth. Miss de Bourgh's impending departure from life made it seem even more necessary to Elizabeth that Mr. Darcy know that he was loved. However blessed she may be in terms of the length of her own life, Lizzy saw quite clearly that it would pass all too quickly with him by her side. There was little for it but to declare herself, and soon.

She could hardly say so now, though, not while he was busy in a flurry of activity making everything ready and doing his duty so diligently. It would simply have to wait. Perhaps she might have a few moments with him once he returned from seeing Lady Catherine and his cousin. Soon Anne de Bourgh would be her cousin too. Elizabeth promised herself that she would not be selfish – she would not begrudge his relatives the comfort that only he could bring. This silent vow made her feel marginally less guilty for her lack of compassion for a very sick woman earlier in the year.

Under the efficient direction of Mrs. Reynolds, who Elizabeth realised was entirely indispensable to the smooth running of Pemberley, trunks were packed and carried down, necessary black gloves were located for Miss Darcy and her brother, and Mr. Darcy's valet was set to industrious activity in ensuring that his master would have suitable wedding clothes to wear upon his return to collect his bride. Mrs. Reynolds suggested that the newlyweds would be well situated at the townhouse in London following the wedding, as it gave easy access to both Kent and Hertfordshire, and requested permission to write to the housekeeper there in order that all should be made ready.

They set off together in two carriages heavily laden with trunks. Mr. Darcy's horse was ridden by a groom for the first leg of the journey; once they reached the posting house at Northampton, its owner would ride the rest of the way.

The roads were good and they made excellent time. It was when they had stayed the night at the amusingly named Inn Sobriety that events took a turn for the coincidentally bizarre.

The whole party had gathered in the private parlour, Mr. Darcy in riding dress and toying with his whip, awaiting the carriage to be brought into the bustling courtyard. Elizabeth stepped out into the bright sunlight for a breath of fresh air to sustain her until she reached home. Travelling was such a tedious business; not even the charming company of her future sister was likely to make it any less of a thing to be endured.

She perched on a little bench near to the wall of the inn. The owners had taken great pains to make the building welcoming. Pretty little baskets were planted with bright flowers and the wall had been freshly painted with lime so that the sunlight bounced off it with cheery effect. Elizabeth found great amusement in watching the passers-by, deriving private enjoyment from unusual mannerisms or oddity of dress. A grand coach pulled up as she watched, and out stepped a splendidly attired older gentleman, his hair powdered and worn long in the old manner. He wore buckled heels and a very full coat with his blue waistcoat on display; the embroidery on that was very fine. What was remarkable about him was not his old-fashioned manner of grand dress but his stature. He was not much taller than Elizabeth herself and the sight of his mincing steps as he crossed the yard made her look away lest her smile be too obvious.

When she did look away, she caught the eye of a man standing but a few yards from her, watching her. She did not, at first, recognise him but after sending him an indignant glower for having the impudence to goggle at her so openly, she realised that she knew him.

Mr. Wickham was not so well dressed as he had been when she had last seen him in Meryton; indeed, he did not look anywhere near so much of a gentleman. His attire lacked neatness and it was evident that he had not troubled himself to be shaved for some days. Mr. Wickham approached her with a meandering walk that spoke of his having been drinking, and sat beside her on the bench. Elizabeth, a little alarmed that he should dare do so without an invitation, especially given the disgraced way he had been driven from Meryton, looked about her for a servant she knew.

"Miss Bennet! I am the most fortunate of men to have met you here. I do hope you are not alone." He smiled, with that same broad grin and easy charm that she had been so used to seeing.

"Good day, Mr. Wickham. No, sir, my party is within. I had not thought to encounter anyone I knew here in Northampton of all places." She slyly added, "I had thought that the regiment had removed to Brighton."

Mr. Wickham laughed, with evidence of neither shame nor embarrassment. "Ah, well, I have been sent by my regiment on militia business to this district. I am afraid I cannot tell you the details – it is important to be discreet in such things."

Elizabeth raised her eyebrows. There was nothing in Mr. Wickham's open face that so much as hinted at his falsehood. He looked directly into her eyes without the least trace of hesitancy nor any obvious signal of a lie. He leant in a little closer to her, and before she recoiled she smelt the stale odour of ale about him and wrinkled her nose.

"How thrilling, Mr. Wickham! I shall not breathe a word of your activities, of course; should a Frenchman approach I shall attest that I do not know you at all. Do tell me, sir, how is dear Miss King? Is she dear Mrs. *Wickham* yet, I wonder?"

"Miss King?" he said, blankly. "Oh! Yes, I beg your pardon. No. *No.* She is not likely to be Mrs. Wickham at all, I fear. She...er...had a change of heart. I cannot fault her at all, you know, however great my disappointment, for it is the female's prerogative to choose where she pleases, is it not?"

"I am very sorry to hear it, sir," replied Elizabeth, quite aghast with the convincing ease in which the man could dispense with the truth. "She was so very enthusiastic when I last spoke with her."

"Well," he said smoothly, attempting to put a brave face on it despite his apparent heartbreak, "I am but a poor soldier, after all. Had things been different...had I been granted all that I had been promised...well it does no good to dwell on these things."

"Elizabeth," ordered Mr. Darcy, in cold fury, "come here."

She very gladly hopped off the bench and stood by him. "Fitzwilliam, how glad I am that you came to look for me," she said in an undertone, "I do not think I have ever met a more accomplished liar than Mr. Wickham. I think I may be quite shocked."

"Has he been bothering you?" asked her betrothed, not taking his eyes off the man, who had realised belatedly that his companion had deserted him.

"He sat beside me without any invitation, and was, I believe, about to repeat the same baseless slander that he spread about you in December. I am very sorry to say I actually believed him at the time."

"Darcy!" said Wickham, with all the sneering courage of a man who has drunk too much, "how is dear Georgiana? She must be fully grown up by now."

Elizabeth watched, fascinated, as anger turned Mr. Darcy's eyes to ice, and tension was evident in every line of his body.

"You have been told once before, very clearly, that Miss Darcy's name was never to be mentioned by you in public ever again, Wickham."

Mr. Wickham's bottled bravery did not fail him and he stood and sauntered nearer. "I do not answer to you, Darcy." A swift glance assured him that Miss Elizabeth was in a good position to appreciate his bravery. "Are you going to challenge me to a duel? Hmm? No, of course not." He then saw how close Elizabeth was stood to his old adversary and his lip curled.

Mr. Darcy lifted a finger, his eyes not leaving Wickham's, and two of his servants who had been watching carefully quickly approached.

"I had not quite realised until now, Wickham, the degree to which you wasted the education my father charitably gave you." Contempt dripped from his words and he looked every bit as haughty and proud as Elizabeth had once thought him. "Gentlemen do not duel servants' brats, Wickham." He put a hand to Elizabeth's waist and turned her toward the door of the inn. His last words were tossed over his shoulder as he led Elizabeth away, as negligently as he would throw a coin for a beggar to catch. "They have them *whipped*. Carter, Mibbs. Mr. Wickham has ignored my warning that Miss Darcy's name is not to be bandied about. Do assist him in sobering up."

Mr. Wickham, seeing the two loyal retainers moving in on him and belatedly understanding that he was very likely to receive a thrashing, backed away, throwing his old friend a pleading glance but seeing only his back as he escorted the lady indoors.

"Darcy!" he called, but received no evidence that he had even been heard. He tried again, "Sir! Mr. Darcy!" Carter and Mibbs each grabbed an arm and Wickham gave a yell that betrayed his fear. Mr. Darcy, having ushered Elizabeth into the dark cool passage of the posting-house, spared him a half-glance over his shoulder before resolutely turning away.

Elizabeth stared up at him. They were quite alone in the narrow entry. Very deliberately, Elizabeth raised her palm to his cheek and gently stroked it with her thumb. His eyes closed and he leaned into the tender caress and put his hand back on her waist.

She swallowed.

"Mr. Darcy," she tried, then summoning up her courage, "Fitzwilliam."

He opened his eyes.

"I should like to tell you something important."

His eyes closed again. "I do hope it is not about Wickham."

"Not really, no."

"Good. I am quite done with him," he said.

"Fitzwilliam, you ought to know that...that when you were in Hertfordshire I did not like you at all."

She softened the blow by bringing up her other hand and, holding his face with both palms, she looked full into his eyes.

Slowly he said, "I suppose, had I troubled myself to, I could have worked that out for myself. Why do you think it vital information, my dear? You have agreed to wed me so your feelings toward me cannot be so unfavorable as all that."

"No, Fitzwilliam." She said it more confidently this time. "I think you are very nice."

His shoulders shook and she grew impatient at his dullness.

"You are very stupid today, sir," she said bluntly. "I am trying to tell you that I do not ever want to be apart from you ever again and that I am very glad we are to be married because my heart is entirely yours so you may as well have my hand too."

A few minutes later, Mr. Bingley, at the sweet behest of Mrs. Bingley, stepped into the passage to find the whereabouts of his new sister and oldest friend.

"Darcy!" he exclaimed, very shocked. "I say, Darcy! You cannot kiss Elizabeth in the passageway of a *posting house,* man!"

Mr. Darcy, raising his head, smiled at Bingley in such a way that his friend swallowed and beat a hasty retreat back into the private parlour to face his concerned wife.

As he did so, another door that led to a parlour opened and out stepped the beautifully attired little man that Elizabeth had seen disembark earlier.

"Can it be possible that I heard that correctly?" effused the man, in a soft lilt. Seeing the young lovers step a little distance from each other, his brows rose. "It seems that I did. I am so relieved – one's hearing is so very valuable after all. My dear nephew! I trust that the young lady is the future Mrs. Darcy that Catherine has been writing of."

Mr. Darcy, his patience with unexpected encounters quite exhausted, nodded tersely. "Miss Bennet, may I introduce you to my uncle Fitzwilliam."

Elizabeth rose valiantly to the occasion and gave a neat, if unsteady, curtsey. "It is an honour, my Lord Fitzwilliam."

The Earl of Matlock bowed with exquisite grace. "Miss Bennet, both my son and my sister have been singing your praises since meeting you in Kent; I am quite enchanted to have met you at last. Do let us move out of this draughty hallway. I cannot at all fathom why Darcy should have kept you standing about when there is such a wind."

They went together into the parlour that Darcy had reserved. The earl was introduced to the Bingleys, and, fondly embracing Georgiana, even condescended to nod to Mrs. Brown.

Darcy, having recovered his senses by this time, turned to the earl. "I suppose you are to Rosings as well – did my aunt send you an express too? You must have come directly from Matlock."

"Certainly she did, nephew. Poor dear Anne – it is a great trial to be sure. Richard elected to ride; he will likely arrive here soon."

"We have thought, Uncle, that we should be married sooner rather than later," said Darcy briefly, thinking that he ought to be kept informed.

His uncle smiled. "Judging by what I overheard a few minutes ago, I should think that very wise," he said gently, and rather enjoyed seeing Mr. Bingley look as uncomfortable as his nephew. To the earl's surprise, Miss Bennet smiled at him in return without a trace of any embarrassment.

"Alas, my brother Mr. Bingley has occasional moments of hallucination – I fear there is no cure for it. Doubtless my dear sister will nurse him through the worst of it," she spoke dryly, but her eyes sparkled with amusement. It was not at all difficult for the earl to understand the appeal of this laughing girl from the country.

"My dear nephew," said Matlock, admiringly, "you must marry this young lady as soon as may be. I should be greatly honoured, Miss Bennet, if you would permit me to attend the nuptials."

Chapter Twenty-Eight

Longbourn, 27th August

*D*ear Cousin Anne,

There! You see how skilled we social upstarts can be at ingratiating ourselves when given sufficient opportunity. The self-same day I am married to your cousin, I have dropped all pretence at formality with you and shall henceforth refer to you as my kinswoman. I am entirely delighted with myself at present. Not one single tear did I shed in the church and neither did I stumble my way through pronouncing even one of Mr. Darcy's plethora of names.

But I must start at the beginning, must I not? Mr. Darcy returned from Rosings yesterday afternoon, quite muddy and tired, and bore with him the good wishes of yourself and your lady mother for our marriage. I was particularly pleased with Lady Catherine's firm instruction that I must write an account of the day to you as soon as I had opportunity and that on no account must I 'swoon at the altar like some low-bred ninnyhammer.' I do believe I shall cherish that advice and pass it on to my children. Lord Matlock, I understand, took particular pleasure in repeating it.

My last evening at Longbourn was a strange one. It is a decidedly odd thing to wander about a house that I have known and loved all of my life – for the last time, in a farewell. The last time I was to sleep in my girlhood bed, the last time I should rise before breakfast and walk out on the familiar pathways that have seen me grow from a gawky, irritable child to a decidedly blessed young woman. Such a sweet melancholy feeling – I declare that I have not encountered the like of it before. How strange it is that such a day of joy should be so poignantly framed with a fit of the dismals.

Your uncle, by the by, was quite the most splendidly dressed personage at the wedding. I would not, you understand, begrudge him his splendour if he had not so comprehensively robbed me entirely of the distinction myself. Until I laid eyes on his beautiful coat, I was so very satisfied that I had turned out very well. Picture, if you please, a very fine silk dress of the palest yellow and ornamented with shades of sunshine ribbons which Lydia had cunningly matched with my bonnet. I have never looked so well, I believe. Your cousin, I am glad to say, was much more soberly clad in a coat of dark blue – it is just as well for I do not think yellow would have looked so charming on him as it did me. Kitty, Lydia, and dearest Georgiana acted as my bridesmaids, and all of them being of a similar height made for a delightful picture when they all stood in the entrance of the church.

My mother has enjoyed my time at Pemberley immensely, and took great advantage of my being away in that I was forced to cede many of the decisions to her with regards to the wedding breakfast. There were ever so many courses to choose from – it is a happy thing that so many of the neighbourhood turned out, else we should not have been able to eat above half of it.

I am sat, just now, in a quiet little corner in the music room. Most of the guests have left us and I, being charged with writing to you as soon as may be, thought that I could not give a better account than one written on the very day that I am wed. My husband (I really must write that repeatedly until it looks less strange) is stood staring out at the window waiting with his customary patience for *me to have done. I feel quite giddy with my joy, dear cousin. I shall make it my task in life to make him as happy as I am.*

Should my sister Mrs. Collins call on you, do tell her that I shall write to her very soon and that my dear brother must bring the family to visit me. I should be quite dismayed if I am the last to meet my very first niece or nephew simply because I must go away to Derbyshire.

Fitzwilliam is impatient to leave soon if we are to reach London before darkness falls. I must bid you adieu.

He has promised me, Anne, that I shall have a little phaeton like yours, to drive about in when we eventually go to Pemberley. He has said that he must first teach me how to drive it safely, though, and I shall think of you whenever I go out in it. I had never been in one before you so kindly extended the invitation, you see, and I do think that I shall tell greatly exaggerated bedtime stories to my children of our illustrious cousin, Miss de Bourgh, who drove at breakneck speeds terrorizing the good people of Kent and who introduced their Mama to the wonders of driving a pair of horses.

I must go now. Mr. Darcy is to send this to you by express, so I daresay that you shall be reading my faithful account by the time I shall be stood in the entry of Darcy House, trying very hard not to be intimidated by the overwhelming stateliness of the housekeeper or the too-great dignity of the butler.

Sleep peacefully, Cousin Anne, and may God bless you.

Elizabeth Darcy.

Heaving a sigh, the new Mrs. Darcy laid down her pen and turned to her husband who had looked away from the view as soon as he heard her do so.

"I have written all that may be written, Fitzwilliam, without turning maudlin – though it is a close-run thing in parts. It is mostly cheerful, I believe; you may give it to the servant knowing that I have obeyed Lady Catherine's instructions as well as I could."

"Thank you, my love. Anne so enjoyed the other letters you sent. Aunt Catherine told me before I left that such light cheerfulness did her more good than any of the medicine the doctors have prescribed."

"I am glad of that then. I feel so wretchedly guilty that I did not do more in Kent. It seems so dreadful that I should be so happy today writing a final letter to be read when she may not live another week."

He bent and kissed her while taking the letter from her to be sent off.

"Run and fetch your bonnet, Mrs. Darcy. We must away – do not think any more on this," he gestured to the neatly folded paper in his hand. "You have done all that was asked of you and need do no more. It is your wedding day; you may enjoy it without sorrow, dearest, loveliest Elizabeth."

"Oh, my dear, I do not think I shall ever cease to grin like a simpleton at my new name." She paused at the threshold of the door, "I suppose I had better bid my family farewell. Jane is already gone back to Netherfield with Georgiana and Miss Bingley." Shaking off the natural sadness that so often came with life changes, Elizabeth smiled impudently at her husband. "Perhaps you will quarrel with me on the journey to London so that I do not miss my sisters quite so much."

He saw the lurking melancholy beneath her lively words and did not tease her.

"Mrs. Darcy, I shall quarrel with you whenever you wish me to."

She smiled at him sweetly in gratitude and departed to find the others. Mrs. Bennet had been looking for her and they walked together toward the drawing room.

"Ah! There you are, Lizzy! Charlotte and the Lucases have just this moment gone; you have been instructed to write very soon. I did tell them that being a married woman now you will have much less time to write long letters than you have done, but I daresay Mr. Darcy has so many servants that you will have some time to yourself."

"I have just come from writing my first letter as a married woman, Mama. Under Mr. Darcy's instruction, no less. Miss de Bourgh wished for an account of the wedding."

Mrs. Bennet looked pleased. "The day went well, did it not, Lizzy? I do not think I ever saw you in better looks, my love. You did me credit. And even the earl commented on the variety of the food laid out – he said that it rivalled anything he had seen in London."

Lizzy impulsively leant in and kissed her mother. "It was a splendid day. I will remember it with fondness and," she added generously, "I will try to rival it should my own daughters or even Miss Darcy require it in the future, but I shall be hard pressed to."

"Oh, Lizzy," sighed Mrs. Bennet, unable to wish for anything else in all the world at that moment. "If only Derbyshire were not so far away. I do not think I like my girls to be so distant from me. It seems so little time ago that you were a jolly ten-year-old and now you are grown so lady-like that I hardly recognise you. Mrs. Darcy! It sounds well on you."

"Remember that we are to London for now, Mama. We shall not travel north until Mr. Darcy has settled things for his aunt."

"Oh yes. I know, I was forgetting his cousin. Poor Lady Catherine."

Kitty and Lydia bounded up. "Lizzy! You will own that we have been the most beautifully behaved, decorous, ideal ladies in all of Meryton today, will you not?"

Lizzy smiled, knowing where Lydia was leading. "I do indeed own it, Lydia. I hope that you will continue to be so. I will keep my promise and speak to my husband. You may need to be patient but I will do my very best to ensure that you may come to visit me. How could I possibly do without my little sisters?"

Evidently feeling a great deal of love for their now rich and generous elder sister, the girls crowded around her in their own sweet affectionate way until Mr. Bennet came upon them.

"Mr. Darcy has called for his carriage to be brought round, Elizabeth. You have a few minutes."

She turned to her father and felt a lump rise to her throat. Memories of quiet moments spent in his company flooded her. There would be no more daily talks or snide interchanges between them; those twinkling eyes that mocked her so lovingly would grow dimmer and more hooded with age, and she would not be there to witness it. It might be months and months before she saw him again.

She could not speak. He looked down at her, seeming quite at a loss for words himself.

"Well now, my little Lizzy," he said at length. "I suppose you think yourself far too grand and grown up to give your poor father a kiss farewell, eh?"

The words fell flat but she dashed away the tears that were threatening to fall and stepped close to kiss his cheek. He brought his arms about her for a moment and held her tightly, kissing her swiftly on her forehead as he so often had done before.

Very much affected, Mrs. Bennet fluttered her handkerchief and clutched onto her nearest single daughter. Kitty, solemn for a moment in spite of the promised hope of visiting London, looked fretful.

Mr. Darcy entered the room, searching for his wife. She noticed him before he spotted her, hidden as she was in her father's shoulder, and she took a moment to admire how tall and handsome he looked. Somehow the habitual hauteur of his expression did not irritate her as it once did, for she knew now that he did not look nearly so proud when she kissed him.

When he saw her, his eyes softened in sympathy and he checked at the threshold. It was very pleasing, she thought, to know that the mere sight of her banished away some of his austerity and stiffness. She pulled away a little from her Papa and kissed his cheek once again.

"Write to me, Papa – even if it is only a line or two to say you are well and that you do not miss me in the slightest. I will send you all a letter when I can."

Her husband extended a gloved hand and she walked over to him and placed her own in it. "Come along, Mrs. Darcy," he said, with pardonable satisfaction. He found his handkerchief and removed the traces of tears that had fallen on her cheeks. "It is a very good thing that I am used to Georgiana's notions of punctuality. If I had not already estimated that we should leave at least half an hour later and so told you an earlier departure time, we might really be in danger of arriving very late. I daresay I shall become used to female timekeeping."

The new Mrs. Darcy did not sputter in outrage at the aspersions cast upon her timekeeping but instead smiled sweetly up at her husband.

"How imperious you are, Mr. Darcy," she exclaimed. "Not three hours have we been married and already I am being ordered about and scolded."

Mrs. Bennet let out a cry. "Elizabeth! You must not run on so as you have been used to doing with your father; husbands must be treated quite differently."

Mr. Darcy, grateful that his mother-in-law had such respect for his person, bowed and agreed with her with a serious expression.

Mrs. Bennet, feeling that her sense of tact was needed to smooth things over for her daughter, continued, "I assure you, Mr. Darcy, that Lizzy has been very well brought up but her papa has well-nigh encouraged her impertinence. I do not doubt that she will not be so with you."

Mr. Darcy, flicking a quick look at his unrepentant wife, did not look as though he shared Mrs. Bennet's confidence in the matter.

Elizabeth grinned. "Should we not be leaving now, sir? I do not wish to arrive so very late, you know."

Her husband ushered her out to their carriage and handed her up into it.

"Do not think I do not know what you are about, Fitzwilliam," she said, once settled against the richly upholstered squabs and waving merrily at her family who had come so far as the door. "You are not at all at ease with females weeping and so sought to insult me instead. For shame, sir."

"I think, my love, that we should have brought your mother along with us. She would be very offended at such accusations as you have cast at me." He was busy, as he spoke, arranging a light blanket about her knees, and smiled up at her once he had completed the task to his satisfaction. His wife laid a hand on his shoulder in silent thanks for his care. He took his gold-topped stick and tapped the roof with it twice before settling himself comfortably beside his wife.

The team of horses strained in their harnesses and the carriage pulled away. Elizabeth clenched her gloved hands tightly in her lap and absolutely refused to look back as they passed through the gate. With a tremor in her voice, she tried to return a witticism of her own. "I suppose you expect that I ought to faithfully follow her advice and refer to you respectfully as 'Mr. Darcy,' and 'sir,' each time you command me to do something."

Her husband, the pity in his eyes suggesting that her courageous efforts were not altogether convincing, replied drolly, "I do not think that I have ever heard you so impertinent toward me as when you are ostensibly being very respectful, so no, madam, I do not at all expect it."

Mrs. Darcy laughed a little at such a description of herself. "And I suppose you think that I will bow to your every edict without question, as Mama suggested that I should only last evening."

"Did she?" said her husband, much interested by this. "I am greatly impressed by such wisdom. No, Mrs. Darcy, I would be very surprised if you did anything without question."

"Oh, how well that sounds!" sighed Elizabeth, rapidly being restored to good spirits, as was Mr. Darcy's aim.

"I imagine, Elizabeth, that you and I each intend to be happy, and so we shall be." Lizzy nodded, serious now. He took her chin in his palm and looked into her eyes. "What has you so rattled, my love?"

His tenderness quite undid her and she felt herself perilously close to tears once more. She sighed. "You are altogether too good at reading my moods, Fitzwilliam. I do not know that there is anything at all amiss with me other than the usual missish nerves that surely accompany most brides. You do understand, do you not, that I can simultaneously love you to distraction and yet still be in low spirits to be permanently leaving my family?"

Releasing her chin, he bent his head and swiftly kissed her. "Quite able to understand it, my dear. So long as nothing has occurred to upset your peace of mind, I am content with that." He bit his lip. "I wish to make you happy, Elizabeth. I am not an ogre."

Lizzy affectionately laid her head on his shoulder and his arm instantly came about her. It seemed so natural and right to sit so, as though they had always done so and that they forever more would travel in such a fashion.

"Oh, I know it, Fitzwilliam! You need not be concerned, my love, if Mama became a little silly last night about you always being given your own way. It is not because I have exaggerated your severity to her – she does not, after all, know you like I do."

This slightly garbled speech deserved another kiss from her husband and it was willingly received with a smile.

"I am almost surprised that she did not advise me to issue thrice daily beatings in the drawing room before we left," said he lightly.

His wife muffled her gurgle of laughter in his shoulder. "Mama? Oh no! She has the greatest horror of brutish husbands. I think it is on account of Mr. Collins's father. She was set to marry him, you know, before Papa intervened. I gather that was the reason for the estrangement between the families. Old Mr. Collins was quite furious."

"I had not heard of any such thing. You have always seemed to be on the best of terms with each other."

"Oh, we are now, Fitzwilliam. Mr. Collins – the present Mr. Collins I mean – wanted to heal the breach by marrying one of us and wrote to Papa after his own father had died. I am told that he was a very…a very hard man."

"And he chose Mrs. Collins?" said Mr. Darcy, his eyebrows raised in apparent bewilderment at such want of taste. He looked down to the woman nestled against his shoulder and saw that she was very carefully smoothing out the folds of the blanket on her lap. He shifted so that he could better see her face. "I had not, before I saw you again in Kent, thought that he would make a match with her. You, as I recall, danced the first with him at Netherfield, did you not?"

Elizabeth attempted to compose her features into neutrality, and apparently failed, for his eyes narrowed.

"I hope that wasn't intended to insult my sister, Fitzwilliam. I am very fond of Mary," she said, trying to avert him.

"Certainly not, but I cannot fathom why any man would overlook you, my dear," replied he smoothly.

"Very pretty, sir!" Mr. Darcy looked inquiringly at her and waited in silence for her to enlighten him. "Oh, very well. He asked me to marry him first but then later proposed to Mary. But you must not tell anyone, Fitzwilliam!"

Fitzwilliam Darcy looked at his wife, very surprised. "I will not, of course, my love but…I do not fully understand. You are on such good terms with him, and clearly he still thinks you are a delight – which of course you are...."

"Mr. Darcy, do you really want to hear this now?" she asked, turning her face up to his.

He bent down and kissed her once more, unable to resist the implied offer, and settled back against the squabs, pulling her in snugly against him.

"Yes, my dear, I really think I do," he said with a slight upturning of the lips, quite ready to listen to his wife speak at length on any subject and feeling as though all future journeys, even the long ones, would be pleasant things as long as the two of them could be seated thus.

Lizzy rearranged herself against him and smiled to herself at the companionable feeling that warmed her to the heart. To think that she had once worried that she might feel lonely, with only him for company.

"Well then, my love, I suppose that the best place to begin would be the morning after the Netherfield ball...."

FINIS.

Made in United States
Orlando, FL
26 June 2022

19168200R00138